"Let me █████████████

A flicker c█████████████

She plante█████████ on her hips. The action brought her loose-fitting tunic snugly across the soft swell of her breasts and the enticing slenderness of her waist.

His body reacted.

"Bossy, aren't you?"

Although her attitude was sassy, he noticed she wasn't actually arguing or telling him to get lost. Maybe because she was suddenly looking really tired around the eyes. Abruptly, it was all he could do not to take her in his arms and offer the comfort he sensed she needed but wouldn't accept.

"When it comes to situations like this, you have no idea," he drawled.

It was exactly how he ended up getting platonically involved with one woman who needed help after another.

"Oh, I'm aware of your reputation as the local Sir Galahad," she murmured cheekily.

"You are?" He had gotten the impression she couldn't have cared less about any of the single men in her orbit.

"Oh, yeah..." Grinning, she took him by the arm and pointed him toward the front door. "Which is exactly why you should save your 'assistance' for someone who needs it and mosey on home."

Dear Reader,

When my husband and I met for the first time, we felt an instant connection. Right away, there was an ability to make each other laugh, an inability to stop looking into each other's eyes, and an immediate, innate understanding of each other. And of course, lots and lots of chemistry...

Cardiologist Claire Lowell thought she had all that with her ex. Until the day he left. Now a single mom of adorable triplets, her life revolves around work and family, and that's it.

Pediatrician Zach McCabe always thought he would have it all: an enviable career, a woman to love and kids. Until he lost his fiancée in a tragic accident. These days, he focuses on work and helping others. Marriage and kids are no longer in his plans.

And that's why for the first year that Claire and Zach work at the same hospital, they steer clear of each other as much as possible. It's not that they don't like each other. Or want to get to know each other. But because they sense that doing so would bring complications to their lives neither wants. That is, until a five-year-old patient with a mysterious heart malady brings them together.

I hope you enjoy reading this book as much as I enjoyed writing it.

Best wishes,

Cathy Gillen Thacker

STAND-IN TEXAS DAD

CATHY GILLEN THACKER

Harlequin

SPECIAL EDITION

ISBN-13: 978-1-335-40233-2

Stand-In Texas Dad

Copyright © 2025 by Cathy Gillen Thacker

 Harlequin Enterprises ULC
22 Adelaide St. West, 41st Floor
Toronto, Ontario M5H 4E3, Canada
www.Harlequin.com

Printed in Lithuania

Cathy Gillen Thacker is a married mother of three. She and her husband reside in North Carolina. Her stories have made numerous appearances on bestseller lists, but her best reward is knowing one of her books made someone's day a little brighter. A popular Harlequin author, she loves telling passionate stories with happy endings and thinks nothing beats a good romance and a hot cup of tea! Visit her at cathygillenthacker.com for information on her books, recipes and a list of her favorite things.

Chapter One

"The question is," Claire Lowell murmured to herself, the way she always did when feeling like there would never be enough hours in her day to accomplish what she should, "do I have time to swing by the express lane and pick up our groceries, or not?"

"I don't know," a sexy masculine voice said from behind her. "Do you?"

Senses tingling, Claire swung around and found herself face-to-face with Zach McCabe, Laramie Community Hospital's most eligible bachelor. And for very good reason. Not only was he a very gifted and compassionate pediatrician, he was handsome enough to be dubbed...*behind the scenes, anyway*...their very own Prince Charming.

"Zach!" Her breath caught in her chest the way it always did when he came near.

His broad-shouldered, six-foot-four-inch frame blocked out the late afternoon sun. Mischief filled his smoky blue eyes. The warm spring breeze wafted over them, mussing his dark brown hair. He came even closer, inundating her with his brisk sandalwood-and-moss scent. "Claire..."

His teasing smile accelerated her pulse even more. But she reminded herself she wasn't interested in him, or any other man for that matter, right now. Not when she already had so much going on in her life. Her body warming everywhere his playful gaze touched, she lifted her chin. "I didn't realize you were there!"

He shrugged. "No surprise, given how fast you were racing across the physicians' parking lot."

Unable to help herself, she felt her eyes irresistibly drawn to the way his pale blue dress shirt clung to his taut abs and muscular chest. It was crazy, how effortlessly he exuded physicality and strength. Even crazier, how much the reckless, romantic side of her wanted to explore just that.

Reminded the triplets' part-time nanny would be leaving in twenty-five minutes, Claire spun around and continued striding in the direction of her vehicle. Leaving him to follow at will. "Fun as this has been, doc, I've got to cut it short. I'm in a hurry."

Zach fell into step beside her. "To get your groceries."

"Yes, so…"

With strides two times the length of hers, he languidly kept pace. "I've been trying to get ahold of you."

Trying not to feel disappointed that the only reason he had apparently chased her down was for work, Claire nodded. "I know about the messages." If she'd had even a second to spare, she would have already phoned him. Reaching the Honda Civic, she stopped and swung back to face him. "Actually, you're at the top of my list of people to call back this evening."

He nodded. Looking happy—yet not. He leaned closer, bartering, "It would be better if we could meet in person."

Taking a deep breath, she found herself focusing on the vivid bear-and-moose print on his necktie. She was sure that had to be a hit with the kids he cared for. Glancing up, she met his gaze again. "We're talking a consult?"

The brackets around his mouth deepened. "At least forty-five minutes."

Claire hit the unlock feature on her keypad, opened the

driver door and tossed her bag in on the opposite seat. "Then it will have to be later in the week."

"Hate to be a pest, but this consult really can't wait. And since you are the best cardiologist in the area…"

So everyone said. Which was great. Except when that took her away from her three kids…

Zach exhaled, worry permeating his expression. "Listen. I know how busy you are, Claire. I wouldn't press you if it weren't important."

Claire knew that to be true. Zach was a compassionate guy, considerate of the situations of others. And renowned for a generous nature that went well beyond his duty to his patients. He was always rushing in to rescue someone from something. Then ducking out as soon as the problem was solved to go on to the next person in distress. So quickly, in fact, that she sometimes wondered what he was running from.

Deciding the grocery pickup was going to have to wait until she could load the triplets in the car, and take them with her to the store, she asked, "How old is the patient?"

"Five."

Such a cute and vulnerable age. Old enough to communicate symptoms yet not mature enough to understand complex medical issues. Especially those of a serious nature. "And you think it's the heart?"

Zach paused. Unsure enough to admit. "I think we definitely need to rule it out…if it's not."

Claire liked the fact he didn't have an ego that made him pretend to always have all the answers. The way some specialists did. She guessed where this was going. "And fix it if it is cardiac related."

"Right."

Well, now she was hooked, too. As she was, every time she came across a patient in need. Especially a kid…

Squaring her shoulders, she returned her gaze to Zach's.

Once again, wishing his eyes weren't such a devastating gray-blue. Swallowing around the parched feeling in her throat, she pushed on. "We can get together if you want this evening, but I don't have childcare past five thirty, so it will have to be at my home. *After* my kids are asleep." Claire calculated errand, dinner, bath and bedtime, then added thirty minutes for good measure. "Is eight o'clock okay?"

Zach flashed another sexy smile. Looking relieved—and relaxed—in a way she suddenly was not. "Sounds good. In the meantime, if you need me to swing by the market and pick up those groceries you were talking about, I would be happy to help out."

Was she about to be added to his damsel-in-distress list? Claire sincerely hoped not! He was way too tempting as it was. "Thanks. But…" The last thing she needed to do was lean on any man. Especially after her last relationship had ended so disastrously. Her hard-won independence kicking in, she adopted a confident stance. "I've got it."

He accepted her refusal with the graciousness the Texas McCabes were known for. Then continued, with a curious lift of his brow as he surveyed the vehicle she was about to get into. "Interesting ride."

And not exactly her style, Claire thought, with the beautifully painted-on landscapes adorning the hood, side panels and trunk. "It belongs to my nanny. She's got my SUV." At Zach's puzzled look, she explained, "Three car seats wouldn't fit in this. Bette and I switch during the days so she can drive the triplets around in my SUV. And I take this to the hospital and anywhere else I have to go to see patients."

Zach surveyed the artistically decorated car panels again. "Makes sense."

Claire slid behind the wheel, glad for the distance between them as she slid the key into the ignition. "Any more questions?" She hoped not, because she really had to run.

He moved away from the vehicle. "Nope."

Claire started the engine and put down the window. "Then I'll see you in a few hours," she said with a small wave before driving away.

Zach parked in front of Claire's home, a few minutes before eight.

The two-story Craftsman bungalow in the heart of the town's residential section was what he expected. Glancing up, he appreciated how the exterior was painted a soothing sage green. The beautiful handcrafted wood door had a transom on either side, and the porch was filled with comfy cushioned wicker furniture that matched the home's snowy white trim. He noted that the thick green grass was neatly cut—probably by a landscaping service—although the generous landscape beds in front were surprisingly empty. A luxury white SUV sat in the drive, in front of the detached garage.

Briefly, a wave of wistfulness swept through him.

Five years ago, he had expected to be living in a place just like this, with the woman he loved, and a couple of babies by now.

But that hadn't happened. He had made a terrible mistake, and lost his chance to have his happily ever after. And now, well, his life was about work, work and more work. And most days, he was happy to have it that way.

As far as Claire Lowell went, he mused, as he headed up the front porch steps, it sounded like she had her hands as full as she had indicated. Of wild children and a barking dog.

Wondering if she was going to be receptive to his presence after all, he rang the doorbell.

The whooping and hollering on the other side increased.

Then stopped completely as the front door was yanked open by a pajama-clad little boy of preschool age. His short blond hair was still wet, smelling of shampoo, and sticking up all over. The tyke's inquisitive green eyes surveyed Zach from head to toe, and back again. "Who are you?" he demanded, with an irritated frown.

A more important question was, where the hell was Claire?

A big, black Newfoundland skidded to a stop next to the boy, and sized up Zach. Deciding he was friend, not foe, the dog immediately began wagging his tail. Zach reached out to pet the top of the pet's silky black head while still addressing the suspiciously glaring, pint-sized sentry. "I'm Zach, a friend of your mom's."

"She's busy. She can't talk now," he retorted, narrowing his eyes even more.

Zach nodded, but before the door could be slammed in his face, he asked, "And what is your name?"

For a second, Zach thought the little ruffian wasn't going to answer, then he said, "Oliver."

"How old are you, Oliver?"

"Three and a half!"

"And who is this?" Zach inclined his head at their pet, and grinned as the Newfie cuddled even closer against him.

Oliver affectionately stroked the Newfie's coat. "This is Lucky. He is our dog!"

Another boy sidled up to join them. He looked ready for bed, too, but his just-shampooed hair, which was several shades darker than his brother's, was neatly combed to one side. His green eyes were analytical and considerably friendlier. "I'm Andrew." He stuck out his hand.

Zach gave it a formal shake. "Nice to meet you, Andrew. And Oliver."

A third child joined them, this one a girl, who was the spitting image of her mom. Her dark curls were cut in a chin-length bob that framed her piquant face. Zach couldn't help noticing her cheeks were pink. Upon further inspection, he saw she had tears drying on her face, a stormy look in her green eyes.

"This is Isabella," Oliver announced. "She is our sister!"

"She's mad at us," Andrew said, looking more accepting than perturbed about that.

"I want my baby doll back!" Isabella shouted, the strength of her lungs at odds with her dainty appearance.

Claire chose that moment to appear in the foyer. She put both hands on her hips. "Boys…give it back to her."

"We don't have it," Andrew said in a way that made Zach suspect his assertion was technically true.

Lucky sized up the scene and exited, heading for the rear of the home.

Claire's brow lifted. "But you know where Baby Doll is…" she presumed. "And I want you to go get her…as well as Giraffe and Zebra…so I can tuck you all in."

Both boys sighed loudly and slowly started moving in the direction that the Newfie had gone. Before they'd taken half a dozen steps, their big black dog was back, carrying a doll in his mouth. He brought it over to Isabella and set it down very gently next to her.

Isabella let out a cry that was part triumph and part aggravation. Snatching it up, she clutched it to her chest. "Thank you, Lucky!" she sobbed.

Claire looked at Zach over her children's heads. Wincing, he wondered if this was what her evenings were like. "Make yourself comfortable. I'll be back as soon as possible," she said.

"You picked up all the toys?" Claire stood in the doorway, her low voice reverberating with shock.

Wondering why she sounded like he had done something wrong, Zach turned away from the last plastic bin of building blocks. It had ended up taking a good twenty minutes for her to put the kids to bed. He had tried sitting on the sofa, but the living room slash kids' play area had been quite a mess.

Not Claire, though.

Even in a loose-fitting, white cotton tunic and faded skinny jeans, she looked absolutely gorgeous. Silky black curls fell just beneath her jaw, framing the elegant features of her face. Her bow-shaped lips were soft and luscious. His eyes drifting up, he noted her long-lashed emerald-green eyes were still wide with surprise. And glimmering with something else, an emotion not quite as welcoming.

Unsure if he'd made a mistake or not, Zach shrugged. And then did what he almost *never* did—he explained his behavior. The why behind his actions.

"I've always had a hard time doing nothing. Especially when there is work…even housework…to be done."

Claire stepped toward him, sizing him up all the while. "I can see that about you." She smiled.

Zach hoped that meant he was forgiven for tidying up without asking permission.

She came even closer, enveloping him with her delicate, feminine scent. And something else a lot more familiar. Baby shampoo, he decided. "Does it have anything to do with your mom being a social worker?" she asked.

"That, and the fact I have a CEO dad, three quadruplet brothers and a sister. The only way our family survived day to day was if everyone pitched in."

"Well, thanks for straightening this room." Claire folded a throw and put it neatly over the back of the sofa. "I intended to have that done by the time you arrived tonight. But the triplets had other plans." She sighed. "They always do."

Zach knew from the talk around the hospital Claire was a single mom who spent all her free time with her kids. Little else. "What about their dad?"

"He's not in the picture. Never has been."

Then her ex was really missing out. Her kids were adorable. Cute, smart and lively. If they had been his he would have been like Claire, with them every spare moment.

He compressed his lips. "Sorry," he sympathized.

Avoiding his eyes, she offered another shrug of her slender shoulders. "It is the way it is."

And she clearly didn't want to talk about why. He could understand that; he didn't like to discuss his own unexpectedly crushed dreams, or late fiancée, either.

Sometimes life just sucked.

"Do you have other family nearby?" he asked gently.

"My sister Gwen and her husband Patrick and their three kids live in Dallas."

Which was a good three-hour drive away. "But no one here in Laramie?"

She shook her head and took a seat in the wing chair, adjacent to the sofa. "So about this patient you wanted my help with…?" she prodded, apparently done talking about her personal life.

"Right." Zach sat on the sofa kitty-corner from her and opened up the file he had brought with him. "Her name is Sasha. Her mom is Harriett Donnelly."

She paused. "One of the hospital dietitians…?"

"Yes. For the last few weeks, Sasha has been having what sound like heart palpitations, and or arrhythmias, in conjunction with periods of wild hyperactivity. Usually in the evenings, after dinner, as bedtime approaches."

Claire frowned. "I can identify with the antics. That is pretty common when kids are overtired at the end of the day. Why does her mom think she's having palpitations?"

"Couple of things. When Sasha makes the complaint, she stops what she is doing. Usually very abruptly. She says she has butterflies inside her chest. Or sometimes something pushing on her sternum. Harriett's taken her pulse when that happens.

Sometimes it is steady and fast but otherwise normal. Other times, it will appear to be skipping a beat, here and there, before going back into normal sinus rhythm."

Her brows knitted together, she looked at Zach. "How long do these episodes last?"

"According to Harriett, half an hour or so."

She pressed her lips together. "Any other symptoms?"

"Not so far."

Claire's frown deepened. "Any congenital heart condition?"

"No. Sasha's been completely healthy up to now. But she fainted today at recess while she was running around the playground. By the time the paramedics got there a few minutes later, she had already come to."

She crossed one slender leg over the other, her foot swinging back and forth. "Any arrhythmia then?"

"When EMS checked, her heart rate was normal."

"But you're still thinking heart," Claire guessed.

Drawing his attention away from her long, sexy legs, Zach nodded. At this point, it was just an instinct. That Sasha's difficulties stemmed from some sort of currently undiagnosed cardiac issue. But his intuition was usually right in cases like this.

"Family history?"

"Still working on getting that," he answered.

She raked her teeth across her lower lip. "Well, let's see what we do have so far."

They spent the next half hour going over Sasha's medical records, from her premature birth and four-week stay in the NICU on. "Everything looks normal," Claire concluded finally. "But that doesn't mean a latent cardiac issue isn't there."

Zach relaxed in relief, glad they were of the same mindset, even though as yet there wasn't much to go on. "What do you suggest?" he said.

"Have Harriett call my office first thing tomorrow and make an appointment to bring Sasha in. We'll do an EKG, get another complete family medical history—in case something was accidentally omitted—and put a heart monitor on her for the next seven days. That way, if there is an intermittent arrhythmia we will have a record of it. And, of course, if she faints again or has more palpitations, you should call me immediately."

"Thank you."

"Glad to help." She rose to show him out, moving gracefully across the living room. "Sorry you had such a hard time getting ahold of me today."

Tearing his eyes from the gentle sway of her hips, he pushed the desire away, reminding himself they were work colleagues. That was all.

"No worries. It all worked out in the end."

They headed for the foyer. Claire opened the front door, but instead of ushering him out and saying good-night, as he expected, she crossed the threshold with him.

Wondering if she'd felt the same unexpected flash of chemistry he just had, Zach grinned. Unable to help himself, he teased drolly, "Walking me out? Cause I think I can find my way to my pickup truck from here."

"Cute, but no," she scoffed.

Claire fished in the pocket of her skinny jeans and pulled out the keypad for her SUV. "I'm finishing my chores." She skipped down the steps of her Craftsman, the denim lovingly skimming her long legs as she moved. "I didn't get all the groceries in earlier. Only the refrigerator stuff."

Sure enough, there were half a dozen bags inside the cargo area. Which meant he was most likely the only one feeling an attraction. Telling himself that was definitely for the best, given their very demanding lives, he offered gallantly, "Need some help?"

Something—surprise maybe—flared in her green eyes as

she opened the tailgate. She turned her attention to the task at hand. "Thanks…but you don't have to do that."

Except for some reason he really wanted to. "Consider it a quid pro quo. You helped me. Now, I'll help you."

She drew in a breath. "Not quite the same thing. But okay." She gestured indifferently. "If you want to carry a bag or two…"

They each took two bags, then brought them into her kitchen and set them down on the island. When she would have gone back for another load, he laid a hand on her arm. "Let me do the heavy lifting while you concentrate on unpacking and putting things away."

A flicker of irritation swept her pretty features.

The kind that told him she wasn't used to accepting a man's help. Because of whatever had gone on with her ex?

She planted her hands on her hips. The action brought her loose-fitting tunic snugly across the soft swell of her breasts and the enticing slenderness of her waist.

His body reacted.

"Bossy, aren't you?"

Although her attitude was sassy, he noticed she wasn't actually arguing or telling him to get lost. Maybe because she was suddenly looking really tired around the eyes. Abruptly, it was all he could do not to take her in his arms and offer the comfort he sensed she needed, but wouldn't accept.

"When it comes to situations like this, you have no idea," he drawled.

It was exactly how he ended up getting platonically involved with one woman who needed help after another.

Which gave Claire just the opening she needed.

"Oh, I'm aware of your reputation as the local Sir Galahad," she murmured cheekily.

"You are…?" He had gotten the impression she could have

cared less about the repute of any of the single men in her orbit. As long as they stayed out of her way, that was.

"Oh, yeah…" Grinning, she took him by the arm and pointed him toward the front door. "Which is exactly why you should save your 'assistance' for someone who needs it and mosey on home," she said.

Chapter Two

The next day Claire met her and Zach's mutual patient. Sasha Donnelly was sweet, smart, and unlike Claire's own children, a little shy. But, as the appointment wore on, she began to relax and open up.

"Looking good." Claire nodded at the heart monitor taped to the five-year-old patient's chest. "How does it feel?"

Sasha considered. "Like a very big Band-Aid. Only there is no ouchie underneath."

Claire grinned at the apt description. "You're going to have it on for one week," she informed gently. "Then you'll come back and we'll take it off, okay?"

Sasha nodded, seemingly okay with that. Which was good. A lot of kids weren't comfortable wearing heart monitors, which made doing pediatric cardiology workups difficult.

Her patient's bespectacled older brother, Tucker—who'd come in to observe so he could write an extra credit report for his AP Biology II class on the use of heart monitors in pediatric patients—asked, "Can you read any of the data the monitor is capturing in real time?"

Claire shook her head. "No. We send it off to a lab. They issue a report back to us, usually in a couple of days." She turned back to Sasha, warning matter-of-factly, "In the meantime, don't get that wet, okay?" Once the child nodded agreeably, Claire addressed Sasha's mom. "The plastic does a pretty good job of protecting the monitor, but you'll still have to be careful when she showers."

"Got it." Looking calm but concerned, Harriett asked, "How soon will you have the results of the blood work?"

Tucker put in helpfully, "Mom's worried Sasha's heart stuff is because of a vitamin deficiency or malabsorption issue." He sighed. "Although I don't know why. Every time we turn around we're having to eat a leafy green vegetable..."

"I hate kale!" Sasha said emphatically, wrinkling her nose.

Her seventeen-year-old brother nodded glumly. "The only fries we're allowed to eat are oven-baked ones—spritzed with olive or avocado oil."

"Okay kids." Harriett flushed. "Dr. Claire has heard enough of our dietary likes and dislikes, thank you."

Claire smiled. "I think it's wonderful your mother is concerned about keeping you all healthy. And she is a dietitian, remember, so this *is* her area of expertise."

The woman shot her a grateful look.

She continued, "We'll have the blood work back by the end of the week. As soon as it comes in, we'll post it to Sasha's online portal."

"If there is any problem..."

"I'll call you to discuss," Claire promised Sasha's mom, before ushering all of them toward the checkout desk to make the next several appointments.

She went on to her next patient. The rest of her afternoon passed swiftly. Before she knew it, it was a quarter after five. And she had fifteen minutes to get home to relieve the kids' nanny.

Zach stood next to his pickup truck, watching as Claire raced out of the building and across the physicians' parking lot, much as she had the day before. He wondered if she was always in a hurry. So stressed in her private life. On the job, she was as reassuring and calm as could be, to patients and colleagues alike.

However, the evening before, at her home, she had simply seemed overwhelmed.

And that made him want to help her. Which was, of course, what his mother, Mitzy, kept warning him about. Telling him not to get so caught up in another's life that he forgot all about his own.

The years were passing. Too fast, she said. If he wasn't open to love again, he really would end up alone. But he didn't want to think about that now. Not when he had to get downtown before the Sugar Love bakery closed.

Luckily, his sister-in-law had his order ready. Ellie handed over the signature pink-and-white cardboard box. "Another damsel in distress?" she teased.

"In case you hadn't noticed, these treats are kid-sized."

"Even more interesting," Ellie said.

Since she and Joe had finally put aside their "we're never getting married" vow, and been blessed with two adorable babies, the two of them had pushed everyone toward a happily married ever-after ending, too.

Zach explained, "I'm just being nice."

"Never said you weren't," Ellie returned airily. Then she got that look in her eye. The same one his parents got when they wished he would pair up with someone again.

But Zach had been there, done that, to heartbreaking result. He wasn't interested in doing it again.

"Thanks for the goodies, Ellie," he said. Not giving her a chance to say more, he headed out the door.

Claire stood on the front porch of her home and stared at Bette, who'd been their devoted part-time nanny for the last seven months, unable to believe what she was hearing. "You... what?"

CATHY GILLEN THACKER   23

"I know." Bette ran a hand through her purple-and-pink streaked red hair. "It's a lot to take in, isn't it?" Her face lit up with joy. "Especially after all these years of trying to get someone... *anyone*...to take a serious look at my work. Never mind that they might be interested in displaying one of my paintings in their next New Artist show."

Sincerely happy for the twenty-six-year-old artist, Claire said, "I know. It's wonderful news!" But the timing for the rest of it absolutely sucked.

Bette pressed her hands to her chest, looking absurdly grateful under the circumstances. "Thank heavens you understand. Otherwise, I'd have to just quit!"

"No. Don't do that," Claire said desperately. Her kids were lingering just inside the open doorway, near the staircase, taking in everything. The last thing she wanted was for them to be upset.

"Anyway," Bette handed over the keys to Claire's SUV and accepted her own in return, "since the gallery owners need to see my work first thing tomorrow morning, I'm going to have to leave now and grab my stuff from my apartment before driving to Fredericksburg. Hopefully, I'll be back by tomorrow night."

And if Bette wasn't, Claire wondered anxiously, what then? "What about tomorrow morning and afternoon?"

Bette shrugged but had the decency to offer a sheepish smile. "I don't know. But I know you'll figure it out! Thanks so much. You're the best!" Bette hugged Claire's frozen form and then ran past her, down the front steps, practically colliding with Zach McCabe.

He had *that* expression on his face again, the one that said he felt sorry for her. And maybe a tad concerned. He took the steps lazily, cradling a pink-and-white Sugar Love bakery box in hand. His eyes lasered into hers. "Everything okay?"

No, it wasn't, Claire thought, doing her best not to show just how upset she was. She inclined her head at the kids who were now coming out onto the porch. "Can't talk about it right now," she murmured softly. Then raising her voice loud enough for the triplets to hear, turned back to him and pointed to the box and asked curiously, "What's that?"

Getting her hint—that a big distraction was in order—he said, "It's a thank-you present. For helping me out on the Donnelly case."

He had to know it wasn't necessary. The physicians in Laramie referred cases to one another all the time. It was part of their job.

Oblivious to her wary attitude, the triplets burst into smiles. Elbowing each other out of the way, they rushed forward to get a better look. Zach lowered the box so they could see what was inside the cellophane window. "Cupcakes!" Oliver shouted with glee.

"Tiny ones!" With scholarly precision, Andrew observed the miniature treats.

Isabella beamed. "Like the ones we get at our preschool parties!" She pressed her hands together in front of her. "Can we have one now, Mommy?"

"Please, please, please…!" Oliver said.

Andrew enthused. "We'll eat all our dinner. We promise!"

Suppressing a sigh, she acquiesced. "Sure." Knowing a little give in this situation would ward off temper tantrums and arguments. Which was the *last* thing she needed right now. "You can each have one to eat at the table, and then after you finish, you can take Lucky out to the backyard and play on the swing set while I get dinner ready."

"Okay, Mommy!"

Claire motioned for Zach to follow them all inside. Even though the mini cupcakes were all identical—vanilla with pastel sprinkle frosting—the selection process took forever. The kids chatted happily with Zach while they ate their treats.

"Don't you want one?" Isabella asked.

Zach declined. "Not right now. Thanks."

"Mommy doesn't eat too many sweets, either," Oliver imparted.

"On account of her waistline," Andrew said.

Claire flushed in embarrassment. Even though, thankfully, Zach managed to maintain a remarkably undecipherable expression on his face.

"I have to be careful with mine, too," he said, winking at her flirtatiously. "It's part of being a grown-up."

Yes, Claire thought, it was.

As was the tremor of sudden awareness rushing through her. He was way too sexy and kind a man to be sitting at her kitchen table...

Making her think about the things she had cut out of her life. Like romance. Or the possibility of simply spending time with a man, one-on-one.

As usual the kids had as much on their hands and faces as they did inside them. She helped them wash up, and then they dashed outside to play, whooping it up, with Lucky stretched out in the grass, delightedly watching their every move. While Claire and Zach stood side by side in the breakfast room's bay window, doing the same.

He turned to her, abruptly apologetic. "Guess I should have asked if they were even allowed to have sweets before I brought these over..."

Yes, he *should* have, but did she really want to quibble over that now? Having learned a long time ago not to sweat the small stuff, Claire turned away from the window and went back to tackle the sticky mess on the table. "It's fine." She sprayed cleaner over the tabletop, then bent forward to wipe it clean with a paper towel. "It got their mind off Bette's news."

His gaze drifted over her, before returning ever so slowly

to her face. Compassion laced his low tone. "She really left you in the lurch just now, didn't she?"

Seeing a spot she had missed, she leaned over to rub it stubbornly. "Yep."

He came closer, reminding her how good he smelled, like sandalwood and moss. "Maybe you need a new nanny."

Trying not to think about what it might feel like to kiss him right now, Claire told him, "It's not that simple."

She opened up the freezer, took stock of what she had, and brought out a box of breaded fish sticks and a microwave kid-friendly mac 'n' cheese, along with some frozen peas.

He moved to the other side of the island, giving her plenty of room to work, then sat down on a stool. "Enlighten me."

Aware how cozy this could be, if she let it, Claire kept her focus on meal prep. Feeling his eyes upon her, she turned the regular oven to preheat. "We have only lived in Laramie for thirteen months."

He kept his eyes on hers a disconcertingly long time, then said sympathetically, "From what I heard, your adjustment from big city to rural Laramie wasn't the easiest one."

Claire nodded. "I went through two nannies in six months, from the premiere Dallas agency that everyone recommended. Both women were perfect on paper, their references impeccable."

"I'm guessing they did everything the way you wanted it done?"

"To the letter. But neither of them really meshed with the kids. Not the way I needed them to..." She paused, searching for the words to explain. But not sure he would understand because he did not have kids of his own. "The triplets were well cared for and kept on a schedule."

A quirk of his dark brow. "But not loved."

Trying not to think what his steady appraisal and deep voice did to her, Claire cleared her throat. "Exactly. So I started looking for someone younger and more flexible. Who didn't want to necessarily live in, the way the other two had, but wouldn't mind staying here whenever necessary."

"Like when you had to take calls at the hospital, or go in to see a patient unexpectedly."

"Right. Anyway, that's when I found Bette, through a friend of a friend. To my delight, she was willing to move to Laramie and take a studio apartment for herself here. But the best part? She was able to accommodate my crazy schedule at the hospital by coming in early to get the kids dressed and fed before doing the preschool drop-off at nine a.m. Then she had the middle of the day to go back to her studio and work on her art before picking up the kids at school in the afternoon, and caring for them until I got home around five thirty. At which point she went off to teach painting classes at the community center." She took a breath before continuing. "And of course, she also comes in to care for the kids when I have to be on call for the hospital ER. Or to do stuff with us on the weekends when I need more than one adult on an excursion."

His sensual lips curved upward. "Not exactly a nine-to-five position."

"No, it's not." Claire paused to look Zach in the eye. Wanting him to understand why she was so forgiving about her nanny bailing on her unexpectedly this afternoon. "But Bette doesn't mind because it gives her more time to work on her art. But even more important than that, she has such an easygoing, unperturbable personality. The kids love her. She's been a godsend."

He flashed another thoughtful half smile. "So what are you going to do about tomorrow?"

Claire got out a baking sheet and lined it with parchment paper. "Call the preschool director this evening and see if the kids can do the before- and after-school programs as well as their regular day, until Bette gets back."

"Seems like your sitter isn't the only one who can be flexible." Zach gave her an admiring glance.

She understood the attraction. He was her type, too. Strong, kind, masculine. She reminded herself he was way too compelling a man to be spending time with. If she wanted to maintain her independence and stay single, and she did. Her heart panged in her chest. With effort, she met his probing gaze. Ignoring the chemistry flowing between them, she said matter-of-factly, "I had the feeling you wanted to talk to me about something when you came over...before we got sidetracked."

He nodded. "Yeah. I heard from Harriett Donnelly post appointment. She was happy that Sasha's EKG and heart rate and blood pressure were all normal today."

Claire sensed where this was going. "But she's still worried."

He shrugged in understanding, his gaze still skimming her appreciatively. "You know how it is when you work in the medical field. You know too much."

Hence, all that anxiety, Claire thought. Remembering how tense Harriett had been during her daughter's appointment. "Well, hopefully, it will turn out to be nothing much at all or something that can be easily fixed."

"That is the hope," Zach murmured, sharing the sentiment, as his phone chimed. He pulled his cell phone out of his pocket and frowned at the screen. "Sorry. I really need to read this."

He thumbed through one screen, then another, his expression getting darker with every second that passed. "Everything okay?" Claire couldn't help but ask.

Zach was normally an easygoing guy, so clearly something had happened to put him so on edge.

He huffed out an aggravated breath. "I just got an email from my landlord. I'm being evicted."

Chapter Three

"Evicted?" Claire echoed in disbelief. "From your office space, or...?" She couldn't imagine he was the kind of guy who didn't pay or was late on his rent.

Zach put the phone back in his pocket. He was still wearing the tie he had worn to work. It featured a pirouetting polar bear in a tutu, accompanied by a rock band of penguins. With a sigh, he undid the knot, and then the first two buttons on his shirt. Finally answering, "The converted garage where I live."

Claire took in the strong column of his throat, his impressively masculine jawline. Ignoring the tingling deep inside her, she lifted her chin. "I take it you didn't see this coming."

Another frown. "Nope."

"How much time do you have to move out?"

He flexed the muscles in his shoulders. They pressed against his shirt. "Thirty days, counting today." Restlessly, he began to pace. He ended up at the window, smiling briefly as he took in Lucky and the kids having a good time.

Intuiting how frustrating this was, Claire edged closer. "Did your landlord say why?"

Zach swung back to face her, inundating her with his brisk, masculine scent. "His mother-in-law is moving in with them, and she wants her own space. It makes sense to put her in the cottage." He shoved a hand through the thick, short layers of his dark brown hair. "So I get the boot." He paused to let his words sink in. "Family trumps tenants every time."

Resisting the urge to give him a comforting hug, she went back to making dinner for the kids. "How long have you lived there?"

"Five years."

Finished layering fish on the baking sheet, she slid it in the oven and set the timer. "You never wanted to buy a place?"

He shook his head. "Initially, my fiancée and I were just going to live there a year."

Realizing how little they knew about each other, and how much she wanted to remedy that, she blurted, "What happened?"

A mixture of grief and regret appeared on Zach's face. "Lisa died in a car crash a few weeks before our wedding. We had just started moving in, and I didn't want to find another place. Plus, you know, we'd signed a lease, although I'm sure my landlord would have let me out of it."

"I'm so sorry." She tried to envision what that had been like for him. Probably even more traumatic than when her ex had voluntarily left. Without any warning.

She slid the mac 'n' cheese in the microwave, but waited to cook it. Lounging back against the counter, she folded her arms in front of her. Wishing he didn't look so big and strong and undeniably sexy, standing next to her, she asked, "Is it a comfort to you, to live where you were going to start your married life?"

"I don't know." He tilted his head, gauging her reactions as carefully as she was measuring his. "Maybe initially. Maybe it made it harder. Like I said, we hadn't even begun to settle in, when Lisa died, so..." His voice trailed off. For a moment, he seemed lost in morose thought.

"And since?" She was being nosy, but she sensed he needed to vent.

He lifted a hand, palm up. "It was just easier to stay. To not worry about that aspect of my life. But instead concentrate on starting and building up my pediatric practice."

Claire understood the therapeutic value of work. Helping others. "You have apparently done a very good job of that."

Crinkles appeared at the corners of his smoky blue eyes. "I definitely love kids and practicing medicine."

She could see that. It was one of the things she admired most about him. "So what are you going to do? Rent again?" Figuring she better get a move on if she wanted the mac 'n' cheese to be ready at the same time as the fish, she began punching buttons on the microwave. She turned back to him with a smile. "Or buy this time?"

"Not sure." He met her gaze, his expression inscrutable. "But I probably better get on it, either way."

Zach stopped by his folks' house to tell them the news. "Well, that's an unexpected push in the right direction," his mom said.

If he had been looking for sympathy, he was apparently in the wrong place. Scowling, he sat down at the dining room table, where his parents were just finishing dinner. "Why do you say that?"

Mitzy McCabe handed him a plate of grilled chicken and vegetables. "You've been in a holding pattern since Lisa passed." She added a hunk of crusty bread. "Continuing to live in the quaint little place where you were going to set up married life hasn't helped you want to move on."

Zach groaned. Why couldn't people believe he had already had the love of his life? That the chance of him ever finding another was next to zero. "Mom. I finished my residency, took my boards, got my license and opened a medical practice. I think I've done all right in the last five years."

"Professionally. But in your *personal life*, you mostly spend time with women you are trying to help out in some way, and when that's over, so is the connection."

Zach knew she had a point. And so had Claire Lowell, the evening before. He did have a type these days.

What was it about a woman who had too much going on in her life that drew him like a moth to a flame? The fact that the damsel in distress seemed to need someone like him to come in and rescue her? Or that the chaos in the aforementioned lady's life kept him from ever wanting to get too close?

All he knew for sure was that every time he helped someone, it felt good.

Until it didn't.

And then it ended.

Aware his mother was waiting for him to answer, he finished swallowing, and said, "There's no point in furthering something that is built on need when the need ends."

"Are you looking for another Lisa?" Mitzy asked.

An all-too-familiar guilt rose up inside him. "No one is going to take her place, Mom."

"I know that," she said gently. "It doesn't mean you can't find someone or something completely different. And go on to have the wife and family of your own that you always wanted."

Zach would do that if he thought he could be what someone else wanted and needed. But he knew better than anyone how selfish and self-absorbed he could be. Especially when his mind was set on a goal.

Yeah, he had been working on being a better person. More giving and selfless, since Lisa passed. But that didn't mean he had what it took to be the kind of husband his dad had always been to his mom. Or the loving partner she had always been to Chase. His folks had something special that just seemed innate to both of them.

He wanted that, too.

And yet...

What if he did get intimately involved with a woman again? And then ultimately let her down, the way he had Lisa? Would he even be able to live with that failure a second time?

Chase cleared his throat, commanding the room with paternal calm. "Not that anyone has asked for my opinion," he began.

No one ever did when Mitzy was doing her social worker thing.

"But I don't think we have to try to find you a wife to jump-start your family right now, Zach."

Thanks, Dad. "Good to know."

"However, I do agree that maybe this eviction is a lucky turn of events, in that it is forcing you to get out of the rut you've been in with your living arrangements."

Zach appreciated the shift from matters of the heart, which he had no wish to discuss, to business, which he did. He buttered the hunk of bread. "You think I should buy?"

Chase leaned back in his chair, as Mitzy brought in a carafe of coffee and began filling mugs with rich, aromatic brew. "If only so you won't be evicted again."

Zach gave his father a droll look. "That's not the only reason you're pushing this, Dad." It wasn't just about him having a roof over his head.

"You're right. Financially, it's better to invest in and own a home than rent one. And you have plenty of money in your trust fund to manage that."

True, but a home signaled permanence. Especially in one's personal life. And Zach had been trying not to get too worked up about what his future held.

Selecting a home and purchasing it would force him to do that, even if he were the only person to ever reside there.

Finishing his dinner, he pushed the plate aside. Sipping his coffee, he said, "A month is not a lot of time to find a place and move in and all that."

Not surprisingly, his parents weren't buying that excuse.

"You have four siblings and the two of us, not to mention countless friends, to help you," Mitzy pointed out. "And if there is a gap in move-out and move-in dates, you could stay with us, in the interim."

Zach loved his folks. But moving in with them again, even temporarily, would feel like going backward.

"Purchasing a home would be a step in the right direction, a step toward your future," his dad added.

Zach knew that. The question was, did he want to take it?

Claire was just getting out of her SUV a little after twelve thirty the next day when she got a text.

The sender—Zach McCabe.

Why was she not surprised?

Her first year or so in Laramie, the two of them had had so little contact, she might have thought he was avoiding getting to know her. Just as she had sort of been avoiding running into him, whenever possible. Because she had known, from the first moment she had crossed paths with him, that he was way too charming and sexy, and she was far too attracted to him. The last thing she had needed, then and now, was another connection with a guy who, at the end of the day, simply wasn't interested in an enduring, permanent relationship.

She had been dumped once. After having very high hopes.

She did not need to be jilted again.

And Zach's reputation indicated he had one casual, or temporary, relationship after another.

Never anything long-lasting. Or even all that intimate.

Not since had had lost his fiancé.

So she had taken that information to heart, and managed to successfully avoid running into him. Figuring it was for the best. Except, now, every time she turned around…he seemed to find some way to command her attention.

Trying not to make too much of what was probably nothing, she inhaled a bolstering breath and read the message:

Do you have time to talk for a few minutes? Need your advice on something. I'll buy you lunch...

Claire texted back: No to lunch today. But happy to talk as long as it doesn't take long.

Bubbles appeared, signaling another message about to be sent. Where are you?

She shook her head, fighting back a smile. The Laramie Garden and Landscape Center.

Great! See you in a few.

The screen went dark.

Claire pocketed her phone. Squinting against the spring sunlight, she grabbed a flatbed shopping cart and moved on into the perennials.

There were so many to choose from! All so beautiful and colorful and fragrant. Claire had never been much of a flower person, but right now, she was in heaven. She picked up a dozen-container flat of starter peonies. Set it down. Then some azaleas...

Before she knew it, she saw Zach striding purposefully through the entrance to the outdoor area, hurrying to her side. Like her, he was dressed for a day of seeing patients, adorned in a pair of dove-gray slacks, dark gray shirt and a necktie with a raccoon in sunglasses. She slowly drank him in. His dark hair was rumpled, as if he had either been running his hands through it, or simply forgotten to brush it after his shower. Hard to tell. A half smile curving his sensual lips, he nodded at the flats of gorgeous perennials in front of him. "For your flower beds?"

As usual his low, sexy voice did a number on her insides. No wonder all the women at the hospital were crazy about him. Which was yet another reason why she needed to keep her emotional distance from him. "Zach." She took a step back, gazing up at him. "You didn't have to come all the way down here."

He made a comical face, subtly letting her know his day thus far had not been all sunshine and roses. "Let's just say…" His gaze drifted over her loose-fitting cotton sheath dress, bare legs and comfortable flats, before returning casually to her eyes, "there are days when I can take my lunch break in the hospital. Others," he winced again, "when I need to get out and breathe in some fresh air."

Claire laughed. He did smell a lot like hospital antiseptic. "Let me guess…"

"Yep." He ran a hand over his clean-shaven jaw. "Three kids with the stomach flu threw up in my office this morning. Janitorial is in there now, sanitizing before the afternoon appointments."

"Kids okay?"

"Oh, yeah. Nothing serious. But you know how it goes. You can't just tell the parents to keep the kids at home. When the fever is over 102 you've got to check to make sure nothing else is going on, too. Hence the in-office sick kid appointments."

Not all physicians could take events like that in stride.

The fact he could made her admire him even more.

Seeing someone was trying to get by them in the aisle, he stepped closer to her to clear the way. Briefly, their arms bumped. "So, what are you doing?" he asked, curious.

Enjoying the warmth of the breezy spring day almost as much as his presence, Claire informed him cheerfully. "I'm knocking two things off my to-do list with one lunchtime errand. I'm buying the kids and I a distraction—from Bette's unexpected absence—and taking care of the empty landscape beds in front of the house." She sighed, recalling the pressure being exerted upon her by her little ones to rectify that.

Another person with a full cart tried to pass, forcing them to move all the way out of the aisle and closer together yet again.

Aware she was way too cognizant of Zach's robust male presence, Claire finished, "The kids have not been happy we are the only ones on the street who do not have flowers in front of the house, now that it's spring."

"Keeping up with the Joneses already?" he teased, seeming to appreciate her dilemma.

"Actually, my sister. We lived with Gwen and her husband, Patrick, and their three kids, from the time the triplets were born until they were almost two and a half and I took the job here in Laramie."

"And Gwen and Patrick always had flowers?"

Claire wished for a bottle of water, aware her throat was feeling a little dry. "They had *everything.* My sister is a full-time homemaker who could put Martha Stewart to shame."

"Oooh. Tough competition."

Deciding bantering with him like this might not be such a good idea, she selected half a dozen impatiens and put them on the bed of her flat shopping cart. "It would be if I cared about stuff like that."

"You don't?"

Claire didn't know what it was about Zach that made it easy for her to confess, "Nope. I'm like my dad, in that sense, I guess."

Zach regarded her, a question in his eyes. Easily and intuitively picking up on all she wasn't saying. "You're not close?"

She steered back into the aisle, continuing to pick up plants as she moved forward. Deciding to add a few annuals in the mix. *Geraniums. Daisies. Petunias.*

With an indifferent shrug, Claire admitted one of the great disappointments of her life. "He was a college professor and an expert on ancient Egypt. That was always his first love. Up until he died a few years ago."

Zach lent a hand here and there, easily reaching things she couldn't quite get. "No room in his life for you?"

Claire headed for the amazingly beautiful Texas sage. "Not really, no."

"What about your mom?" Zach queried, making room for the bigger pots of sage.

"She was wonderful. Very loving and supportive." A wave of tenderness sifting though her, Claire reflected. "She made both me and my sister feel like there was nothing we couldn't do if we set our minds on it. Unfortunately, she was diagnosed with MS when I was a senior in high school."

When he noticed the cart getting hard for her to push, he took the handle and steered it forward. Making light work of what she had been struggling to do.

"Sorry to hear that."

Claire nodded. The depth of Zach's compassion helped her open up more than she usually would. *With anyone.* She drew a breath. Let herself meet the kindness in his gaze. "It was hard, watching her decline. Anyway, she eventually succumbed to the disease when Gwen and I were both in college. My dad couldn't handle either the illness or the loss, and as soon as my mom passed, he told us he needed a change and took a visiting professorship overseas."

Zach pushed the cart in the direction she was going, toward the edge of the store's fenced-in outdoor gardening area. "That's really rough," he said.

It had been. Claire swallowed around the sudden lump in her throat. "Anyway, Gwen married Patrick as soon as she graduated, that same year, and went on to have three amazing kids. I went on to med school and residency."

"Sounds like you both made the right choice."

"We did."

Claire glanced at her watch. She had twenty minutes to get back to the hospital for afternoon appointments, if she didn't want to be late. "If you wouldn't mind helping me," she consulted the list Gwen had sent her, "could you grab four bags of that potting soil—without getting it all over your clothes?"

She scanned the area. She would have gotten an employee to help her. Unfortunately, all seemed to be busy.

"No worries," Zach said, with a confident wink. "I know how to do things neatly." His muscles flexed as he did as she asked, as adept as he was strong.

Near the checkout, she picked up three sets of sturdy plastic tools, meant for kids. A real set for herself. And a shovel.

She headed for the shortest checkout line. Just as she approached, another opened up and she was waved over. "I'm going to want these delivered by this evening," she told the clerk.

And quickly hit a snag. "We can deliver," the young kid told her, "but not until Monday."

Claire blinked. *"Monday?"*

"It's a holiday weekend. We have half the staff off tomorrow, because it's Good Friday, and we're closed Sunday for Easter. Saturday will be a madhouse."

Claire watched as all her carefully made plans went up in smoke. "But I was told you had same-day delivery when I called yesterday."

The clerk nodded. "And that's true, during the week. Unfortunately, all the delivery slots we had available for today were taken earlier in the week. So Monday is the next available."

Claire looked at the big bags of dirt, and all the plants. "Well, I guess I'll put them in my SUV…" Although it would probably make quite a mess.

Which would probably cause her vehicle to need to be detailed.

"My pickup truck would probably be better," Zach told her, while the clerk rang the items up.

Claire thought about how hot the metal bed of a truck could probably get, when parked in an asphalt parking lot. She bit her lip. Appreciating Zach's gallant offer, but…"I'm not sure all this should sit in the full sun, out in the open like that."

Full of solutions as always, he said, "It wouldn't have to. You don't live very far from here. We could park my truck in your driveway, which is shaded by trees if I remember correctly—"

"You do."

He smiled. "—and you could give me a ride back to the hospital. Then after work, we'll go back to your place, and I'll unload my truck and put the stuff wherever you want it."

That was a lot of imposing for her to do. Claire didn't like leaning on people, or being in a situation where she seemed to be doing most of the taking, little of the giving.

He read her mind. "It's not a problem."

He really was a Sir Galahad.

"And I'd still like to talk—if you have time."

She *did* owe him. Giving him the time to ask her whatever he had wanted to ask her when he had tracked her down would even the playing field. "Okay. Sounds like we have a plan, and very few moments to spare. So…let's go."

Chapter Four

"Sounds like I didn't need to worry about you being all by your lonesome when you moved so far away," Gwen teased, her cheerful voice coming over the car speakerphone while Claire drove to the preschool to pick up the kids from aftercare.

Glad to have at least a few minutes to talk to her sister, Claire smiled. "It's just the way the McCabes are. They have a reputation for helping everyone who crosses their path." Especially Zach…

"Hmmm…" Gwen teased. "Sounds like this handsome doctor went above and beyond."

Claire flushed. "I never said he was handsome."

"*Is* he?"

Gosh, yes. With his big, strapping six-foot-four frame, chiseled masculine features, mesmerizing gray-blue eyes and dark brown hair, just the sight of him made her catch her breath. But sensing her big sis didn't need to hear that, she merely acknowledged, "He's all right. I guess…"

Gwen's knowing laugh filled the interior of Claire's SUV. "I'm going to go right to the hospital directory and look up his picture, you know."

It was all Claire could do not to groan. Fortunately, duty called, making further dissection of the handsome doctor in question, out of bounds. "I'm at the preschool pickup line. I have to go."

"Call me later. And let me know how the flower-planting goes with Doctor McCabe."

"He's not going to be part of that." Although she secretly wished he would be.

Gwen laughed again. "We'll see. Just remember. When a guy is interested, he never leaves one date without arranging for the next."

"We're *not* dating," Claire said in irritation, annoyed at how attractive that sounded to her, too. But her sister had already hung up.

The kids were as cranky as Claire expected when they got in the SUV. "I don't like extra-long days at school," Isabella huffed.

"I miss Bette." Oliver kicked his legs against the back of the passenger seat. "I like it better when she picks us up."

"When is she coming back?" Andrew whined.

"As soon as she can," Claire said.

Which, as far as her kids were concerned, was not going to be soon enough.

Happily, there was a distraction waiting for them when they pulled into the driveway at her house.

"What's Doctor Zach doing here?" Andrew demanded.

Claire had offered him a ride from the hospital, but he hadn't been able to leave when she needed to go, to pick up the kids from school, so he had told her he'd catch a ride when he was finished and be by later. She just hadn't known exactly when that would be.

"And why does he have so many flowers?" Oliver wanted to know.

Isabella gaped in admiration. "He must be *really* strong to lift those big bags!"

Yes, indeed, Claire thought. His back and shoulder muscles were flexing beneath his cotton shirt, as he lifted two at a time, and carried them over to the empty flower beds. He set them down gently, and then turned to face them, watching as Claire's kids hustled out of her SUV and headed his way.

"Hey there," Zach said in greeting, a warm smile creasing his handsome face.

The three-year-olds gathered around him, smiling exuberantly. "Where did you get all that stuff?" Andrew wanted to know.

"Is it a present for us?" Oliver's eyes widened.

"Like the cupcakes?" Isabella squealed.

"Yes, it is a present, from me, for all of us," Claire said quickly, before the triplets could embarrass her further. "Remember, I told you all that we were going to get our flowers planted this weekend? Well," she turned toward them expansively, "here they are!"

The children moved toward the array of blooms, still in the little black plastic pots. Isabella clapped. "They are pretty! So many different colors!"

Andrew nodded thoughtfully. "Just like the ones Aunt Gwen has."

Oliver asked, "Can we start now?"

Claire shook her head, hoping this didn't trigger a meltdown with her overtired kids. Especially with Zach there to witness. She wasn't sure why exactly, but she wanted him to think she was a good mother. Or at the very least, respect how hard she tried to be.

With a gentle look, she informed her kids, "No, it's going to take several hours and a lot of work, so we're going to have to wait until tomorrow morning. But that's okay, because it's a holiday and you don't have school and I don't have work. In the meantime, can you all get your backpacks out of the car and take them up on the porch for me?"

As her kids dashed off to do as asked, Claire turned back to Zach. With his tie off, the first couple of buttons on his shirt undone, his sleeves rolled up to just below his elbows, he was the epitome of masculine efficiency. Ignoring the shiver of awareness pooling inside her, she said, "Thank you for unloading the gardening stuff. But you didn't have to do this all by yourself. I would have helped."

Seeing that Andrew was struggling to get his backpack out of the SUV, he went over and untangled the strap from the edge of the rear floor mat. "It's okay. I didn't mind."

"Thanks." Andrew gave Zach a look of pure hero worship, then joined his siblings, who were already up on the porch, taking turns sitting in the wicker furniture.

Hearing Lucky bark on the other side of the front door, Claire gestured for Zach to follow her, and headed up the steps, too. "And we still need to talk about whatever you wanted to discuss, don't we?" She tossed the words over her shoulder.

He nodded. "If you wouldn't mind."

Zach knew there was a chance he was intruding. He also knew Bette wasn't here and Claire probably needed a little help. Not that she seemed to ever ask for it, for herself anyway.

He watched as she got out her keys and unlocked the front door. "Mommy, I'm hungry!" Oliver complained. And so were his brother and sister.

"Lunch was a long time ago!" Andrew said.

Isabella looked near tears. "So was afternoon snack!"

Tail wagging, Lucky came out to say hello, getting petted by everyone before going back inside the house. "Not to worry. Dinner is almost ready." Claire shooed everyone after their Newfie. "So let's all go inside and I'll have it plated up in no time."

Zach was wondering if he should offer to come back at a later time, when she turned to him with a dazzling smile. "Would you like to join us? We're having Asian."

He hadn't expected a dinner invitation. Yet he wanted to accept it, with an enthusiasm that surprised him. "Would love to."

"Great." Her attitude as casual as his, Claire led the way inside. While the kids raced ahead to let Lucky out back, she dropped her things on the foyer table and walked toward the rear of the house.

A perplexed frown curving her lips downward, she headed straight for the Crock-Pot sitting on the kitchen counter and lifted the lid. Then let out a gasp that quickly turned into a muffed groan of utter defeat. "Oh, no…"

Zach didn't think the contents could be burnt. They would have smelled scorched. Then again, he really didn't smell much at all. Which was strange, for a dish that had been slow-cooking while she was at work. "What is it?" he asked.

Claire checked the front electronic panel—where Zach now noted nothing was showing on the screen. And then behind it. The appliance was definitely plugged in. "I think I forgot to set the timer and push start. Damn it…"

Isabella corrected swiftly, "Don't say '*Damn it,*' Mommy!"

"Yeah," Oliver added, with just a hint of facetiousness, "it's not nice."

Claire's hand flew to her mouth. "I know. I'm sorry. I meant, *Oh my…*"

It was all Zach could do to stifle a laugh.

"Can we eat now?" Looking bored by all the talk about manners, Andrew climbed up onto a stool at the counter.

"Actually…" She looked down at the raw chunks of chicken and fruit and sauce that had been sitting at room temperature all day, with a mixture of misery and disgust. "What's in the Crock-Pot isn't good, kiddos. We're going to have to have something else."

Isabella, who had been near meltdown since arriving home, fisted her little hands. "I don't want something else! I want pineapple chicken!" New tears appeared in her eyes.

"I could run to the Chang's downtown," Zach offered.

Claire shook her head. She moved closer, lightly touching

his bicep. "They won't eat that," she said under her breath. "Too authentic."

Oblivious to the effect her brief touch'd had on him, she turned back to the kids. "How about pineapple pizza instead?"

Isabella's lower lip stopped quivering. "Can we make our own?"

"Yes. Just the way you all like it."

Claire turned the oven to 400 degrees. Then, reaching into the fridge, brought out two tubes of premade dough, mozzarella cheese, various toppings and tomato sauce. "You're still welcome to join us," she told him before slipping on a chef's apron over her work dress. "I just have to get these into the oven ASAP."

Zach went to the sink and washed his hands, after the kids and Claire all did the same. "What can I do to help?"

She brought three individual kid-sized pans out of the pantry. "Assist wherever needed."

It was obvious they had done this before.

Claire portioned the premade dough into rounds and flattened them on the metal baking discs, creating pinched edges to keep the ingredients on the pie.

Once that was done, she put a dollop of sauce on each pie and handed it to a child. They used a spoon to carefully spread it across the dough.

Cheese followed, then they added whatever ingredients they liked. Isabella preferred cheese and pineapple. Oliver liked pepperoni and pineapple and cheese. Andrew wanted ham, pineapple and cheese.

Afterwards, Claire slid the individual kid pizzas in the oven. "How long till it's done, Mommy?" Andrew asked.

"Ten minutes."

Oliver asked, "Can we go outside and play with Lucky and swing while we wait?"

"I think that's an excellent idea," she said with a grateful sigh.

The kids bolted out.

As soon as they were gone, Claire's shoulders slumped in fatigue. It was all he could do not to take her in his arms and pull her against him for a long, comforting hug. Only the thought of what that could very well lead to kept him in place, opposite her. "Very good crisis management," Zach praised. He would have expected her to be frazzled beyond belief about now.

Claire got a couple of cold sparkling waters out of the fridge, handed him one, and opened the other for herself. Lounging against the counter, she lifted the bottle to her lips and took a long thirsty drink. "I can't tell you how many times I've put dinner in the Crock-Pot in the morning, and then come in and made noodles, rice or instant potatoes as soon as I walked in the front door." Her eyes lit with self-directed fury. "*Never* have I forgotten to turn the Crock-Pot on!"

So she was just as much a perfectionist at heart as he was. He wondered how that translated when she made love. Not that he should be considering *that*…

He took a drink, forcing himself to cool down, too. Albeit in a different way. "You had a lot going on today. Especially with Bette not here." He recalled what her nanny had said as she left. "But she's supposed to be coming back to Laramie tonight, so—"

"Actually," Claire interrupted, suddenly looking even more frustrated, "I haven't told the kids yet, but she called me this afternoon, right after I got back to the office. She's not coming back tonight after all." She inhaled deeply, the movement lifting and then lowering her soft breasts. "The gallery is going to display one of her paintings, and they want her to be at the showing. So now, she's not going to be back until Sunday evening."

Not cool, Zach thought, wondering just how bad it was likely to get for Claire. "Are you on call this weekend?"

"No, thank goodness," she said with obvious relief. "You?"

Suddenly, he wished the opposite were true. "Yeah. Friday night."

"I'm guessing you volunteered…"

She was making him out to be some kind of hero: he wasn't. "Well, a lot of people had Easter plans with their kids, so I volunteered to step in."

Her gaze warmed appreciatively. "That was nice of you."

More of a way to avoid being lonely, Zach thought, or think about what was missing in his life, in terms of love and a family of his own.

Claire straightened. "Okay, I know I asked you to dinner…"

Not about to let her back out now, he said, "And I'm holding you to it."

"That's not what I meant!" Claire went to the window and checked on the kids, then swung back to face him. "I just wanted to make sure you're okay with homemade pizza too. Cause otherwise I could make burgers or something like that for us just as quickly."

Zach countered with a grin. "And miss the pineapple pizza?"

"Well, that's the thing. I don't have any more small round pans, so we'll have to split the rest of the dough on a rectangular sheet pan. And then top it strategically. Your half on one side, mine on the other."

Wow, this family came with a lot of negotiation. Not that he minded. It was kind of nice, the way she tried to take everyone's wishes into account, and make them happy.

He joined her at the island. "Works for me. And I'll just have whatever you want on yours on mine to make it simple."

"Uh-uh, mister. You're the guest here. I'll at least give you first dibs."

She was serious.

"So, I'll ask again." Her green eyes sparkled. "What do you want on yours?"

Chemistry sizzled between them. He pushed aside yet another impulse to take her in his arms and kiss her. Telling himself she was exactly the kind of sexy, complicated woman he should stay away from, at least on an emotional level, he retorted, "What you got?"

She gestured at the counter. "Everything that is already out." Which was shredded mozzarella, sauce, pepperoni, ham and pineapple. "There is also already prepped Italian sausage and salami in the freezer. Plus probably whatever other topping you want except anchovies. My fridge and pantry are pretty well stocked with items for any Plan B."

He imagined that was so. Claire wasn't the kind of woman who left anything to chance. He thought about what would go with what the kids had already selected. "Green pepper? Onion?"

Claire went to the fridge. "Yes, to both." She returned, veggies in hand.

He sprinkled cornmeal and began to spread the dough onto the sheet pan she handed him. "You good with Italian sausage, pepperoni and ham on the pie—in addition to everything else we've got here?"

"Yeah. And thanks." She went to the freezer for the container of crumbled Italian sausage. "For intuiting how it would be seen by the kids if you chose just ham or just pepperoni." She brought a mandoline out of a top cabinet and made short work of slicing the veggies.

Meanwhile, he spread sauce and sprinkled cheese onto the dough. "Like I was playing favorites?"

"Uh-huh." She moved in beside him, as they added meat to the rectangular-shaped pie. "This way it just looks like an adult specialty pizza."

"I can go for that."

The oven timer dinged. While Claire brought out the three pies and set them to cool enough to be cut up and eaten, he added the final ingredients to their pizza.

The kids burst back in through the rear door.

"Ours is ready!" Oliver shouted happily.

"Okay kiddoes, wash up…" Claire said.

And once again, Zach lost the chance to talk to her.

"I can't believe you stayed through all that," Claire said two hours later. Not really surprised her kids had fallen asleep almost the moment their heads hit their pillows.

What had been amazing was the way Zach had helped out with everything that needed to get done. And, even more importantly, really seemed to enjoy doing it.

Together, they finished the dishes and wiped down the kitchen counters.

Smiling affably, he admitted, "It was fun. I needed to learn how to build the tallest, most rickety structure imaginable, and then knock it down with one loud rebel yell and a kamikaze kick. And dinner was delicious, by the way."

"Thank you. Maybe next time you're over, you can have the real pineapple chicken," she said before she could stop herself.

The way his blue eyes gleamed indicated he looked forward to another invitation to dinner. Wondering what had gotten into her, Claire babbled on, "Which by the way, is actually sweet and sour chicken without the onion and green pepper."

"Ah." He seemed impressed by her cleverness. "They *think* they don't like Asian."

"Let's just say they can be very suspicious and finicky when it comes to food."

"Like most three-and-a-half-year-olds—if what I hear from the parents of my patients is any indication."

Claire grabbed a pair of scissors and a black permanent marker from the kitchen drawer. Aware the kitchen was suddenly feeling way too intimate, and that she owed him something for all his effort, she drew a breath. "Want a beer?"

"If you've got one, sure."

Aware her heart was beating way too fast, she opened the fridge and handed him one.

His eyes darkened with an indecipherable emotion. "You're not having one?"

"Um, no." Her defenses were lowered enough as it was. Which made it imperative she find something else to do to occupy herself. "I still need to prep for tomorrow morning's planting extravaganza."

Grabbing a small trash sack, she headed out the front door, leaving him to follow at will. The evening was still pleasantly warm, the sun disappearing behind the horizon, shades of pink and gray streaking the blue sky.

She placed the marker and scissors on the side table, gathered up the three kiddie gardening kits she'd bought earlier, and sat in one of the cushioned wicker chairs. He took the seat on the other side of the white porch table.

She swiveled toward him. "So what did you want to talk to me about?" she asked.

Once again, he surprised her. "My immediate future," he said.

Chapter Five

"I decided I want to buy a house," Zach said. Something flickered in his expression, then disappeared. "I don't have a lot of time. And since you recently went through the process yourself, last year, I hoped you could advise me on how to get it done quickly and efficiently. Because there is no doubt you picked a great place to live."

Claire cut the tags off the kiddie tools, and worked them out of the packaging. "I do like my house. But I'm hardly the expert on real estate in Laramie County."

His gaze narrowed. "And yet you managed to find yourself and your kids a great place to live nevertheless."

As always, his ultramasculine presence made her acutely aware of him. "I was just lucky enough to find a Realtor who understood my needs and found me a place fast."

He sipped his beer, relaxing in his chair. "Who did you choose?"

Claire waved at her neighbors, across the street, setting off on their evening walk with their two Goldendoodles. "Mary Lou Andrews of Premiere Realty."

He leaned toward her curiously. "Why her?"

Claire continued working the tools out of the packaging, glad she had something to do other than look at Zach's handsome profile. "Mary Lou was the top salesperson for Laramie County the last couple of years. She was a working mom and a professional woman with as many demands on her time as I had on mine so she understood the concept of time crunch and multitasking."

He flashed her a sexy, sidelong look that turned her insides to mush. "How long did you look?"

She took a deep breath. "I saw three properties on one day. And made an offer on this place that same afternoon."

"Wow."

Wondering why she felt such a flood of overwhelming attraction and desire whenever she was around him, when she had *never* reacted like that to any man before, Claire shrugged. And swallowed around the knot of emotion in her throat. "It was late January. I needed to be in the home before the end of February to start my new job. The spring and summer boom hadn't started yet, so there wasn't a lot available that met my requirements."

"Which were...?"

As their eyes met, she felt warmed through and through.

"Four bedrooms. Two and a half baths. Two thousand square feet or so, and a backyard that could hold a playset and be fenced in. Everything else was negotiable."

"Did you have to do any updating when you moved in?"

"Oh yeah." With effort, she babbled on. "The entire interior and kitchen cabinets had to be painted a neutral color, the kitchen needed all new appliances. A swing set put up."

"So..." Claire wrote the names of all three kids on the tools in big bold letters, so they would know what belonged to whom. "What do you want in a place?"

He squinted. "Honestly? I'm not sure."

That she could believe. Particularly if he had never even considered taking the leap of faith purchasing a home required, until now. "Mary Lou should be able to help you figure it out. If you choose her, that is."

"Oh, I'm going to ask her to help me." The husky timbre

of his voice sent a thrill up and down her spine. What was it about this man that made her so cognizant of his presence? All she knew for sure was that it was hard to concentrate with him around!

"You seem awfully sure." Finished with her task, Claire stood, hoping he wasn't aware of the effect he had on her. But he looked so handsome in the fading light, it was all she could do not to move closer.

Zach stood, too. "What can I say?" He took a step toward her. "When you know, you know."

Only suddenly, he wasn't talking about Realtors or purchasing property. But something more personal and intense.

Her heart skittered in her chest. She stayed where she was, gazing up at him. The next thing she knew his hands were coming up to frame her face, his head was lowering, her lips parted, ever so slightly. Their breaths mingled, and then his mouth was on hers. Kissing her ever so tenderly. Instinctively, she found herself rising on tiptoe, wreathing her arms about his shoulders, kissing him back.

Again and again.

Until she tingled all over and lost her train of thought. Until all she could feel was the sweet, hot, impossible yearning welling up inside her. Making her want. Making her *need*.

Zach hadn't come over here intending to hit on her, or kiss her. But when she had looked at him like that, with the same yearning he felt, the reserve that he'd erected around himself the past five years faded. Replaced by a need to explore the red-hot chemistry between them.

Desire roaring through him, he flattened a hand across her waist and brought her closer. Until the length of her body was against the length of his.

The world narrowed to just the two of them. Feeling the softness of her surrender, he returned her kiss with every ounce of pent-up passion that he had. Letting the kiss deepen, all the while savoring the sweet and womanly taste of her. Her warmth and tenderness.

He could have stayed there all night, just holding her and kissing her. Until she stopped suddenly, a helpless sound escaping her throat. With a deep inhalation of breath, she pushed him away. "I'm sorry. I can't do this. Not again."

"So that's how it ended?" Gwen asked a short time later, when Claire called her on the phone. "You just kind of pushed him away and ran inside the house, and left him to leave on his own? Without another word?"

Needing her sister's input, Claire curled up on the sofa, an afghan drawn across her lap, a cup of hot Sleepytime tea by her side. "Pretty much."

"How did he react?"

The heat of humiliation burned her face. Glad her sister wasn't there to witness it, Claire said, "I have no idea. I didn't look back to find out."

"Hm."

She straightened in indignation. "What do you mean, *hm*?"

"Unless I missed something... Isn't he the first guy you've kissed since you and Sebastian broke up?"

Claire rubbed at the knee of her pajamas. "Yes."

Ever the romantic, her sister chuckled. "Was it good?"

"Gwen, come on..."

"Claire, *you* come on! Tell me how it was!"

"Fine." She huffed out a breath. "It was good. Really good." *Too good for comfort, as a matter of fact.*

"Well, then I don't see the problem."

Claire forced herself to take a sip of tea. "I like him. I think he'd be a great friend."

"But you don't want anything more?"

"I...no, I don't." Even as the words were out of her mouth, Claire knew that wasn't quite true.

She could see herself with a man like Zach.

And that scared her.

Because if she went down that path, she also opened herself up to the possibility of being hurt again....

She went back to rubbing at the knee of her pajamas. "I have so much on my plate right now..."

"Is Bette back yet?"

Claire sighed. "Not until Sunday evening."

"She's gone *all weekend*?" Gwen sounded aghast.

"Yes."

There was a pause on the other end of the connection. "Do you want to put the kids in the car and come here for the holiday?" Gwen asked kindly. "Patrick's parents are coming in from Arkansas to spend Easter with us, but we can make it work..."

Claire knew that was true. Patrick's parents were wonderful people. She also knew that she had created enough havoc in her sister and brother-in-law's life, when she had been living with them. "I think we need to be here, to have our first Easter weekend in Laramie." The previous year, they had gone back to Dallas. "One that they will hopefully remember anyway. You know how important the holidays are for the kids."

"For us all. But if you change your mind, you-all are welcome here. Just remember that."

Sisterly love flowed between them. "I will," Claire promised.

"And one more thing. The reason I wanted to talk to you earlier today..."

This sounded suddenly ominous. Claire stiffened. "I thought you were just checking in."

"I was," Gwen said slowly, "but there was also something else. I didn't want to get into it while you were picking up the kids from school."

Panic ensued. "Everything is okay with you and Patrick

and the kids, isn't it?" Their marriage had hit a brief, rocky patch before Claire had moved out on her own.

"Absolutely. Everything is wonderful between us. Promise!"

"Then...?"

"I had a phone call from Sebastian."

"My ex?"

"The one and only Dr. Sebastian Miller. He said he's been trying to contact you via email, but the messages keep bouncing back."

That was not surprising. "My old email was shut down when I left the job in Dallas." There had never been any reason to give him her new one.

"Well, he wants to talk to you."

A shiver of unease went down Claire's spine. "What about?"

"He wouldn't say."

She swallowed. "You don't think he suddenly wants to be part of the triplets' lives, do you?" She couldn't think of a worse move.

"It's possible." There was a long pause. "He is their biological father, after all."

Fury mixed with fear. "I don't want them hurt, Gwen."

"I know," her sister countered gently, practical as always. "But I think you still have to listen to whatever it is he has to say."

The next day, as Zach and his brother were getting ready for a run, Gabe asked, "Why are we going this way?"

Zach stretched. "Thought we'd change it up."

Gabe snorted. "Wouldn't have anything to do with that pretty cardiologist, would it?"

Damn. Was he that obvious? Maybe, Zach acknowledged silently, it had something to do with that smoking hot kiss he and Claire had shared the previous evening, before she had pushed him away. And bolted. Not about to discuss that with anyone except Claire, however, Zach turned his attention to the street and began to run at their usual warm-up pace. "Don't know what you're talking about."

Still grinning, his brother fell into step beside him. "Well, you should because everyone else in town likely does. My paralegal's cousin works at the garden center. She said you were there with Claire Lowell, at noon yesterday, doing your Sir Galahad act."

"I wish people would stop saying that."

Gabe laughed harder. "That you were with Claire?"

"That I'm trying to be a knight in shining armor," Zach muttered, picking up speed.

Gabe raced to catch up. "So you admit you're into her."

Was that what it was? A couple of days ago he would have said no, but after that kiss last night… He shrugged, pretending an indifference he couldn't begin to feel. "I'm just trying to give her a helping hand."

Gabe began to slow. He reached out and caught his brother's arm. "Well, if the chaos in the yard up ahead is any indication," he said drolly, "the pretty doc needs your assistance. Now, more than ever."

Zach looked ahead. His brother was right. There *was* chaos in Claire's front yard. More than the first night he had arrived at her home.

Happy about the excuse to see her, and learn if there was going to be any fallout from his move the night before, he quickened his pace. As did Gabe. "Let's see if we can help."

Oblivious to their approach, Claire continued to try and use an adult-sized shovel on the flower bed in front of the house. It was clear she didn't have either the upper body strength or the weight to push the blade through the rock-hard dirt. But she sure looked cute trying, Zach thought, as they stopped short of her.

"Doctor Zach!" Oliver said. "What are you doing here?"

"Did you come to help?" Andrew hoped out loud.

Isabella tossed her kiddie spade down in frustration. Then propped her hands on her hips just like he'd seen Claire do on many occasions. "Cause we can't do this. *At all!* Mommy, either!"

That was obvious, Zach thought wryly, as their Newfoundland got up from his place in the grass and walked toward him. Once there, Lucky leaned against Zach, and gazed up at him adoringly as he settled in for a pat on the head. With a smile, Zach indulged the pet.

"Sure, we can help," Zach told the kids. If Claire agreed, that was. Right now, the stubbornly wary look on her face seemed to indicate otherwise…

"Kids…" Claire warned with a chastising shake of her head.

The triplets ignored her the way they always did when they had other plans.

"It's okay, Mommy," Isabella soothed. "The big men want to help."

He actually did, Zach realized.

As usual, his generous quadruplet brother was on board, too.

"Who are you?" Oliver asked, looking at Gabe.

"This is my brother, Gabe," Zach explained.

Claire's cheeks were bright pink. She tilted her head to one side, regarding Gabe intently. "The family law and business transaction lawyer?"

"Yep. That would be me. Nice to meet you," he said, shaking her hand, and smiling as Zach introduced the kids, too, one by one.

"So. What's going on?" Zach asked. It didn't look like they had made much progress, but all three kids were covered with a fine dusting of dirt. Their mom also had smudges on the knees of her jeans. The flats of flowers had all been removed from the planting beds, and were scattered across the grass on the other side of the brick edging.

"I thought we were going to have time to get this done before the kids go to their playdates this afternoon."

"I'm going to play with my friend Alice," Isabella informed him.

"And me and Andrew are going to play with our friend Bart," Oliver said.

"What time?" Zach asked.

Claire sighed. "I drop them off at noon and pick them up around four thirty. So at the rate we're going…"

They weren't going to get anything done before the kids had to leave, Zach thought.

Isabella complained, "Our shovel doesn't work. Our spades, either…" Her lower lip went out into a petulant pout. "Mommy's not strong enough."

"But you've got muscles, because you are guys," Oliver said, as direct as usual.

"So maybe *you* can dig." Andrew regarded them both.

Claire held up a hand, looking reluctant to impose. "Kids, I don't think that's going to work, either. The soil in the planting beds is way too compacted." Abruptly she looked as miserable and frustrated as her triplets. She shook her head, admitting, "Which is something I obviously should have thought about before we got started."

Andrew studied the problem with a wisdom that seemed beyond his three and a half years. Reporting, "Mommy was going to wet the dirt with the hose… to see if that would work…but then she said it would be way too messy."

"Probably right about that," Zach said solemnly.

He and Gabe exchanged looks. They were of the same mindset. Zach turned back to Claire. "Got another adult shovel or gardening rake?"

"There is a complete set in the garage, hanging on the wall. The previous owner left them."

"I'll get 'em." Gabe strode off.

Claire was still blushing. He sensed she was embarrassed to have been caught looking less than efficient. Although he found her adorable, looking all mussed and overheated. She ran a self-conscious hand through her silky black curls. "Don't you have to finish your run?"

"We'll get there," Zach promised.

Gabe returned. He set down the spade and the rake, and handed Zach the other shovel—which was obviously too big and heavy for Claire to use.

Figuring they could knock this out in no time, Zach stepped to one side of the front steps. "You take that side of the walk, and I'll take this one," he told his brother.

Ready for the challenge, Gabe laughed. "Ready...set...go!"

They each stepped onto their shovel, the packed dirt no match for their weight and upper body strength.

"Wow," Andrew breathed, as they readied the flower beds in short order.

"You're good at this!" Oliver agreed, totally impressed.

Zach turned back to Claire. Knowing she and the kids were still out of their league if the kids had a playdate to go to. "Want us to put out the planting soil, too?"

She bit her lip. "Would you mind?"

"Not at all," Gabe said.

They ripped open the sacks and poured. Claire showed the kids how to take the plants she worked out of the plastic containers and arrange them in the furrows Zach and Gabe had created.

"This is so pretty, Mommy!" Isabella said, when all were laid out, in a symphony of shape and color. Zach and Gabe followed along, with spade and rake, flattening out the furrows of dirt. Then Claire demonstrated to the triplets how to gently pat the soil around the plants, before bringing out the hose with a watering attachment so the little ones could each take a turn giving their thirsty new plants a drink. Which was, as it turned out, about the time the kids' attention span ran out.

"Mommy, can we have some Popsicles in the backyard?" Oliver asked.

"Sounds like a very good idea." Claire turned to Zach, gratitude shimmering in her eyes, along with something indecipherable. Like she suddenly wanted more from both him and Gabe. Although he couldn't imagine what that was.

"What do you think, fellas?" she asked after several palpable moments had passed. "You-all want to join us?"

Chapter Six

Claire watched as Zach and Gabe exchanged looks, clearly as of one mind about this, as they had been about everything else.

"Sure," Zach said with a shrug, speaking for both of them.

Wondering if she was making a mistake, bringing them into her dilemma, but knowing because of the gravity of the situation that she had little choice, Claire pushed down her nervousness and smiled. "Meet you out back then."

Seemingly oblivious to her worry, the guys headed off with Lucky and the kids, going through the wooden gate to the backyard. She went inside to get the box of treats from the freezer and a couple of big bottles of chilled water for the guys. "Thought you might be thirsty since we caught you in the middle of your run," she said as she handed them over.

Gabe grinned appreciatively. "Good call."

The kids all chose pineapple Popsicles. Zach took a mandarin orange, and Gabe a mango-flavored one.

Enjoying their treats, her children wandered over to the playset and took seats on the swings. Lucky followed.

"Aren't you having one?" Zach asked.

"Um…no."

He studied her. "Everything okay?"

His husky question sent a thrill down her spine.

Her cheeks hot with embarrassment, she pulled up a lawn chair, kitty-corner from where they were sitting. Then, knotting her hands in front of her, she drew a bolstering breath and looked both brothers in the eye. "Well, actually, I've got a problem. And I need some advice." Briefly, she told them about her ex suddenly wanting to get in touch with her, after four years of radio silence.

Zach's gaze turned briefly to the triplets, who were still playing on the swing set at the other end of the backyard, well out of earshot. He seemed as protective as she felt. "Do you think it's about the kids?" Zach asked.

Feeling a little unsteady, she replied softly, "I don't know what else it could be. Except, Sebastian's never wanted anything to do with the triplets."

"Nothing?" Zach seemed simultaneously shocked and pissed off about that.

Which had pretty much been how Claire had felt at the time. With difficulty, she related how distant and dismissive her ex had been. "When I found out I was pregnant, a few months after he left, I called him. Sebastian told me to do whatever I wanted. But kids weren't and never had been his thing and he didn't want to be involved. He wished me good luck. Whatever I decided." She huffed out a breath as the painful memories washed over her. "I asked him if he wanted to see the kids, or be at all involved, and he said no. He was staying on in his medical research job in Antarctica and had no plans to come back to Texas, ever. So, that being the case, I never put his name on the birth certificate. Or asked him for child support."

"And you weren't legally married at the time of the triplets' birth," Gabe ascertained, abruptly in attorney mode.

"Nope. Never engaged or married. We never even lived together," Claire confirmed. Maybe if they had, she would have known Sebastian better and wouldn't have been so shocked by his cold behavior. Instead, all they had ever talked about was their medical school classes and labs, problematic diagnoses and the development of new medications.

Zach held her glance, letting it linger. A thoughtful silence fell between them. Even though he was letting his brother take the lead in the impromptu conversation, she could see the depth of his concern for her and the kids, and somehow that made her feel safer.

Zach made her feel safer.

Something else she wasn't used to feeling.

She swallowed, looking at both men once again. "What do you suggest I should do?"

"Depends." Gabe frowned. "Do you think Sebastian might have had a change of heart and is going to go after custody?"

Zach's eyes glittered with thinly veiled fury, while Claire's insides trembled with nerves. She knit her hands together even more tightly. "I don't know what else it could be."

"Well, then, to be on the safe side, you probably need to get some family law representation," Gabe said solemnly. "Then set up a meeting with Sebastian and have your lawyer present, to document everything, and protect your interests."

"Could you do that for me?" Claire asked hopefully.

He nodded. "Of course. Send your contact information to my office, and I'll have my paralegal work with you to set something up for early next week."

"Thank you," Claire said, relief pouring through her. With a plan of action set, Zach looked a little more relaxed, too.

Gabe's phone buzzed and he checked the screen. "A client. I need to take it. Okay if I step inside for a moment?"

"Sure. Go ahead," Claire said.

"Thanks."

An awkward silence stretched between Claire and Zach as Gabe disappeared inside the house, phone pressed to his ear. "I'm sorry. I kind of feel like I took advantage of you and your brother twice this morning," she murmured.

Zach didn't answer at first. Instead, he turned and waved

at the kids, who were gesturing wildly toward him from their perch on the swings.

Finally, he returned his attention back to Claire, his tall frame radiating barely leashed energy. "First, I didn't mind helping you and the kids get those flowers planted. And neither did Gabe. Not for an instant." His sexy grin widened, laying bare the truth to that.

His eyes turning an even smokier blue, he continued softly, "And second, if you're scared of what your ex might be up to, I want to be there for you. The way any friend would," he added.

Was that what they were now? *Friends?* Instead of just work colleagues?

Claire liked the idea of that. Even as she realized in her nervousness, she might have given the wrong impression. She rubbed at a smudge of dirt on her knee. "It's not so much that I'm scared of Sebastian, and what he might do…"

"Then?"

She slanted her glance to the playset, where the kids were still horsing around and giggling merrily. Relieved that they were lost in their own whimsical world and had no clue what she was potentially facing, she picked up a piece of Popsicle wrapper that had fallen on the ground and placed it in the small waste container she had brought outside with her. "I guess I'm afraid I might make *another* mistake where Sebastian and the kids are concerned."

Zach edged closer, his voice dropping a notch. "You regret not holding him responsible when the triplets were born?"

Realizing her fingers were now a little sticky, Claire removed the small bottle of hand sanitizer she had tucked in her pocket and squirted some on her palm. "If I had, it would certainly make it easier now. Because then everything would already be legally settled." Aware of his eyes upon her, she rubbed in the sanitizer until the residual stickiness disappeared. "With visitation…or not. As well as child support, legal rights and so forth."

Zach held out his hand. She offered up the small patio waste can for his trash, then gave him some cleanser, too. Holding her gaze, he worked the antiseptic smelling lotion into his fingers. "You think you'd have trouble sharing?"

Hitching in a breath, she tried not to think about how dexterous his big hands were. Or how sensual they'd feel on her body…

No doubt he made love as well as he did everything else. Pushing the ardent thoughts away, she returned her attention to the conversation at hand. "More like… I worry I'd accept Sebastian's desire to be a daddy at face value and welcome him into the kids' lives. Only to have them really devastated if he changed his mind about being a parent. Again."

He sat back in his chair, his broad shoulders flexing against the clinging fabric of his athletic shirt. "What do the kids think about their dad now?"

"Um." Claire sighed and shut the lid on the plastic bottle with a snap. *Now it was really time to feel guilty.* "They don't know they have one."

Zach's handsome brow furrowed. "Come again."

Reminded he was a pediatrician and might have strong feelings on this matter, Claire shrugged. "I didn't want them to grow up thinking they'd been rejected." The way she and her sister had been after her mom passed. "So, when they were old enough to start asking why they didn't have a daddy, I said there were some families with just a mom, and some with just a dad. And some with a mom *and* a dad. And some with two moms and two dads. And we had the kind of family where there was just a mom."

Zach smiled, understanding in his McCabe blue eyes. "That's a good way to put it."

"For now, yes," Claire agreed. "It simplifies things." Then

she bit her lip as her anxiety rose. "But eventually, they will know there had to be a male involved in their conception, and that he chose not to stick around, at least for the first three and a half years of their lives."

Leaning toward her, he reached out and covered her hand with his. "And that's probably going to hurt."

"Eventually, it will." Claire sank into the warmth of his touch. Appreciating his understanding. Holy moly, could the guy *get* any dreamier? Too bad she wasn't looking for anything long- or even short-term. Wary of the kids seeing, and making something of this that it definitely wasn't, she moved her hand away. Swallowing around the parched feeling in her throat, she continued, "When the abandonment sinks in. And whatever sugarcoating that I do wears off."

He nodded, seeming to get she'd been doing the best she could under less than ideal circumstances.

Claire paused to wet her lips. "I was just hoping that when that happened, the kids would be a lot older," she finally confessed. Then forced herself to predict, "Plus, they'll probably be angry...whenever they do find out...that they had a daddy all along. And I just kept that information from them."

Zach tilted his head, considering. "Then maybe it's better that whatever happens with your ex, the truth about their paternity comes out before they get too much older."

"Maybe. Although I still think it would be better to wait until they can understand the science of it." *Or better yet, already had a daddy figure in their life, absorbing and returning all their boundless love. Someone who was strong and dependable. Kind-hearted and easygoing. Like the man sitting next to her...*

Of course that man would need to love her, too, Claire thought on a beleaguered sigh.

Waiting for her to continue, Zach looked into her eyes. Claire bit her lip. "I just wish..."

"What?"

She could tell by the way he was looking at her, he wanted to take her in his arms. The hell of it was, she wanted that, too. His gaze still locked on hers, he waited for her to finish.

Figuring as long as they were talking this intimately, she may as well finish honestly, Claire confessed, in a low voice laced with regret, "I wish that I hadn't done what I always do, when I let my heart lead the way. Which is to see what I want to see in someone, instead of who or what that person really is."

And just like that, a tiny wall went up between them.

He studied her closely. "Is that how you got involved with Sebastian?"

If Zach can't understand I have and will continue to make some mistakes, there's really no point in us getting closer, Claire told herself. *Because the last thing I want is to be judged.* She stood, and grabbing the broom she kept by the back steps, began sweeping a few errant leaves to the edge of the patio. "Sebastian was—is—truly brilliant in terms of medical science, but sometimes short on social skills." Claire could see Zach still didn't understand. "We were great study partners in medical school. Eventually that led to a more romantic connection, too."

He nodded. Seeming to think that at least made perfect sense.

Claire explained further. "I thought Sebastian never said he loved me because it wasn't in his lexicon." The heat of embarrassment spread across her face, and she sat down beside Zach once again. So close they were practically touching. "But instead it was because he *didn't* love me. And even worse," she added miserably, "I only loved who I *thought* he was, not who he actually was."

"A family man?"

With a shake of her head, she corrected, "The kind of guy who would always be there for me, come what may." The kind of guy who would never abandon her. "Anyway, I never want to make that kind of mistake again."

This time, Zach took both her hands in both of his. Attraction sizzled. "For the record," he told her gruffly, looking very much like he wanted to shift her over onto his lap and kiss her again, "Sebastian was a damn fool. Any man would be incredibly lucky to have you in his life."

He meant it.

She felt it.

And her kids were just yards away. Within plain view.

Knowing she couldn't bring them into this, any more than she could hurt them with their biological daddy's rejection, she moved away again and released a quavering breath.

Gabe chose that moment to rejoin them again. "Sorry about that," he said. "A bit of a work emergency." He looked at his brother. "I'm going to have to go."

"I'll go with you," Zach said, standing, too.

Claire tried to feel relieved. That they wouldn't end up rushing into something crazy, like kissing again. After all, she couldn't afford to give in to her impulses, especially with the kids around to witness.

Zach turned back to her. "Is there anything else you need?" he asked.

Besides moral support and plenty of it? Claire thought, forcing herself to be reasonable. Feeling like she had imposed enough on the charming McCabe brothers for one day, she shook her head. "No. Thank you."

Isabella, Oliver and Andrew ran toward them. They placed their sticky Popsicle sticks in Claire's palm. "Is it time to get ready to go yet, Mommy?" Isabella asked.

Claire checked her watch, realizing it was nearly eleven. And the kids were going to need to take turns in the shower, rinsing off the flower bed dirt before they left. "Yes, it is." She asked the triplets to thank Gabe and Zach for their help.

Then the two men took off shortly thereafter, to finish their run. And, her mind still awhirl with the unheralded feelings that were threatening to upend her life, she herded the children inside to get ready for their playdates.

An hour later, Claire was kid-free for the rest of the afternoon. Her first order of business? Identical thank-you gifts for Gabe and Zach.

She called a mutual friend at the hospital to get their addresses, then went to the best barbeque restaurant in town to purchase two gift certificates. Added some local craft beer in the insulated gift bags, along with thank-you cards. And then went to drop off the presents.

Gabe lived in a shotgun house close to historic downtown Laramie. She left the gift by his front door, then headed over to the converted garage apartment where Zach lived. She had just set his gift bag down when the door swung open, and she came face-to-face with her sexy colleague.

Barefoot, clad in shorts and another T-shirt, he looked like he had just gotten out of the shower. "Whoops," she said, straightening slowly. "I didn't mean to disturb you."

"And yet…" He grinned. "So what is all this?"

"A thank-you for your help today."

He peeked inside the insulated bag. "A gift card for barbecue. And beer." The corners of his lips curved upward. "Nice."

Shyly, she handed over a book and a stack of printed articles. "I also brought you some materials that helped me when I was making that first home purchase. It talks about all the things you need to consider before putting in an offer."

The familiarity and ease between them deepened. "Thanks," he said, his strong masculine presence like a port in the storm.

Warmth flowed upward into her face as she prepared to bid him adieu. "You're welcome."

"Want to come in?"

Now, that was a dangerous idea, she told herself, even as she felt an even stronger urge to explore and strengthen their connection. "I don't want to impose..."

"First—you're not. If you hadn't guessed by now, I'm always happy to see you. Second. Aren't you curious to see what my place looks like?"

Actually, she was.

She paused on the threshold, tempted to go in despite all the warning bells clanging inside of her. "Okay, but just for a minute. I know you're on call tonight, and you probably want to rest or something."

"Or something..." He winked, ushering her inside. Claire looked around while he put the six-pack of bottles in the fridge, and the gift card and stack of books on the kitchen counter.

It looked like it had once been a three-car garage, and was now basically two rooms and a bath. The first held a kitchenette and a living area with a long leather sofa big enough to nap on, a matching club chair and ottoman perfect for reading. Scanning the space, she noticed the bedroom held a king-sized bed, and a narrow closet that ran the length of the room. The bath sported a shower, no tub. Area rugs covered a painted concrete floor. Not surprisingly, it was a very solitary kind of place, for a solitary kind of man. There was no art on the walls, or decorative pieces of any kind. Books, however, were everywhere. Stacked against the wall, by the chair, the sofa, the bed. "Read much?"

"When I need to relax, or get out of my own world."

She turned her head sideways, to scan some of the titles. "Looks like a lot of military history..."

"Yeah, I got into that when I was in med school."

She swung back to him. "Really? That's interesting."

All she had wanted to read were comedies. Satire.

He came closer, inundating her with the clean, masculine soap-and-shampoo scent of him. "It started out with me wanting to understand my brother Joe's life in the military. So initially, I picked up a lot of firsthand accounts. Of training. Battle. And then, when I got deeper into the genre, I became fascinated with how people survive trauma and tragedy." His gaze darkened, as did his mood. "And still find the courage to go on."

Clearly, he felt a connection to someone in those straits. And the emotional struggle that always followed.

Before she could stop herself, she moved closer, too.

Reminded of how much he had helped her earlier in the day, by allowing her to talk about things that were painful to her, she studied his haunted expression and asked softly, "Did you have trouble with that when your fiancée died?"

For a second, she thought he wouldn't answer. Finally, he nodded noncommittally. "Mostly because I felt responsible."

It was hard to imagine that was even possible. She touched his forearm gently. "Were you driving the car?"

"No." His denial sharp, angry, he swung around to face her. "But I should've been."

Chapter Seven

Zach didn't know why he had opened the door to this. Especially since he had worked so hard to put it all behind him.

"I don't understand," Claire said.

Maybe it was time he talked about it. At the very least let her know what she'd be getting into, if she ever got that close to him.

"Lisa and I were a few weeks out from our wedding. We were both finishing up our residencies, and had our board-certification exams ahead of us. Plus, we had both taken jobs here in Laramie, and still had to finalize the move from Houston, a few weeks after we were hitched."

Her green eyes glimmered with compassion. "That's a lot to handle."

Just remembering made him tense. "Yeah." He began to pace. "Which is why I didn't want to do a lot of the extraneous stuff related to the wedding."

She perched on the back of the sofa, ankles crossed, delicate hands braced on either side of her. "Like…?"

The list had been endless. And at times mind-numbingly ridiculous, at least to him. "Choosing a calligrapher and font for the place cards. Picking out the exact shade of pink table linens for the reception. Purchasing wedding favors for the guests to take home with them. It seemed like every time I turned around, there was something that hadn't yet been done."

Basically the kind of things that he doubted anyone would remember, even a week after the ceremony.

The soft curve of her lips tilted downward. "You didn't have a wedding planner or trusted family member to handle some of those arrangements for you?"

"We did. In fact, both our moms volunteered to take over some of the tasks, multiple times."

Frustration mounting, he began pacing the room. Then after several long beats, he stopped just in front of her, hands shoved in the pockets of his shorts. "But Lisa couldn't cede control of any of it."

"Nothing?" Claire, who had been through residency and board-certification exams herself, seemed surprised. Which made him realize she was the type of woman who would accept help.

The realization made it easier for him to go on.

"Lisa wanted to do everything herself. Except she kept changing her mind about stuff. All the time."

"And she couldn't settle on anything?"

"Not for long." *The menu for the reception dinner had been altered half a dozen times. Always with some sort of financial penalty.*

"And that morning, when she wanted to go to the florist for what seemed like the umpteenth time, to tweak the flowers for the bouquets, *again*, after working all night at the hospital, I finally just lost it. I told her she was running herself ragged focusing on things that were superficial, at best, and that there was no reason why either she or I had to take on all those pre-wedding errands ourselves. When we had family ready to pitch in."

"What happened?"

The pain of that last fateful conversation hit him like a blow to the solar plexus. "She blew up, too. *Accused me of not caring about her or the wedding.* Told me she didn't want my help and stormed out." The ache in Zach's throat matched the one in his heart. "I was exhausted and too angry to deal with any of it. So I went to bed." Grief and guilt welled up inside him. "Thinking we would deal with it all later, when we had both calmed down…"

Claire reached out and took his hand in hers, the warmth of her skin pressing against his palm. "Is that when the accident happened?"

He nodded. "Lisa didn't see an oncoming car as she went through an intersection, and was hit square on the driver side. She was killed instantly."

"Oh, Zach." Claire's voice was thick with emotion. Stepping closer, she wrapped her arms around him. "You're not to blame." She hugged him tightly. "It was an accident."

Without warning, Zach's face was wet from the moisture leaking out of his eyes. He scrubbed a hand over his face. "One that could have been prevented," he gritted out, hating himself for his failure all over again. "If I had just either convinced her to stay home and catch some zzz's with me. Or gone with her. Then all our quarrel ever would have been was just that. A silly premarital argument. Instead," he said bitterly, "it was the last words we ever said to each other…"

And he still had a hell of time forgiving himself for that.

Claire's expression turned stern.

If he had expected her to blame him, too, he had been wrong. She glared at him, her emerald eyes fierce. "You don't know that you being in the driver's seat would have changed the trajectory of events. No one does. What we do know is that Lisa is gone, and you're still here, and you have to go on. No matter how hard it can be at times."

There were times—like right now—when that seemed like an impossible task. "Let me guess. You're volunteering to help me."

His sarcasm was usually enough to push a woman away.

Not Claire. She somehow managed to see straight through his pain, his agonizing worry that if he ever let himself get that close to a woman again, that the same thing would happen. He shoved a hand through his hair, knowing deep down in his gut how things would play out. Everything would be wonderful... for a while. During the infatuation period. Then their agendas would differ and change. He'd put walls up to protect himself, and make the worst kind of mistake, and it would all end badly. "Yes," she said. "I am. Because I've been stuck, too."

Zach blinked in surprise. "Stuck?" he echoed. "What the hell are you talking about?"

Claire passed a hand over her eyes. What was it about this guy that had her spilling her guts every chance she got? He already knew more about her situation with her ex than she would have preferred. Knees weak, she perched on the back of the sofa. "As I told you earlier, I found out I was pregnant two months after Sebastian left for Antarctica. I was in the middle of my residency and petrified of going through it all alone. So Lucky and I moved in with my sister and her husband and their three kids. I was only supposed to be there until the baby was born."

"But then you learned you were having triplets," Zach guessed.

"Gwen and Patrick insisted the babies and I stay with them, until the kids were toddlers, so I did."

He moved to perch beside her. "How did that go?" He gave her a casual, sidelong glance, which she suspected was his attempt to try to camouflage the grief and regret that were still roiling through him.

"Good—for the kids," Claire was pleased to admit. "Because the pediatric nursing students I hired to help out were under Gwen's direction."

"And yet...?"

"By the time I finished my residency, their marriage was showing the strain of having to deal with six kids under seven, all the time. Even with the help I brought in, it was a lot. And I knew, no matter how much I did not want to reconfigure my life, never mind how hard it was going to be able to do so, that I had to let Gwen and Patrick go back to focusing on their family." She released a quavering breath. "Which meant I had to move on. Really start over instead of continuing to live life in half measures. So I found the job in Laramie."

Zach's gaze gentled. "Because of the slower pace?"

Claire nodded, his intuitiveness rendering her temporarily speechless. "I'd heard Laramie County was a Texas utopia. That the cost of living was a lot less. The people in the community were wonderful. And I wouldn't have the problems I had in Dallas, like wasting so much time commuting and sitting in traffic. But mostly," she admitted, briefly closing her eyes against the crushing weight of her own guilt, "I did it so I wouldn't be tempted to run back to Gwen and Patrick."

"How are they doing now?"

"Great." She opened her eyes and smiled. "Their twins, Seth and Sam, are finishing up third grade this year. And their five-year-old daughter, Regan, is in kindergarten. They finally have time to be a family again. As do the kids and I."

He stood, legs braced apart, and flicked a glance her way. "And you are telling me all this because...?"

Aware she might be crossing a line with him, she pushed on. Albeit calmly and carefully. "I think...although for different reasons...you're just as emotionally stuck as I was. And that as hard as it is to move on after heartbreak, if you ever want to have the kind of life you were planning with Lisa..."

He winced. "Marriage. Kids."

Claire nodded. "You have to open yourself up to the possibilities. And stop blaming yourself for things that can't be undone."

His dark brow lifted. He guessed where she was going next. "Start taking risks?"

She stood, too. Thinking maybe it was time to be on her way. Before she felt any more fragile and or inexplicably connected to him. "Big ones."

He put a light hand on her shoulder. "Like this?" he asked her huskily, guiding her toward him.

The next thing Claire knew, instinct was taking over. She was all the way against him and her arms were lifting to wrap around his neck. His head slanted, dipped, as he cuddled her against his strong, steady warmth. And then there was no stopping it. They were kissing. And everything she had ever wanted, everything she needed right now, *in that moment*, was happening.

In this kiss.

Zach had promised himself he wouldn't kiss Claire again. But the moment she turned her pretty green eyes to his, all previous resolutions were off.

He was going to pursue her the way he wanted to pursue her, no holds barred. Because she was right. He was wasting his life. At least the personal side of it. Telling himself he didn't deserve a wife and family. Not allowing himself to want more than what he had right now.

Had she not told him otherwise, or confessed her own romantic mistakes, he might not be ready for an affair. He also knew that surrendering to their passion was the surest way to bring both of them back to life. And Claire needed to admit that she was a flesh-and-blood woman who had her own life ahead of her. If she would only allow herself to want more.

Claire broke free, grinning in pleasure and gasping for breath. "Well, not exactly…like this…"

"Then how about like this?"

She made a sexy little sound in the back of her throat. Her

mouth opened to his once again, allowing him deeper access. "Nice, but…"

He felt the need pouring out of her, matching his own. "You're right," he said solemnly as she dug her fingers into his shoulders and kissed him back with wild abandon. He savored the taste and feel of her, satisfaction roaring through him. "You, *I*, can do better…"

Looking slightly dazed, she sucked in an impatient breath. "Zach…"

Worried, though, that she would regret this, he groaned softly and lifted his head long enough to look into her sultry eyes and rasp, "I feel like I'm taking advantage…"

She went up on tiptoe, rocking against him, making him hard. "You're not." She kissed his jaw, his cheek, his mouth with searing passion. "I'm a grown woman. I know exactly what we are doing here…"

Did she?

He had to wonder.

Until she tugged her T-shirt over her head, toed off her sneakers, and eased off her shorts, then slid them down her long, silky thighs.

He watched her. Mesmerized. She was without a doubt the most beautiful woman he had ever seen. He caught her hand before she could undo the clasp of her bra. "Let me…"

Her breasts were full and round, the nipples taut and rosy against the paleness of her skin. He slid her panties off, too. Pulling them down, past the damp curls, over her knees. He knelt to help her step out of them, and once there, decided to stay.

Claire gasped as he buried his face in her sweet, warm softness. Giving him a glimpse of what it might be like if she really let go.

She held on to him, quavering now. He dropped gentle kisses on her thighs. Determined to help her find release.

Slowly and deliberately rubbing the pad of his thumb along the delicate feminine seam. Coaxing her to let all her inhibitions ease away, to open for him even more. His body pulsed and she melted against him, shuddering with need.

Experiencing her climax was almost his undoing.

Still quaking with aftershocks, she took charge. "My turn now…"

She drew him to his feet and led him toward his bed. Keeping it light and easy, she eased off his shirt and shorts, then his boxer briefs. She ran her hands over his pecs. And shoulders. Eagerly exploring the trail past his navel, lower still. Then, as long as she was down there, she spent time pleasuring him, too…

Not about to finish without her, he brought her back up, laying her onto her back. Excitement ricocheting through him, he found a condom, rolled it on, slipped between her parted thighs and covered her with the length of his body. As he did so, the delicate floral scent of her inundated his senses. They kissed as their bodies joined. Then he was going deeper, slower, until he was as enmeshed in her as he could be. She whimpered low in her throat and rocked against him, taking him more fully still.

The climax came hard and fierce.

As they clung together afterward, still shuddering, Zach knew this was more than a fling. Or an arrangement borne out of mutual loneliness.

It was the beginning of much, much more.

Claire lay still, her head on Zach's chest, trying to catch her breath. She felt so cozy and good. And completely sated.

"Wow," she said. Aware this was absolutely the best sex she had ever had.

"Yeah. Wow," he agreed, his body still quaking with reaction, too.

She rolled onto her back, feeling the mattress beneath her. The only time she had ever slept in a king-sized bed was when she was in a hotel. She had a queen at home. Which was fine for one person. But this…this was idyllic for her and Zach….

She put her hand over her eyes. Not quite sure how to go from sheer ecstasy to normality with a man she actually didn't know all that well. Yet, anyway. So she did what she usually did when she was ill-at-ease, she concentrated on the mundane. She wiggled around in the sheets, testing the give of the surface beneath her, and found it…amazing. "This is such a wonderful bed, Zach. It must be so great to come home after a night on call and crawl into this."

"I wouldn't know. I'm usually asleep two seconds after I hit the pillow."

Claire laughed, as she knew he meant her to. She sent him a flirtatious glance. "Well, you *are* very lucky to have such a cozy bed," she said.

"Perfect, huh?"

So perfect, Claire thought. He had no idea.

As was he.

She'd never made love so magnificently.

If it hadn't been for the soft chime of a phone text, interrupting, she might have been in for round two. Sighing regretfully, she moved away as it chimed again. "Sorry. My kids. I have to get this." She pulled it from the back pocket of her shorts and looked at the screen. Read: Confirmation Needed.

She groaned.

Zach sobered. "What is it?" Clearly, he thought the worst.

She waved off all his anxiety, explaining, "It's from the organizers of the Easter egg hunt at the town square park, tomorrow afternoon. I signed up all three kids."

He rolled onto his side, looking deliciously disheveled, and sated, too, at least momentarily. "And that's a problem because?"

He watched her tug the sheet a little more snugly beneath her arms. "There are supposed to be around 200 kids, in four different age groups, participating. I thought I'd have Bette with me. There is no way I can keep track of the triplets on my own. The hell of it is, I've already promised them. A lot of their friends from preschool are going, too." She drew her gaze away from the flat plane of his abdomen. A distracting shiver moved through her. "They're going to be so disappointed." She moaned in frustration.

He sat up against the headboard, the sheet draped low across his hips. "They don't have to be. I can go with you-all."

It was a tempting offer, especially given how much she and the kids all enjoyed spending time with him. Except…"You're on call tonight, remember?"

His broad shoulders lifted in an affable shrug. "I'm off at six a.m. I'll come home, catch some zzz's and shower then come pick you all up." He continued to study her as if trying to figure something out. "What time does it start?"

"Two p.m. They're asking us to show up by one forty-five though."

"Then I'll be at your house at one thirty," he told her.

She worried her bottom teeth with her lip. "You really want to do that?"

He pulled her toward him for a long, thorough kiss that had her tingling from head to toe. Lifting his head, he smiled. "I really do."

"I don't know why you've got your knickers in such a twist, if all you've done is share a couple of kisses," Gwen teased later that same evening, when Claire called her after the kids were asleep.

Except this time they had done a lot more than that, she thought. And she was still wildly aroused every time she thought about it!

"This Doctor Zach sounds like a keeper."

Claire sipped her tea. "A keeper I'm way too attracted to."

"So? Nothing to say it can't or won't work out."

Nothing to say it *would*, either, Claire reminded herself. And could she really put herself through another heartbreak? Especially with someone she was going to have to continue to work with?

All she did know was that their hot, sexy lovemaking had turned her world upside down. And that she had never wanted or felt as wanted as she had today.

Never felt such instant intimacy.

"Besides, I thought you were into taking risks these days. To get yourself on a path to a better future."

That was true.

It just hadn't included sex. Or being on the verge of falling head over heels for someone… "I didn't plan to date anyone until life was a little less crazy busy and the kids were older."

"Well," Gwen said, laughing, "you know what they say. Never put off until tomorrow what can be done today."

Which was exactly what she had done, by hitting the sheets with Zach. "Haha."

"Seriously, sis, just follow your heart. It won't steer you wrong."

Claire hoped not. Because already she wanted Zach way too much.

And if things went south it could be a disaster of epic proportions. For them both.

Chapter Eight

Claire greeted Zach when he showed up on Saturday afternoon to go to the Easter egg hunt. She looked gorgeous in a pair of hot-pink walking shorts, and a lacy white top that showed off her slender shoulders and taut midriff. She leaned up to give him a light hug. "Prepare yourself," she whispered in his ear, soft enough so her trio of preschoolers couldn't hear.

He hugged her back, just as affectionately, before letting her go, promising, "Sure thing."

Seconds later, he found out what she meant.

"*You're* going with us?" Oliver huffed out an aggravated breath and stood on the bottom stair step, a scowl on his face.

"I want Bette," Andrew agreed.

"Me, too," Isabella harrumphed.

"And I told you-all," Claire countered sternly, "that can't happen since Bette isn't back from her trip yet. And we can't go unless we have an extra adult with us, to help make sure no one gets lost. And Doctor Zach has kindly offered to help out." She paused to look each child in the eye. "So what do we say to him?"

More sighs. And a reluctant chorus, "Thank you."

He smiled, as if they meant it. "You're welcome."

"Now everyone please go and find your sneakers," Claire continued. "We don't want to be late."

They darted off, up the stairs. Claire looked around, searching the floor. Noting she, too, was barefoot, and that her feet were as pretty and feminine as the rest of her, he spied a pair of slip-on white sneakers next to the sofa. He ambled over to get them. "Are these what you're looking for?"

"Yes." She hurried toward him, a pained expression on her lovely face. "Thanks. And sorry about the sulkiness just now."

Zach shrugged. "I figured they'd resent me at some point."

Claire did a double take. "Why?"

He watched her put on one shoe, then the other. "Because you like me."

Mischief lit her eyes. "You think so, do ya?"

He didn't want to come off as too cocky. He shoved his hands in the pockets of his shorts, forcing himself to dial it down. "Hope so."

One thing was certain, Claire was not a woman to be taken for granted.

"Well, then, you'd be right." Her smile bloomed slowly. "I do…like you…"

He was standing so close, they were practically touching. Their eyes met and held. "Good. Cause," he dropped his voice to a whisper, "I like you, too."

Thundering footsteps sounded on the stairs. The kids came down, en masse. "We're ready, Mommy!" Andrew announced.

"Then let's go," Claire said.

Zach rode shotgun while Claire drove. They had to park several blocks from the park in the middle of town. She took the hands of both boys, while Zach held Isabella's hand. As they moved closer to the activity, the kids got quieter and shyer. Zach realized it was probably nerves making them so cranky. He looked down at Isabella. "Is this your first Easter egg hunt, sweetheart?"

She shook her head, her ribbon barrette slipping slightly, to one side, making her look even more adorable. "We did one last year."

"With our cousins," Oliver said.

"At their house," Andrew explained.

"In Dallas," their mom clarified. "But this will be our first big event here."

They slowed, and following the instructions of the event runners, herded the kids toward the line for the three-to-five-year-olds. As they did so, they ran into Sasha Donnelly, and her dietician mom Harriett. Her teenage brother did not appear to be with them.

Sasha waved merrily, her shyness of the other day all but forgotten. "Hi Doctor Zach! Doctor Claire!"

"Hello Sasha," Claire and Zach said in unison.

"Tucker's not here," the child announced. "Mommy wanted him to come, but he says there is no point if we can't eat the candy in the plastic eggs." Something, Zach noted, Sasha didn't seem to mind.

"And besides," Sasha informed them, "he has to study. Which is what he does all the time!"

That, the little girl *did* seem to mind.

Harriett winced slightly at the recitation. "Tucker has two more Advanced Placement exams coming up."

Which meant the teen was stressed, Zach thought.

Wondering—not for the first time—if the goals the ambitious teen had set up for himself were too much, he asked, "Has he heard from any colleges?"

Harriett nodded. "Princeton accepted him. So did his safety school—UT-Austin. But as you know, he really wants to go to Yale, and he won't hear from them for at least another week or so."

"I'm sure he will do well wherever he goes," Zach said. Meaning it.

Harriett nodded.

Claire looked at Sasha. "How is the monitor doing?"

The little girl tugged the neck of her T-shirt down, to show them. "I haven't got it wet! Or tried to take it off!"

"That's really great, honey." Claire smiled.

"I've been telling her, it will come off on Monday afternoon, after school," Harriet said. She paused as an event worker walked down the line, handing out cloth bags for all the kids to put their plastic eggs in. All four kids took them gratefully, testing them out, and opening up the handles to peer inside.

Harriett continued, "Any word on when the blood work will come back?"

Claire reassured kindly, "The lab promised me Monday morning. So we should be able to talk about it when you-all come in."

"Great." Harriett smiled.

Shortly thereafter, the line was divided again. The kindergarteners were escorted to one cordoned-off area of the twenty-acre park, the preschoolers another. Then the rules for the hunt were explained, and they were off.

"Are you sad, Doctor Zach?" Isabella asked, an hour and a half later, as Claire parked her SUV in the driveway of her home.

Claire sent him a perplexed look. But left him to answer.

"Uh, no…" Zach got out of the passenger seat. He assisted Isabella, and her brothers, onto the ground. They all needed help since they all would not let go of their Easter bags.

"Why would you ask that?" Claire asked her daughter.

"Because you didn't get to hunt for any eggs!" Andrew explained.

"So we want to know if you and Mommy are sad about that," Oliver continued solemnly.

Claire and Zach exchanged the kind of glances parents gave each other when their kids said something cute or interesting.

Claire explained, "I got to go to plenty of Easter eggs hunts when I was a kid."

"So did I," Zach said.

"So no, we're not sad about that," she assured the triplets as they all walked up the steps. She opened the door, and Lucky let out a happy bark, then came out onto the porch, tail wagging, to escort them into the house.

As they walked inside, Zach smelled something delicious cooking. Like fruit. And chicken, maybe...

"What about Sasha?" Andrew asked. "Is she sad?"

"Cause her mommy said she couldn't eat any candy," Oliver chimed in.

Isabella frowned. "Why would she do that?"

Claire tried to take the observation in stride. So her kids would, too. "Different families have different rules. We've talked about that."

"Are we going to be able to eat our candy?" Oliver asked.

"A little at a time. After dinner."

"When is dinner?" Isabella queried.

"Not for an hour." Claire went over to peer into the Crock-Pot on the counter. Fragrant steam rose up when she lifted the lid.

"Can Doctor Zach stay and eat with us?" Oliver asked.

"Yeah, we want him, too!" Andrew said.

Zach looked at Claire, letting her know she didn't have to feel obligated to extend an invitation.

She held his eyes, her expression benign. He couldn't figure out what she was thinking. He realized he wanted her to *want* him to stay. That he didn't want to leave any more than the kids wanted him to. And that it would be all too easy to get used to this. Which could definitely be considered a warning sign. Since neither he nor Claire were in the market for a broken heart or botched romance.

On the other hand, nothing risked, nothing gained.

"Well, Doctor Zach, how do you feel about pineapple chicken and rice?" she asked.

"Love it."

Almost as much as he loved hanging out with the four of them.

"Mommy," Isabella said, an hour later, as dinner came to an end. "When is Bette coming back?"

"Will she be here tomorrow to see us get our Easter baskets from the Easter Bunny?" Oliver wanted to know.

Good question, Claire thought. "Probably not tomorrow morning but hopefully the following day." Their sitter had assured her in her last text that she'd return to Laramie *at some point* on Sunday.

She exchanged a worried look with Zach. Could she trust Bette to follow through on her latest promise? One thing was certain—she didn't want her kids to have to endure any more lifted hopes and crushed expectations. "I'm not sure she'll be able to come in on Monday morning but I'm hoping she will be here after school."

"Then...does that mean," Andrew said, his eyes squinting as he analyzed the situation the way he always did, "we have to go to early care at school again?"

She nodded. "If Bette's not here, then yes."

The kids considered, their emotions mixed. Extra playtime with friends was always great, but having to get up earlier than usual and rush to get out the door was not something they enjoyed. Claire couldn't blame them. She liked mornings to be easier and more relaxed, too.

"I ate my dinner. Can I have some candy now?" Oliver asked, already moving on.

His siblings looked at each other and chimed in that they'd eaten their dinner too.

"Then you can each open up two plastic eggs and see what's inside," Claire told them.

It turned out to be pastel mini-marshmallows, yogurt-covered raisins and miniature bunny graham crackers. The kids were delighted with their find, and traded off 'til everyone had at least one of each. When they were finished, they were all yawning.

Zach looked a little tired around the eyes, too. "Got any coffee?" he asked.

Claire showed him where everything was. "Help yourself. I've got to get these kiddos in bed before they crash right where they are."

"Need any help?"

She shook her head. "Got it."

The kids said good-night to him and led the way up the stairs. Claire got them into their pajamas, helped them brush their teeth, and tucked them in.

A short time later, she smelled freshly brewing coffee as she descended the staircase. Walking back into the kitchen, she saw Lucky was sprawled out on the tiled floor watching Zach put the last of the dishes in the dishwasher. "You didn't have to do that."

He turned, looking totally chill. "You didn't have to invite me to dinner. But you did. Want some coffee?"

Claire realized she was dragging a little, too. Ignoring how much she liked having him here, like this, she nodded. "Please."

He poured two mugs while she got out the cream and sugar.

Ignoring the river of emotion running through her, she observed, "You look like you want to ask me something."

"That obvious?" Laugh lines bracketed the corners of his eyes. A day's growth of beard gave him a rugged, manly appearance. Their gazes locked and she felt another moment of tingling awareness.

"Mmm-hmm."

They carried their mugs over to the island and both took a seat. "Mary Lou Andrews sent me the specs on a couple dozen properties that might work for me. She wants me to pick out three to go see on Tuesday evening."

"And you need me because...?"

He lifted a shoulder in a careless shrug. "They all look pretty good."

Ah. She was beginning to see where this was going.

She cleared her throat, in an attempt to clear her head of all the ridiculously romantic notions his request was conjuring up. "You want my opinion." More a statement than a question.

"Yeah. Would you talk it through with me?"

Claire paused, aware her feelings were still a little confused, about what exactly they were to each other, and where all this was heading.

To just platonic friendship?

Friends with benefits?

Or something...deeper?

She didn't know.

They hadn't discussed it after they'd impulsively made love.

And, most important of all, it was too soon to know or really dissect. Therefore, it was best to continue to take things one moment at a time.

She smiled at him. "Sure. I'd be glad to listen to your thoughts on the matter. But can I ask something in return?"

"Lay it on me."

Would you mind helping me put together the Easter baskets for the kids first."

He seemed happy not to have their evening end anytime soon. "You strike a hard bargain, woman," he teased. "But how can I resist?"

Despite their lighthearted banter, the weight of being a single parent felt heavy on her shoulders once again. "Thanks. I want to make sure I haven't forgotten anything."

They went into the garage and brought back two big bags from the superstore in town. After she set all three wicker baskets on the kitchen table, Zach opened up the bags of synthetic green grass and layered the bottom of each basket. Meanwhile, Claire divided up the mini-jelly beans, marshmallow chicks and yogurt-coated granola treats. Instead of the usual solid chocolate candy bunny, there was a vanilla cake bunny, coated with pastel frosting, from the Sugar Love bakery in town.

Once they'd arranged the treats inside all three baskets, she added an Easter story for each child, along with bottles of bubbles, a coloring book and a small pack of crayons. Finally, Claire tied a ribbon and a name tag on each handle.

"Well, what do you think?" She offered him a couple of the extra jelly beans and stepped back to admire their handiwork. "Will they be happy?"

He popped a few candies into his mouth, clearly savoring the fruit-flavored treats. "Very. You did a great job."

"Thank you for helping thread all the treats into the grass." Claire helped herself to a few jelly beans, too. "It went a lot faster." She cleaned up the trash and put it in the bottom of the trash bag, for taking outside later.

He gave her another long look. The kind that said he wanted to kiss her again. "My pleasure."

Was this what it would be like if she had someone to share all this with? Knowing she was entering treacherous waters, Claire shook off her daydream. "So, about those homes you want me to look at…"

Realizing it would be a lot more comfortable in the living room, they sat on the sofa together. She got out her laptop and he pulled up his email on it. Then zeroed in on the message—with all the attachments—from the Realtor.

It didn't take long to veto a shotgun house close to the hospital as being way too small. Even though his brother Gabe lived in that area.

Two other properties were too far outside the town limits. Most of the rest were fixer-uppers that, while priced appropriately, were going to take way too much work. "I just can't see trying to live in a place where a lot of renovation is going on."

"I get it," she said. "Plus, when a property hasn't been updated in a good while, you never know what you are going to find when you start to rip out a bathroom, or kitchen."

Lucky came over and put his silky black chin on Zach's knee. The Newfie stared at him adoringly while he reached over and petted him.

Claire pointed to another selection, and sifted through the pictures. "What about this townhome? It's brand-new. Move-in ready with three bedrooms and two baths. You wouldn't have to worry about lawn work or exterior maintenance. Which is always a plus for someone who is single and works as much as you do."

"There's no real privacy, either, though. The decks are side by side. I wouldn't even be able to grill a steak without hearing what my neighbors were talking about."

"True." Claire moved on to the next. "Well, this home has been updated and is in a new subdivision just outside of town."

"Those homes have almost no yard, either. Which would be bad if I ever wanted to get a dog."

At that, Lucky's ears perked up and he wagged his tail vigorously. Claire grinned at her canine's obvious approval. She turned back to Zach, who was still petting Lucky and rubbing him behind his ears. "Do you *want* to get a dog?"

"I hadn't really considered it, but your Newfie here has me realizing what I've been missing out on."

"Well, then you probably need to look at something not too far from the hospital, so you can run home at noon, to let your dog out."

He opened the final attachment. "Here is a home like yours."

"The hundred-year-old Victorian down the street."

"Yeah, it's bigger than I think I need though." He furrowed his brow. "With six bedrooms and three and a half baths. And a big downstairs. Nice large yard too."

He showed her all the photos in the listings. "There are no pictures of any of the bathrooms in the listing."

"Which could be a warning sign if they are all in bad shape." Claire scrolled through the rest of the images thoughtfully, doing her best to assess. "And the kitchen appliances are definitely outdated, but the rooms are all freshly painted in a neutral color, the wood floors refinished."

He shifted closer for a better look, the sinewy warmth of his shoulder aligning with hers. "Yet it's been on the market for several months."

The intimacy of the moment caused a jolt of electricity to whip through her. "With a price that seems reasonable." She studied the specs, trying to keep her focus on the matter at hand and not on her wildly beating heart.

But then Zach shifted away, and immediately, she felt bereft. "So what do you think is going on there?" he asked her with a puzzled frown.

"There's something they aren't telling you about this house. It could just be all the bathrooms are awful, and it's going to be a lot to remodel them, both in terms of expense and time." She crinkled her forehead, contemplating. "It could also mean the roof needs to be replaced. Or maybe the house requires new wiring and plumbing, to bring everything up to code, which would be a huge undertaking too."

"That's true." He continued looking at the handsome exterior, the homey wraparound front porch. "But I still think I should look at it…"

Claire agreed. "That is definitely the only way to know if it is right for you, or not."

Sometimes selecting a home was more tied to a feeling

than physical attributes. At least it had been for her. She had known this bungalow was the place for her and the kids the moment she walked in with the Realtor.

She returned her laptop to him, so he could close out his email and all the links. When he handed it back to her, their fingers brushed. Another zing of chemistry filled the air.

Zach seemed aware of it, too. As well as the sleeping children upstairs. He looked at the clock above the mantel and saw it was close to 10:00 p.m. "Guess I better be going."

She stood with him. As they walked to the door, she smiled over at him. Working to keep things casual, she slid her hands in the pockets of her shorts. "Thanks for everything today. I don't know if I could have managed this afternoon without you."

His gray-blue eyes glimmered down at her. "Thank *you* for dinner. And inviting me to tag along. I haven't been to an Easter egg hunt since I was a kid. Brought back a lot of memories."

A sense of contentment drifting over her, Claire switched on the outside lights. She paused to look at him again. "Hopefully the event made new ones for you, too."

"That it did."

Another awkward moment ensued. He stepped across the threshold onto the porch. She was surprised to realize she was as reluctant to see Zach leave, as he appeared to be to go.

Lucky went past them, galloped down the front steps and headed for a patch of grass. Normally, Claire didn't let her dog out front without being on a leash, but he'd obviously had a mind of his own this evening. So she came out to stand beside Zach in the yellow glow of the porch light and watch over her pet.

"So. Big plans for tomorrow?" he asked, lingering beside her.

The moon shone in the star-filled sky overhead, and a cool spring breeze drifted over them. Claire wrapped her arms close to her body, not sure where he was going with this. "No. None actually."

Zach smiled, his gaze suddenly filled with tenderness. "Then I only have one more question."

"Okay..." Her breath hitched. "W-what is it?"

"Would you and the kids be my plus-four for Easter dinner at the Knotty Pine ranch?"

Chapter Nine

For a moment, Claire looked shell-shocked. Wary. Which, in turn, made Zach wonder. Too much, too soon? Just like the lovemaking the afternoon before had been?

Not that either of them regretted it.

Or said they did.

He just wasn't sure what the impetuous hookup meant for them. Or if she did, either. Although he knew what he *wanted* it to mean.

More closeness.

More time together.

With her kids.

And without...

Claire tilted her head to one side. She looked so pretty, standing there in the soft glow of the porch light, her cheeks flushed from being out in the spring sun, that afternoon. "Isn't that a family thing?" She bit her lower lip.

Remembering all too well how soft and giving her mouth felt beneath his, Zach said, "Mom always invites newcomers to the community, for holidays."

"So the invitation is coming from her?"

Zach nodded. Glad now his mom had made the offer yesterday evening, when they ran into each other at the hospital. "And me. And *all* the McCabes, actually. You and the triplets are still relatively new here. We want you all to feel welcome. ..."

"The thing is, I'm not sure how well my kids will behave at a formal dinner."

Her concern for others was endearing. He smoothed a stray curl from her cheek, tucking it behind her ear. "Then you're in luck," he told her, dropping his hand back to his side before looking into her eyes. "My brother Alex's quadruplets always have trouble with that, too. Which is why my parents keep it casual and set up long tables outside for the meal. And have activities for the kids to do. Dress is informal, as well. Everyone will be in jeans and boots."

She was starting to capitulate; he could see it. "And...where is their ranch?"

"About half an hour outside of town. If you-all want to go, I'll pick you up and take you. Plus, everyone brings their dogs. So Lucky can come, too."

Now, she was really tempted.

He could see that.

"Are you sure you-all are up for this?" she asked softly.

Zach nodded, aware he hadn't felt this happy and optimistic in a long time. And it was all due to Claire. He lifted her hand to his lips and lightly kissed the delicate skin of her knuckles. "Positive."

"Look, Mommy, cows!" Oliver shouted excitedly the following afternoon.

"Lots and lots of cows!" Andrew added.

Isabelle clapped her hands. "And horses, too!"

Because the triplets' car seats were already installed in her SUV, and she didn't know her way around the rural parts of Laramie County, Claire had asked Zach to drive her vehicle. As she relaxed in the passenger seat, she realized she was glad she had. It gave her a chance to fully take in the scenery, in a way that would have been impossible had she been driving. "Your parents' place is incredibly beautiful," she murmured.

A black wrought-iron archway framed the entrance to the Knotty Pine ranch. Split-rail fencing lined the long drive from the highway into the wildflower-strewn property.

It was easy to see where it had gotten its name. The beautiful Texas landscape was a combination of rolling hills and flat pasture, interspersed with handsome stands of woods that seemed to consist primarily of towering pine trees.

She turned to Zach, noting how strong and capable he looked behind the wheel of her SUV. He seemed as content and happy here as he was in town, or at the hospital. As eager to see his family as she always was to see hers.

Glad he valued his familial connections in a way her ex never had, she turned her attention back to the surroundings. "How big is the ranch?"

Zach drove slowly along the wide gravel lane. "Now?" His brow lifted contemplatively. "About five thousand acres, give or take. Although it started out about three hundred acres, years ago, when my dad first bought the place."

Talk around the hospital was that Chase McCabe was a self-made businessperson, as were most of the iconic Texas McCabes. "Did he always want to ranch as well as work as a CEO?" Claire tried to imagine what kind of childhood that would have made.

Zach shook his head. "Although my dad grew up on a working cattle ranch, the Knotty Pine was more of a retreat, and an investment for him. A place to learn basic ranching skills, hone our work ethic, and blow off steam for us kids."

Claire could see how that would benefit growing children. Her own would love it.

"Although lately my mom and dad have talked some about selling their home in town and moving out here, when they retire in five or six years."

They passed more pastures and several well-maintained

barns. Zach gestured at more livestock. "Right now, my brother Alex runs some of his herd here."

"Nice," Claire murmured, as the ranch house came into view.

Turning toward the rear of the vehicle, she said, "Kids, we're here!"

Big grins broke out. "Yay!" they shouted.

They parked at the end of the circular drive in front of the sprawling adobe structure with the red-tile roof.

"Your parents place is beautiful!" Claire enthused.

"Thanks." Zach cut the engine and got out of the SUV. "My mom said you've met her and my dad?"

Claire stepped out, too. "Yes, after we first moved to Laramie, at a party for Eleanor Fitzgerald."

"Who is my sister-in-law, Ellie's, grandmother," he noted as he helped her with Lucky and the kids.

"Right. Eleanor Fitzgerald was one of my first patients here, so I've met Ellie and Joe, and their two adorable babies, too."

All were wonderful people. Warm and welcoming. Incredibly kind and principled. Just like Zach…

"And of course, Gabe." Who was going to help her with her Sebastian problem.

"And Sadie—who used to work at the Sugar Love bakery. But recently bought a ranch, where she intends to grow lavender."

They unsnapped seat belts and lifted the kids down from the SUV onto the ground. "And I know your brother Alex from the preschool. Although his boys are a good year older than my kids."

Zach smiled. "Well, that will make things easier."

Still in awe of their surroundings, the kids walked with them to the front door. His parents, Chase and Mitzy, greeted them warmly and ushered them inside. There was an arched roof over the big central living area, with kitchen and dining on one side, and seating and fireplace on the other. Glass walls overlooked a sunny central courtyard, which was situated between two long wings.

The tables outside were already set up for dinner, just as Zach had promised.

Inside, Mitzy had prepared a play station for the kids, at the kitchen table. Alex's four quadruplet sons were already there, decorating pastel Easter eggs with stickers, markers, edible icing-glue and various kind of sprinkles. Claire's triplets happily joined in, and the celebratory afternoon began.

Of course, it didn't take long for the little ones to get restless. Thirty minutes for a craft project at that age was a long time. So the men took all the youngsters outside, while Ellie, Sadie, Mitzy and Claire put the finishing touches on dinner. Giving the beautiful ham one last pineapple brown sugar glaze. Sautéing big pans of spring vegetables. Checking on the scalloped potatoes, and sliding the homemade yeast rolls in to bake.

As they worked, Claire couldn't resist peeking out the windows from time to time. Observing, Mitzy smiled, like the astute social worker she was. "Everything okay?"

"I can't get over how well my triplets are playing with Alex's quadruplets. Even Isabella. Usually, they are intimidated by older kids, at least initially, or a little shy in new situations. But it's like they've known each other all their lives."

"There's something about kids who are part of multiple births. It's why the Laramie Multiples Club is so successful, and has been for so many years. Having to share everything, in the way single birth kids don't, can make for quick bonds."

Claire felt a pitch coming on. "Hm."

"Has anyone talked to you about joining LMC?" Mitzy continued.

"They have," she allowed carefully, not wanting to offend. "I just haven't had time to really look into it…"

Sadie came over to join them at the window. Together, they watched the game of Statue being played. With the men taking turns calling it, while the other men goofily participated along with the kids, making them giggle uproariously. "What amazes me," Sadie said, "is that Claire got Zach to finally come out of his shell again."

Claire pivoted toward Zach's only female sibling. "What do you mean?"

"He hasn't brought a woman to a family gathering since Lisa died. Actually dated, either—if you don't count his Sir Galahad act, and yet from what I've heard, this weekend he hasn't been able to stay away from you."

We haven't been able to stay away from *each other*, Claire thought wryly.

But not wanting to make too much of it, especially this early in the game, Claire waved off the attention. "He was just helping me with the triplets, while we worked on a patient case together. Initially, it was the only way we could get together. Then my nanny had to go out of town suddenly." She felt her face fill with self-conscious heat. "And things got even more complicated."

Not because of the case, but as Sadie had correctly intuited, because they couldn't seem to stay away from each other.

Claire continued matter-of-factly, "I think he invited us here today because he knew we didn't have any family nearby or anywhere to go this weekend. And he thought the kids and I would really enjoy celebrating the holiday with you-all. Which we are. Bottom line, he was just being kind."

The other women nodded at what she said.

Yet, at the same time, she got the feeling they all believed there was more to her relationship with Zach than Claire wanted to admit.

And that, she realized belatedly, could turn into a very big problem if Zach was uncomfortable with the assumptions being made.

A feeling of contentment unlike anything he had ever known filled Zach as he drove back to town, three hours later.

The triplets had fallen asleep in their car seats almost as soon as they were latched in. Claire was focused on the early April scenery. Which, he admitted, with all the Texas wild-flowers in bloom, was pretty darn amazing.

Still, he sensed something was on her mind.

"You've been awfully quiet this afternoon."

She turned to him. "Have I?" She flashed a cordial smile, the kind you gave at a business gathering you were being forced to attend.

His alarm upped another notch. "Did my sister Sadie give you the business? She's known for her unsolicited romantic advice, you know." Which in Claire's case, would not have been welcome. Even if she was too polite to say so.

The emotional shield that had been up around Claire, the first time they had met, was suddenly back. She gave him an-other placid smile that did not reach her eyes. "Everyone was very nice, while we worked to get dinner on. Which was in-credibly delicious, by the way."

He knew she was being sincere about that at least. "Yeah. My mom is a fantastic cook. She loves having us all together." Resisting the urge to pull over to the side of the road, so he could take her in his arms for the rest of the conversation, he said, "So." He tightened his hands on the steering wheel. "What did Sadie say?"

A really awkward silence fell.

For a moment, Zach thought Claire wouldn't answer.

Finally, she swallowed and turned to look at him. Hands knotted in her lap, she admitted in a low voice, "She said you hadn't brought a woman to a family gathering since you lost your fiancée."

Zach swore silently to himself.

Realizing too late that he should not have started down this path. Especially while he was driving and the kids were asleep in their car seats.

Since he had, however, he needed to discuss this. He gave her a quick, deliberate look. "That's true." Then turned his attention back to the road.

"Your sister also said you hadn't actually dated anyone since Lisa. All the helping out damsels in distress stuff aside."

He winced. "Also true."

Exhaling softly, Claire took a moment to absorb that.

Unable to read her emotions, he muttered, "I haven't met anyone I wanted to date." *Until now.* But aware now was not the time to ask her out, lest she think he was being forced into it by the meddling women in his family, he said, "I haven't wanted to put myself out there that way again. Not when I already had the love of my life." And then blew it…

Nodding, Claire turned toward him, as much as her safety belt would allow. "I can understand that. My bad breakup with Sebastian left me feeling the same."

He watched the self-conscious pink blush her cheeks. But wasn't sure how to comfort her. "Did you tell the women that?" he asked her gently. Thinking it might have helped if she had.

"No." Shaking her head, she looked out the windshield, at the country road in front of her. "We didn't talk about my romantic past."

"Then what's bothering you?" Zach prodded, because she still seemed uncomfortable.

Claire placed a hand over her heart, as if thinking how to respond to that. "Sadie and…well, everyone else I guess…seemed to think that meant you were romantically interested in me. And me, you."

And they were right, Zach thought. *Even before you and I made love, Claire, and rocked each other's worlds.* Figuring it was too soon to say that, though, he said instead, "What did you tell them?"

Claire continued looking out the window, as if she were afraid to meet his eyes. "That you were helping me out while my nanny was away, so we could work on a medical case together."

Seeing they had breached the town limits, and her home was only a few blocks away, he slowed down. "And you inferred that we'd been doing that all weekend?"

She seemed to know that was stretching facts. She shrugged. "I didn't really get into that. Fortunately, the food was ready, and we had to call you all in, and we never got back around to that topic again."

Good. Whether or not Sadie and the other women had meant to cause issues, they had. He reached over to touch her hand. "Sorry they made you uncomfortable."

Claire removed her hand out from beneath his but finally turned to face him. "They were just curious. Trying to figure out if there was something going on with us." Uneasiness filled her pretty green eyes.

Zach knew Claire well enough to guess, "You assured them there wasn't."

"I didn't really say, but I tried to give the impression that we were just colleagues and friends, and it had been an unusual weekend, with my nanny gone."

Nice and vague. A good smokescreen for feelings, whatever hers were. Obviously not as intense as his.

"And you felt sorry for us, not having any family nearby to be with at Easter, and so on."

Zach noted the familiar Honda Civic with the landscape-painted exterior up ahead. "Well, you're not alone any longer."

"What?"

"Looks like you've got company."

Bette was finally back.

Which meant, Zach thought, surprised by the depth of his disappointment, by Claire's calculations his help was likely no longer needed. And he'd be able to be on his way.

Chapter Ten

Claire followed the direction of Zach's gaze, wondering what had him on such high alert. Then she saw Bette sitting on the top step, her head bent, her attention on the phone in her hands. She looked up as Zach turned Claire's SUV into the driveway. A broad smile crossed her face, as Isabella yawned and sleepily opened her eyes.

"Bette?" Claire's little girl said sleepily. "Bette's back!"

Andrew and Oliver woke up, too. "Hey," Oliver said. "It *is* Bette!"

"Yay! She's here!" Andrew noted.

Zach cut the engine, and got out to help Claire unlatch the kids' seat belts and get Lucky out of the cargo area, while Bette bounded down the steps, her arms outstretched. The kids piled into her waiting embrace, hugging her fiercely, all talking at once.

"I missed you, too," Bette was saying, hugging them back, as Claire approached.

Bette glanced at Claire. "Sorry it took me so long to get back to Laramie," she said.

Claire nodded in response, aware her emotions were all over the place. "Hi. Bette. We weren't expecting you until tomorrow. Change of plans?" She was being polite but the conversation she really needed to have with her employee could not happen in front of Zach and her children. Because an upset to their schedule like this could not happen again. That had to be made clear.

"Yeah, well, since I missed a lot of hours this week…" Bette smiled with youthful exuberance. "I'd like to make it up to you by being here this evening. Maybe give you a much-needed break? I could feed the kids dinner."

"Actually, they've already had their main meal this afternoon, but they probably will need a little something—like cereal and milk—later," Claire said.

Bette beamed. "Well, I can handle that. And do the whole bedtime routine, the way I usually do when you're on call at the hospital. Get their lunches ready for tomorrow. The whole spiel."

"Please, Mommy!" Isabella said.

"We want Bette to take care of us tonight," Andrew agreed.

Oliver burst out, "Yeah, we've missed her!"

Bette looked at Zach. Seeming to conclude that there was something going on between the two of them, too, she said, "You could go on a date…or something."

Claire turned to Zach, ready to tell him he did not have to worry—he was off the hook when it came to helping her out—and instead found his eyes were twinkling. "*Or something* sounds good to me," he said.

Zach was pretty sure Claire was going to turn him down. Even though he would very much like to accept her nanny's offer to watch the kids, so they could have some time alone, to cap off what had been a pretty damn fine holiday weekend. At least according to him.

Then Bette smiled again. "Please, Claire. Let me make it up to all of you," she implored.

"Yeah, please Mommy!" the triplets cried in unison, jumping up and down.

"Okay." Claire led Lucky up the porch steps and unlocked

the front door. She unhooked his leash and let him inside. He trotted off in the direction of his water bowl and she turned to hug her kids, one by one. "I want everyone to promise they will be very good and cooperative with Bette this evening."

"We will, Mommy!" Isabella said, as her brothers chimed in, agreeably.

She pulled her phone out of her pocket. "Call me if you need me."

"Stay out as late as you want!" Bette advised cheerfully.

As if not trusting herself to say much else, she nodded again. And started down the steps, toward her SUV. Zach's pickup truck was parked at the curb. When she reached her driver door, she turned to him, her spine as stiff and unyielding as the expression on her face. "You really don't have to entertain me," she told him stoically.

Like spending time with her was an unpleasant chore. When nothing could be further from the truth.

She inhaled deeply. "But I do need some time to get my thoughts together…"

"I can imagine," he murmured back, thinking about all her part-time nanny had put her and her kids through. "And I don't mind keeping you company. Or listening to you vent about the situation, if you want. So…" Zach sucked in a deep breath, wishing deep down they *could* have a real date. One not borne out of crisis. "Want to go to dinner or…?"

She blinked in surprise. "Are you seriously hungry? Because that dinner your mom served us was really something."

He smiled at her gentle teasing. "Actually, I'm not." He let his gaze drift over her face. "I'm just not sure what else there is to do, given it's a holiday. There's very little open on Sunday evenings in Laramie anyway, and given it's Easter, too…" He inhaled the sweet and lovely scent of her, resisting the urge to take her hand. "But we could go for a walk. Drive out to the lake…"

Claire reflected a moment, then pulled herself together. "That sounds nice. But how about we do something practical and helpful to you instead?"

Taken aback by her sly smile, he asked, "And what would that be?"

She sent him a challenging look. "How are you doing on packing up all those books in your place?"

Fortunately, Zach had purchased a dozen medium moving boxes and packing tape, the day after he'd found out he was being evicted. He hadn't done anything with them yet. Claire must have seen them, sitting unopened in a corner of the living room, when she had been there on Friday afternoon. "Trying to light a fire under me?" he teased.

There were chores he loathed and delayed whenever possible. Packing up to move was one of them.

Not that he had any place to go yet.

The only place he had seen he really liked was Claire's bungalow, and as she would have been quick to point out, it was occupied.

"More like," she chose her words carefully, "burn off a lot of my fury."

He watched the quick rise and fall of her chest. "You're ticked off?"

A quick, terse nod. "I didn't realize how much so until just now. Which is why I need to do something to blow off steam."

He understood. If it had been him, he would probably have gone for a long run. A woman with as much on her to-do list as Claire would blow off steam with something practical, like chores that had to be done anyway.

He touched a light hand to her elbow. "Then let's go…"

Not surprisingly, she wanted to see herself home later, so they both drove to his garage apartment and parked next to it. "Want something to drink?" he asked, after they had walked inside. "I have a bottle of wine. And that craft beer you gifted me with…"

She shook her head, more tense than he had ever seen her. "I'd rather just get started," she replied.

Knowing it would be dark in an hour or so, he forewent opening the blinds and turned on all the lights instead.

As he surveyed the number of books he had collected over the past five years, he realized a dozen boxes was not going to be nearly enough.

From the look on her face, she was thinking the same thing. "Where do you want to start?" she asked, hands on hips.

Not with packing up books, he thought.

Not when they could cuddle on the sofa and just talk…get to know each other better.

That clearly wasn't happening. Not tonight, anyway.

So, he might as well help her do what she wanted to do. "Why don't we assemble a bunch of moving boxes first and get the bottoms taped up. Then we can just fill them all at once, label and close them."

"Sounds like a plan."

For fifteen minutes or so, they worked in silence. Despite the constant physical exertion, she seemed no less tense when they had arrived. "You want to talk about your disappointment in Bette?"

Her expression grew conflicted, and the corners of her lips turned down. "I know she's only twenty-six. And ambitious. And that it is very hard to get a start in the art world. Never mind make a living selling paintings." She sat down on the edge of the sofa, the hem of her denim skirt riding up above her knees. "But…"

He caught a glimpse of silky bare thigh and forced his gaze back to hers. "She also has a job taking care of your kids."

"Yes." Claire touched the triple birthstone necklace, nestled in the V of her floral-print blouse. This time inadvertently drawing his attention to the soft womanly curves of her breasts.

Her lower lip quavered. "And she let them down!"

Truth to tell, Zach was ticked off, too. He didn't want anyone, or anything, hurting Claire or her kids. Putting the roll of tape aside, he went over to her.

He didn't know why this was suddenly so difficult for Claire. "So tell her it can't happen again."

"Believe me, I'd like to but…" She swept both her hands through her black curls, pushing them away from her face, before dropping them back to her lap, "if I do that, Bette might quit on the spot, and then where would the kids and I be?" She let out an anguished groan and buried her face in her hands. "I should have known this would happen! That I would do it again…as soon as another difficult transition hit…"

"What are you talking about?"

Claire leapt to her feet. She threw her hands in the air and stalked away. Then swung back to face him, her emotions in turmoil. "I lean on people, way too much, whenever life starts to get too tough!"

"You are saying this is a pattern?"

Abruptly, she looked as wary as she had the day he had chased her down in the physicians' parking lot, trying to get her to agree to an immediate consult. He hated seeing her like that. As if she needed to keep her guard up at all times. "Yes. When my mother died, I leaned on my older sister Gwen, to get through college."

The slight catch in her voice revealed more than she knew. Once again, she was being too hard on herself. Expecting perfection when perfection wasn't possible. "Everyone does that when they're grieving," he told her gently, closing the distance between them once again. "I wouldn't have gotten through my initial grief over losing Lisa, if it hadn't been for my family and friends."

"Yes," she told him miserably, "but with me it continued even after I had accepted that loss. I did it again with Sebastian, when I was in medical school, letting a study partnership turn into something it never should have been. And then when he left, and I found I was pregnant, I leaned on Patrick and Gwen so hard to get through my pregnancy and the rest of my residency and the first few years with the kids that their marriage almost imploded." She released a breath. "And now I've done it with Bette. Letting her become an integral part of our family, without taking into account that nanny-ing had never been her dream job, and that she could decide to up and leave at any minute. Which she kind of did this last week, at least temporarily." She shook her head remorsefully. "And then there's you…!" Her voice broke.

"Whoa! What?" He girded himself for the worst.

She stared him down, growing even more agitated. "I've leaned on you all week, Zach. Unfairly!"

He could not quite keep the exasperation from his voice. "I'm not complaining, Claire."

She tilted her head to one side and kept her eyes on his. "But maybe you should be," she told him softly. Regret turned the corners of her soft lips down. "My life is so chaotic and demanding, Zach."

"I know that."

With a weariness that seemed to go soul-deep, she said, "I'm not sure I even have room for a friendship."

Friendship?

Whoa again!

He definitely did not want to be put in the friend zone with her. Especially not after they had made love once. And he hoped to do so again.

With a shake of her head, she allowed in a low, strangled voice, "And I've got three kids."

She wanted to believe in him, in them. He could see that. She just wasn't sure she should.

It was almost comical how far off the track she was. He wrapped an arm around her, bringing her body against him. "Three *adorable* kids."

She sighed, resting her face against his shoulder. "And a dog."

He stroked a hand through her glossy black curls. "Whom I also adore."

"Not to mention a medical practice..." she added in a low voice.

He turned her so she had no choice but to face him. "Well, there we have something in common," he said, still holding her close. "I've got a medical practice, too."

"I'm serious, Zach." She splayed her hands across his chest, gazing up at him. Her breath hitched in her chest. "I have been letting you swoop in and rescue me and the kids and make all our lives better...*happier*...all week long..." Her slender body trembled. "I've been taking such unfair advantage of you..."

And she clearly loathed herself for it.

He frowned as she slipped out of his arms. "Is that what you think has been happening here?"

"Don't you?"

"No." His heart filling with all he felt, he tugged her back into his arms, lowered his head and let his lips brush the softness of hers. "I don't..."

And if this was the only way to show her something else... something incredible...was happening between them, then so be it.

"Zach..." She let out a soft moan of desire, mingled with restraint.

"Claire." He kissed her again, his body hardening.

She yielded a little more. Arguing breathlessly, between soft and tender kisses, "I...can't... use you...like this, too..."

He tunneled his hands through her dark hair, lifting her face to his. "Use me all you like… I mean it, darlin'. I want to be here for you. Tonight and whenever—*however*—you need me."

Even if it was a gamble for him, too. And the cautious side of him was just as afraid as she was to take a leap of faith. Worried that history might repeat itself. But damn it, she… they… this… was worth the risk…

She put a hand on his shoulder, drawing in another breath. "Oh, Zach, the last thing I would ever want to do is hurt you…"

He took her by the hand, leading her toward his bed. When they stood beside it, he wrapped his arms around her, reveling in her sleek feminine warmth. Once again, he let his actions do the persuading. "You're not going to do that." He dropped kisses along her temple. Waiting for her to decide.

She trembled in response. Lifting her head, she gazed deeply into his eyes again. "You…we…don't know that."

Trouble could come, whether they did anything to prompt it or not. He couldn't allow himself to worry about things they couldn't control. Or even anticipate. Nor could she.

"What I know," he told her gruffly, running a hand down her spine, letting the other cup the soft weight of her breast, "is I want you, and you want me and that is all we have to worry about right now. Finding a way to bring each other the closeness we both need…"

Her nipple tautened against the center of his palm. Their gazes meshed. And the surrender he had been waiting for finally came. Claire surged against him, kissing him deeply and passionately.

He kissed her back in exactly the same way. Enjoying the soft, sweet, tender ministrations of her hands and lips.

Their coupling could have been just sex. It wasn't. He couldn't get enough of her softness and warmth. The silk of her bare skin. The dampness between her thighs.

She wanted him, as much as he wanted her.

Before they knew it, they were all the way undressed. Dropping onto the mussed sheets of his bed. Finding the condom they were going to need. While he held her right where he wanted her to be, their lovemaking turned to an all-encompassing need. A connection that brought them breathtakingly close. Capitulating more with every stroke, every touch, every achingly tender caress. Until finally, they surrendered to the blazing passion, the heat and the soul-deep intimacy.

Claire lay with her head on Zach's chest, her body still feeling the aftershocks of their encounter. She knew she should pull away. Force herself to be practical again. But she couldn't seem to make herself do that.

Not after she had just experienced the hottest, most wonderful lovemaking of her life again.

She didn't know what it was about this man. It felt so good to spend time with him. Share confidences. Snuggle into his solid strength. Let herself feel adored. And protected.

Finally realizing the truth of the situation, she eased away from him and sighed. "We're not going to be able to stay away from each other, are we?"

Zach rolled onto his side, guiding her to do the same. They were still close enough to touch, facing each other. His lips turned up in a satisfied smile. "Doesn't seem like it, no."

Exactly what she had thought.

Which meant they were going to have to be really adult about this.

He traced her cheekbone with his thumb, amusement tugging at the corners of his lips. "You don't seem to know if that is a good thing or a bad thing."

Maybe because she didn't have the inner confidence he seemed to have right now. Wincing at the accuracy of his observation, Claire forced herself to admit, "Well... I've never been a friends with benefits kind of gal."

He wrapped his brawny arms around her, tenderly nuzzling her temple. "Same with me. I have to be in a relationship to be intimate."

Excitement roared through her and her breath hitched. "And yet here we are, Zach. Not in a relationship." She shrugged, warning herself not to get ahead of themselves, no matter how badly she wanted to do just that. "Not likely to be in one."

Zach shrugged. "That doesn't mean we can't take our time, see where this whatever-it-is between us goes."

He had no idea how tempting that sounded to her. Or how quickly she would jump on it if she didn't have her children to worry about. She raked her teeth across her lip, warning, "I wouldn't want the kids to get hurt."

"Me, either."

"So," she confirmed lightly, doing her best to keep it as casual as they had just agreed it was going to be, "as far as our public persona goes, we are just friends who occasionally go places together. Right?"

"Sure." Something inscrutable came and went in his smoky blue eyes.

Another wave of anxiety sifted through her. "You really want to do this?"

"Take it moment by moment? And do whatever we feel is right?" Looking impossibly handsome and determined in the muted light of his bedroom, he kissed her and said ever so softly, "Yes, Claire, I do."

Chapter Eleven

Claire's schedule was packed Monday morning, so Bette took over with the kids, as per usual, and she left early for the hospital.

Harriett Donnelly, Sasha's mother, was waiting outside Claire's medical office door. She looked very stressed-out. Claire knew why.

"Did you see the results of Sasha's blood work?" Harriett asked immediately.

Sympathizing because she knew how hard it was to have a child sick, never mind with an as yet to be fully diagnosed malady, Claire unlocked the door. "I did. The labs were posted in the portal an hour or so ago."

"Her blood glucose was elevated," Harriett continued anxiously.

Claire ushered her in. "I know." She switched on the office lights.

"You don't think she's diabetic, do you?"

Claire waved the woman into her private office, then gestured for her to take a seat. After unloading her belongings, she settled behind her desk and turned on her computer. "I think it's far too early to rule anything out. We do need to do a fasting blood test, to find out the A1C, or average glucose levels in the blood over the last three months." After logging in, she paused to pull up Sasha's chart. "So I was going to ask if you could reschedule this afternoon's appointment and bring your daughter in first thing tomorrow, before breakfast, instead, so that we could do the necessary blood draw at the same time we remove her monitor and get another EKG."

"Sure. Absolutely." Harriett's body slumped.

"It's going to be okay," Claire soothed.

Even if Sasha was becoming diabetic—and it was far too early to even be thinking that way—there were medical treatments that would allow her to live a pretty normal life.

More likely this abnormality was linked to whatever had caused the little girl's intermittent heart palpitations and occasional arrhythmia.

And they were still working to diagnose that. One step at a time. All the while keeping a careful eye on the little girl.

Harriett remained fixated on the blood work results. "But her glucose level was so high!"

"It was also the middle of the day. She'd had lunch at school, right?"

Harriett nodded. "But… I pack her lunch! Every day! There's no sugary items in there."

True. Claire nodded. "But we don't know what was in the other kids' lunches. Things like triple jelly and bacon sandwiches, or high-fructose gummy snacks, or well, anything that would create a spike. Sasha could have traded or shared with a friend. And not thought a thing about it, except that it was fun. I did that when I was a kid."

Harriett paused. "So did I."

"So let's not jump to conclusions. Or worry unnecessarily. Especially if there are no other symptoms that would point to diabetes."

"You're right." Harriett exhaled and sat back. "I'm just on edge because I'm not used to handling this all on my own."

"Is your husband still in Alaska, working?"

The woman nodded. "Geoff thought he was going to be

able to get home this weekend, but now it looks like it might be another month or two. He's not even sure he can get home to see Tucker's high school graduation."

"Oh, boy."

"Yeah."

Claire's receptionist came into the office. She stuck her head in to make sure everything was okay, since no patients were scheduled that early.

Claire indicated it was.

Jolted into awareness, Harriett looked at her watch. "Well, thanks for talking to me."

"No problem. We will see you and Sasha tomorrow morning, at eight o'clock."

"We'll be here," Harriett promised.

Claire told her receptionist about the change in Sasha's appointment time and went back to her desk to check her email. She had a message from Gabe, along with forms that needed to be filled out and signed, including a letter retaining him. He also wanted to know if she wanted to come in to his office to talk more about Sebastian first, or if she just wanted him to try and set something up. Needing to get that taken care of ASAP, she chose the latter.

She heard back from him almost immediately. He said he would get on it, and let her know.

Relieved that much seemed to be in control, she got on with her morning. Seeing patients, one after another, until noon.

She was just headed down to the cafeteria to grab a bite, when she ran into Zach. He was dressed for seeing patients, in the usual nice slacks, button-up and crazy tie. His face was freshly shaven but she noted his dark brown hair looked a little rumpled, as if he hadn't bothered to style it after getting out of the shower.

Her heart skipped a beat as he came toward her.

"Hey."

Trying not to notice how masculine and undeniably sexy he looked, she said, "Hey…"

He sent her a bemused look. Turning, he let his glance drift over her lazily. "Fancy meeting you here," he quipped.

"Same."

He fell into step beside her. "Want to have lunch together?"

Why not? It was likely the only time she would see him today. "Okay." Bypassing the long lines at the deli and hot entree counters, Claire headed for the refrigerated section that held freshly made salads and sandwiches. Zach did the same. After they had paid for their purchases, they headed for a table for two near the back.

He sat down opposite her, bumping knees.

A thrill went through her.

He unwrapped his ham and swiss on rye. "So you talked to Harriett Donnelly, before she talked to me," he said.

"Yes." Claire eased the lid off her chicken Caesar salad. Poured on the low-fat dressing. "I told her we will know more by the end of the week, when the heart monitor results and A1C labs come in. But since Sasha seems to be doing well, and hasn't had any more arrhythmia incidents in the last week, we should table the worry for now."

Zach sipped his water. "That's exactly what I said." He paused, to look her over candidly, as if wanting to make sure she'd had no more crises in her personal life since they had last seen each other.

He shifted in his seat, the hardness of his knee brushing up against hers. "How's the Bette situation?"

Tingling all over, Claire shrugged and took another bite. "Fine…"

"Did you talk to her?"

Unexpected emotion simmering inside her, she drew a breath. "Not yet. We were both exhausted when I got home last night, and she had to be at my place very early this morning, which she was, so… I let it go for now."

Claire's phone went off. She stared at the screen, hardly able to believe what she was seeing.

"Got to go?" His voice was a sexy rumble in his chest.

"No. It's from Bette. She said she is in the hospital and on her way to meet me!"

"Actually," Zach said, glancing toward the cafeteria entrance. He lifted his hand in a wave, catching the nanny's attention. "She's here."

Claire's heart leapt to her throat. "I hope nothing is wrong with the kids." Although if it had been, Claire would have been notified, wouldn't she?

Bette headed to their table. "I'm sorry to interrupt your lunch, but we need to talk. And it can't be in front of the kids."

Zach rose, like the gentleman he was. "How about I get us both a specialty coffee? That usually takes a while. Mocha Frappuccino?"

"Venti. Thanks."

Bette sat down. Face pale. Expression determined. "This isn't going to be easy, so I am just going to say it. I was offered a full-time job at that gallery in Fredericksburg. In addition to showing my work—I already sold two paintings, believe it or not!—they are going to let me teach amateur painting classes. They wanted me to start right away, but I told them I had to give you at least two weeks to find another nanny. And they said fine. But then I have to be there, because summer tourist season is almost upon us, and they always have a lot of traffic in the gallery then."

Feeling like she had been run over by a bus, Claire nodded, taking it all in.

Bette continued softly, "I don't want to tell the kids until we have to—or we know who is going to take my place."

She finally found her voice. "Agreed." This was going to be hard enough as it was, without causing sudden chaos.

"So you're not mad at me?" Bette suddenly looked like a kid.

Mad? *Heck, yes!* Disappointed. Stunned… Claire's feelings ran the gamut. She also knew there was nothing she could do. She couldn't force Bette to work for her. Even if she offered her a significant raise, the young woman would not stay on. The opportunity she had been offered came along once in a lifetime.

Her appetite gone, Claire pushed her food aside. She chose her words carefully. "I'm sad for us, because we are going to miss you, but I know this is the career path you want. So I'm glad you have this opportunity." *Even if it temporarily blows my entire life to smithereens.*

Bette jumped up out of her seat. She came over to give Claire a hug. "Thank you so much! I knew you'd understand!" Promising to see her later, Bette rushed off.

Zach returned, coffees in hand.

He took in her numb state. "Everything okay?"

"No," Claire said, aware it was all she could do not to burst into tears. In a low, discouraged tone, she filled Zach in on the news.

"Want me to come over tonight? Either before or after the kids are asleep?"

Claire had promised herself she wasn't going to lean on Zach so much. That vow went out the window, too. "Yes, I do."

Zach wasn't sure what he expected when he arrived at Claire's home, around eight thirty that evening. Bette's car was gone, which meant she likely was, too. Most of the lights on the second floor were dark. But the first floor was still all lit up.

He rapped softly, hoping Lucky wouldn't bark an alarm.

Silent seconds passed.

Claire swung open the door, looking very much like the harried mom of three that she was in her off hours. She was barefoot, in a loose shirt, and shorts that came to the middle of her sleek thighs. Her curly dark hair was tousled, her pretty face pink with exertion. Just as it had been the very first night he had stopped by her place. To talk.

"Come in." Her voice was barely a whisper.

"Kids asleep, I take it?"

"Yes, but it was wild, getting them bathed and in bed."

He cocked a brow. "Bette didn't offer to stay and help?"

Claire wrinkled her nose in that cute way he loved, admitting ruefully, "She did. But I realized that upping the time they spend with her, right before she leaves for good, might not be the best idea. So I told her I could handle it."

And she apparently had, Zach thought, impressed.

"So how can I help?" The living room, foyer and kitchen were all disaster zones.

She pointed to her laptop, which was open on the kitchen counter. "Use your expertise as a pediatrician to go through some of those profiles to see if you think any of those nannies might be a good fit for us."

Zach recognized the name of the premiere agency. It was the largest in Texas. They were always sending out promotional brochures to pediatricians, advertising their services. "Have you used them before?"

"Yep. It's the place I got my first two nannies."

Which hadn't exactly worked out for them, he remembered. "Where did Bette come from again?"

"A recommendation from a friend of a friend, who mentioned she had a real way with kids, and knew she was looking for a part-time job that would pay the bills while she got her career off the ground. I called her on a whim, and it worked out. Unfortunately, only for about seven and a half months, but—" Claire inhaled deeply, her breasts rising and lowering seductively "—we are where we are, right?"

Zach nodded. Glad she was being strong about all this.

She indicated her laptop with a nod of her head. "So if you could just go through those profiles and pics and see if anything or anyone jumps out at you...?"

"Sure."

The next fifteen minutes passed in silence, while Claire quickly put her kitchen back in order and assembled three school lunches for the next day, while Lucky lounged on the floor between them.

Finished, she came over to slide onto the stool next to him. She looked over his shoulder. "You've been through *all* the candidates? That was pretty quick."

He inhaled the scent of lavender baby shampoo clinging to her. "Yeah."

She also had a few wet places on her clothes that he figured were splashes from the bathwater. Which made him wonder how far down the dampness went.

She tapped her delicate fingertips on the counter, oblivious to the sensual nature of his thoughts. "Okay, out with it. What are you thinking?"

Zach exhaled and turned his attention back to the profiles he had been perusing. "You really want me to give you my honest opinion?"

"I really do."

"Well, first, I'm not sure why you're going the agency route when it didn't work out before."

Indignant, she sat up straighter. "It sort of did."

Treading gently, he asked, "In what sense?"

She lifted her hands, palm up. "The nannies were career professionals. And the kids were well taken care of, when I wasn't home, and I never had to worry that someone would walk out without notice."

"I thought there was a certain lack of simpatico."

She acknowledged that to be true, with a tilt of her head. A flash of worry came and went in her green eyes. "I'm hoping the third time will be the charm."

His heart going out to her, he fell silent.

She studied him unhappily. "Obviously, you're finding a problem with these candidates."

A glaring one. Still...the last thing he wanted to do was fight about this. "You sure you want my opinion?"

"Yes."

Okay, then. "None of these nannies list any experience with multiples. And having been a quadruplet myself, I can tell you it takes a unique skill to be able to handle multiple birth kids like yours, or my brother Alex's boys."

Claire seemed abruptly taken aback. Her brow furrowed. "He's divorced, isn't he?"

"Yes."

"How long?" she asked.

"Since the boys were a year old."

"Does he share custody?"

"No. His ex-wife didn't want responsibility for the kids. She said it was too much for her. So he's had sole custody for almost four years."

She raised her brows. "Wow. How did he manage them *and* a cattle ranch?"

"By leaning on family. And the volunteers from the Laramie Multiples Club."

"You think I should go to the club for help?" Claire guessed in a pinched voice.

Zach nodded, elaborating kindly, "According to my mom, none of us would have survived the first couple years of quadruplet-hood, if it hadn't been for the club volunteers. And in fact, my parents believe in the group so much that they've continued to be members after all this time."

"The problem is, my kids have already been through so much. We moved here last spring, and since then, they've had three different caretakers, in addition to me." She blew out a breath. "Now, I've got Sebastian somehow back in my life, wanting what I don't yet know—except to talk about the kids. And while it might be nice to have experienced volunteers here, I don't know if a rotating group of helpers would bring more continuity and stability to our life, or less. In any case, it seems like a lot for me to juggle."

Zach covered her hand with his. "That's the beauty of the club. You don't have to juggle. They have schedulers who take care of all that for you. And who knows? Maybe one of those volunteers might end up being interested in coming to work for you. Or you could hire a couple of them, and that way you wouldn't be reliant on only one person to help you care for the triplets. Plus, all of them live in the county, so you wouldn't have to try and convince anyone to come and live in rural west Texas."

She wove her fingers intimately through his. "You really have thought about this." She stared down at their entwined hands.

"I know your kids. I know the people in the Multiples Club. They are all wonderful, Claire. And if you got them involved now, Bette could help train whoever is going to be watching your kids to the way things work in your household."

Claire rose and began to pace. Swiveling back to him, she propped her hands on her hips. "What if it doesn't work?"

"What if it *does*?" He drew her all the way into his arms, loving her softness and warmth. "At least talk to my mom about the idea," he said. "She's been a social worker in this community for the last forty years. I guarantee she'll know what possible solutions are out there."

Uncertainty shone in Claire's eyes. "I'm not sure I know her well enough to impose on her that way."

"You're in Laramie County now, remember? Helping a neighbor is never an imposition." He kissed her. As they drew apart, Zach volunteered, "I'll even call Mom for you, help set something up."

Finally, the smile he had been waiting all evening to see spread across her face. Relaxing against him, she splayed her palms across his chest. "You are a very persuasive man, Zach McCabe."

"You don't know the half of it," he murmured. Then, drawing her close again, he couldn't resist kissing her one more time before heading out the door.

Chapter Twelve

"I didn't know you were on call tonight," Zach said that Tuesday evening, his low, sexy voice rumbling over the phone.

Claire stepped outside into the courtyard outside the cafeteria for her fifteen-minute break. The stars shone overhead, and a quarter moon gleamed against the black velvet sky. A warm spring breeze, scented with flowers, filled the air. Claire took her coffee and sat down at one of the tables. "I traded with a colleague, at the last minute, so I wouldn't have to do a night soon after Bette left."

"So she is with the kids?" Zach asked.

His voice cloaked her like a cozy blanket. Making her feel all cared for and comfy inside. "Yeah. All night. She'll sleep in the guest room. She stays over whenever I'm on call or have to be at the hospital after hours. So, the kids are used to it."

Claire tried not to imagine how nice it would be if he were sitting here with her. Even for just a few minutes. She also knew that wasn't likely to happen, since he had been looking at houses all evening. "So what's up?"

"I wanted to know if you and my mom had touched base."

The depth of his concern warmed her from head to toe. "Yeah. We're having coffee tomorrow afternoon."

"Great."

Claire hoped so. She was still a little nervous about it for reasons she didn't quite understand. It wasn't as if Mitzy was the type of woman to judge her. Quite the contrary.

Yet it seemed somehow important for Zach's mother to like and respect her. Even when she'd made a muddle of her kids' childcare situation.

Zach didn't seem nervous about it, though.

"I also wondered if Gabe had ever been able to get in touch with your ex," he said.

Claire didn't mind him asking. In fact, she was glad she had him to lean on right now. "Gabe and Sebastian finally talked by phone." She huffed her frustration. "Sebastian said he wanted to talk to me directly, that there was no need to get lawyers involved."

Zach made a disgruntled sound that mirrored her mood. "What did Gabe say to that?"

Claire reported with satisfaction, "Gabe said, if there was no legal representation for me, present, there would be no contact with Sebastian. And he also suggested that if this had anything to do with the kids that Sebastian get an attorney for himself."

"Sounds like my brother," Zach mused. "Ethical to the end."

"Yeah." And it was a good thing, Claire thought. Having a competent, ethical lawyer would make whatever this was go a whole lot easier for everyone.

"So what did Sebastian do then?"

He sounded so relaxed, Claire could imagine Zach leaning back in his seat. Arms folded across his big, brawny chest. She wished she felt nearly as chill about the whole thing. But instead, she found herself pinching the bridge of her nose, recalling, "Sebastian said he didn't know why I was making such a big deal about something that should be nothing, then said he would have to think about it and hung up on your brother."

"Hm. What was Gabe's take on all that?"

"He thought that Sebastian definitely wants something from

me, and will likely contact us again as soon as he's ready to proceed."

"Probably true." Zach sounded as unhappy as Claire was about that possibility.

"So what about you? How was the house-hunting?" she asked, in an attempt to change the subject to something a lot more cheerful. Like where he would be living next.

Zach paused. "I've got some thinking to do."

Claire waited for him to go on; he didn't. "So you found something that might work?" Even though she knew technically it was none of her business, she was frustrated the handsome doc wasn't more forthcoming.

"Yeah. Anyway, I was on my way home. Do you need anything? I'd be happy to drop something by the hospital if you haven't had dinner yet."

Claire could only imagine how tired Zach was given he had taken overnight calls over the weekend. And then spent hours celebrating the holiday weekend and helping her with the kids. "Thanks. But not necessary." Although Claire would really love it if it were. "I ate with Bette and the kids." Her pager went off. "Listen, gotta go."

"Understand. Catch you later." He hung up.

As Claire headed back to the ER, she couldn't help but think how good it had been to touch base with him. Hearing his voice. Feeling his tender concern. Which was kind of crazy, actually. It had only been twenty-four hours since they had last seen each other. But until he had called, it had felt like an eternity.

Was she head over heels for him, or what? And if she was losing her heart to him, as she half suspected, did that break their agreement to keep things casual between them?

Claire and Mitzy met in the park across the street from the Cowgirl Bistro on Main Street, the following afternoon.

They took a seat at one of the picnic tables under the picnic shelter roof. Claire had showered when she got home from her overnight hospital duty, and slept six hours before getting up again and fixing herself something to eat. So, she felt better overall, but was still dragging a little. Which was why she usually took the day after call off from patient appointments.

"Thanks for agreeing to brainstorm with me," Claire said.

"Happy to help. So give me a quick history on the problem, and the triplets' childcare experiences to date…"

Claire did. Starting with their two-and-a-half-year stint with her sister Gwen and her husband Patrick and their three kids, then the two agency nannies, neither of whom really clicked with the kids emotionally, and Bette, who had, but was now leaving.

Mitzy sipped her chai tea. "Do the kids know Bette is going to take another job soon?"

"No." She took a sip of her vanilla latte. "And I'm dreading telling them, after the way they took her unexpected absence last week."

"Yeah, that definitely wasn't responsible on her part, but you can suddenly lose your current childcare for all sorts of reasons."

Claire supposed that was true. "So what do you think?" She looked Zach's mother in the eye, appreciating her sensitivity and compassion. "What should I do?"

"Well, I have to tell you, I don't think my son's idea to enlist a rotating cast of volunteers is a solid one."

Glad they were on the same page about that, Claire said, "He shared that with you?"

"Oh yes. Trouble is, he doesn't really know how the Laramie Multiples Club operates, other than they take great care of kids."

"So you don't think I should use a bunch of different volunteers?" It kind of helped to know she and Mitzy were instinctively on the same page about that.

"Not in your situation, no. We do that a lot for parents of multiple infants who need help twenty-four hours a day, for the first six months to a year. In that case, we try to pair one adult to every child and rotate caregivers. So the babies are not just well-loved but well socialized, too."

Made a lot of sense. Maybe then, kids wouldn't get so attached to any one person they couldn't accept a replacement? "What happens to kids like mine that are three and a half years old? And don't have a lot of experience with babysitters? How are they helped by the Laramie Multiples Club?"

"Depends on their background. If the family had LMC helpers from the get-go, they continue to get help as needed from the many volunteers. Although in some cases, especially in two-career families, the parents will permanently hire a person or two to assist them. To make things more settled. Which is what I would suggest you do."

That sounded good to Claire, too. "Did you have anyone specific in mind?"

"Yes. I think Charlene Parker and Danielle Reyes would both be a good fit. They are both empty-nesters, and have raised multiples themselves. And volunteered with the LMC for years. But now are looking for part-time employment. Would you like me to see if they are interested in meeting you and your kids, and if so, set something up?"

Claire felt a wave of enormous relief. She was so happy Zach had set this meeting up for her. "That would be great!"

Mitzy opened up her notepad and took out a pen. "Then I'm on it. Don't worry, we will get it worked out ASAP."

They talked a little more, to choreograph what that might look like for the kids, as well as the best timeline to tell them about their sitter leaving, as Bette's time in her employ came to an end. And all the while, Claire couldn't help noting that Mitzy was so much like her son, and indeed like the entire McCabe family. Gentle. Kind. Practical. Zach was lucky to have them, and now, crazy as it was, she couldn't help but wonder what it would be like to actually be a part of their amazing family.

"How come you're here to pick us up, Mommy?" Oliver asked.

"Yeah, where's Bette?" Isabella echoed with a frown.

Claire made sure the kids were all buckled in, then navigated her SUV through the school pickup lane. When she got back out on the street, she answered, reminding them, "I had to work last night, remember? Bette was with you for dinner and baths and bedtime, and then again this morning, when I got home from the hospital. To help you get to preschool."

"So where is she *now*?" Andrew persisted, still unhappy their nanny wasn't the one in the driver's seat.

Claire paused at a stop sign. Wondering if all parents felt as unappreciated as she did at this moment. "At her apartment, I think."

"Is she coming to help us with dinner?" Isabella asked hopefully.

Claire drove on through the quiet streets. "Not unless I get called in to the hospital." Which she hoped did not happen. She could use a night with just her and the kids. To get them settled down again.

Unfortunately, her best-made plans went awry. No sooner had they sat down to their evening meal, than her cell phone chimed. It was the hospital. "Do you have to go to work?" Andrew asked, as soon as she got off the call.

"I'm sorry. Yes, I do."

"Yay! Bette's coming!"

Luckily, their sitter was there in ten. Cheerful as always.

Wondering what she was going to do at times like this, when Bette was no longer in her employ, Claire headed out.

The patient situation was as complex as expected, and the next few hours passed swiftly. She was still in one of the viewing rooms, looking at film and waiting for the last of the lab reports to come back in so she could finish up the final orders for the night, when there was a knock on the door.

Zach poked his head around the corner. He strolled in, looking every bit as happy to see her as she was to see him. No goofy tie tonight though. She imagined he had "lost" it at the same time he opened up the first couple of buttons on his cotton dress shirt. And rolled up his sleeves. She decided he was way too sexy, no matter what time, day or night. Way too capable and masculine and kind. He smiled over at her and sank down in one of the other swivel chairs and flexed his broad shoulders. One colleague to another, he asked, "What's going on?"

"One of my patients overdid it with the spring yard work and had a heart attack. Fortunately, he was in the front yard when he went down. The neighbors saw and called 911, and the paramedics got him to the hospital quickly."

Zach considered the ramifications. "Is he going to be okay?"

"I believe so. It doesn't look like there is any permanent damage but we admitted him for observation, and will probably run some more tests tomorrow, just to be sure. What about you? Why are you here?"

"For an admission," he answered. "Bronchial pneumonia complicated by asthma and seasonal allergies."

Claire thought about how much she liked hanging out with him, and how easy it would be to really start depending on him. "How old?"

"Seven." A mixture of empathy and concern colored his low tone. "She's a sweet kid, but she hates taking medicine, and her parents hate making her do what she doesn't want to do, so…" A muscle ticked in his jaw. "We've got to get a little bit better at that, so she doesn't end up in the hospital again."

"I feel everyone's pain in this situation." Claire frowned when her phone vibrated. "Hang on. Got to get this. Hey, Bette."

"Hi Claire."

"Kids asleep?"

"For a couple of hours now. Listen, would it be okay if I crashed in the guest room tonight? I'm exhausted and this way I will already be there in the morning when it's time to get the kids ready for school."

"Sounds like a plan." Claire paused, almost afraid to ask but needing to know the assessment when little ears weren't listening. "Were the kids well-behaved for you?"

"Are you kidding? They were angels! I can't remember when we had a better night!" They chatted for a few more moments, then Bette signed off.

Claire put her phone away.

"Everything okay?" Zach asked.

The viewing room suddenly seemed awfully small. Trying not to be too aware of his soothing, ultramasculine presence, Claire nodded. "Yeah, Bette's sleeping over in our guest room. Which is great. Because now I don't have to worry about when I'm going to get those lab results." She widened her eyes in exaggerated glee. "I can stay out 'til…gosh… I don't know, almost midnight?"

He chuckled, as she meant him to. "Cinderella, huh?"

"Sure feels like it sometimes…" she said, rolling her eyes.

Claire looked at the computer screen. "Aha, here they are! And the results are excellent. Just as I had hoped…" She typed in a few more orders for the CCU staff, and then signed out.

Zach rose, his tall frame towering over her. "Done?"

Darn, he smelled good. Like soap—and man. Memories of how wonderfully he made love came flooding back. "Yep," she said hoarsely. "You?"

He nodded. She watched him take the work badge clipped to his shirt, turn it around so only the back was showing, and slide it into his shirt pocket. "Did you have dinner?"

Claire took her badge off, too. Sliding hers into her bag. "Almost."

He narrowed his gray-blue eyes at her. "I'm not sure that counts."

Claire would have said the same thing had she been fishing for a dinner invitation—she wasn't.

Aware things still seemed to be moving awfully fast between them, and in this case fast probably wasn't good, she shrugged off his concern.

"I can have a bowl of cereal or something when I get home."

"How about I do you one better, since I didn't eat, either?" He surveyed her with his trademark compassion. Something sweet and lovable in his gaze. "Want to split a takeout pizza from Lugazzi's?"

A nice piping hot, fresh pie sounded pretty darn good right about now. Especially since she actually was starving.

Claire decided to stop fighting the desire to spend more time with him outside of work and kids. Maybe this was what they needed for her to feel a little better about her impulsively hooking up with him—twice. More time together getting to know each other. Platonically, of course.

"Sure," she agreed lightly, assessing him right back, friend to friend. "Where do you want to eat it?" Either of their offices would work, this time of night.

Or even the town park, which was just down the street from the tiny, busy take-out restaurant.

He quirked his brow. Clearly having something entirely different in mind. "My place."

Chapter Thirteen

The hesitation on Claire's face when he suggested going back to his apartment was not what Zach wanted to see. Although he supposed it was understandable. She was trying to limit the times they hooked up, to keep their relationship within certain casual parameters and not get emotionally involved with him. Yet every time they saw each other, the intimacy between them grew.

Knowing pushing her into something she either wasn't ready for, or didn't feel she had time for, would be a mistake, he continued offhandedly, "Or we could go to your place." Where chaperones…albeit sleeping ones…abounded.

She grabbed her bag as she headed for the door. "I'd rather not chance waking up Bette or the kids."

"Then my place it is." He followed her to the elevator, stepping inside with her.

"So what do you want on your pizza?" he asked. The doors slid shut, confining them in the quiet space.

She leaned against the wall, her hands behind her, as the cage slid downward. "You don't want to do half and half?"

Only the fact they were at work kept him from pulling her in for a kiss. "Nope. What you're ordering is what I'm eating tonight."

This seemed to please her, as he had hoped it would. Her soft lips curved into a sensual smile. "Chivalrous."

Chuckling, he returned her compliment with a wink. "Or lazy."

Too soon, the doors opened again. They walked out through the employee-only exit, to the physicians' parking lot. He got out his phone and brought up the number for Lugazzi's.

She pursed her lips together, as if still trying to decide what to request. Squinting at him, she asked, "Exactly how hungry are you?"

For you? Zach felt a wave of heat slide through him. His body ached with the need to make love to her again. "Very."

She relaxed. Unlike him, her mind was only on the meal ahead. "Okay then. A sixteen-inch extra-thin-crust Meat Lover's."

"Ah. A carnivore after my own heart," he teased, pausing to call in their order. She waited for him to finish on the phone, then continued walking across the asphalt until they reached her SUV.

"See you there?"

Wanting her with him, but knowing for a lot of reasons it would be better if they both took their vehicles out of the work lot now, when they appeared to be headed home, instead of out on a private rendezvous, he nodded. Claire was a woman who had a ton of demands on her and needed a lot of personal space.

They met up again at Lugazzi's. By the time he paid, their pizza was boxed up and ready to go.

She followed him to his place. They walked inside.

Looking around, she remarked, "Somehow I thought you'd have more packing done. Instead, it looks exactly the way it did when we left off Sunday night."

Including the rumpled covers on his bed, that still smelled enticingly like the two of them.

Wishing he'd thought to tidy up a bit before he left for work that morning, he set the pizza box on the coffee table in front of the sofa, then went into the kitchenette.

"That's because it is," Zach said, not sure which he admired more, the purposeful sexy way she moved, or the way she looked in her notch-collared blouse and knee-length skirt. "I was with you Monday night. Tuesday, I was out house-hunting. And now it's Wednesday, and we were both at the hospital, seeing patients and now we're here."

"Good point." Claire's soft lips twisted in a sympathetic moue. "You haven't had much time."

Certainly not enough to pursue her the way he wanted, anyway, with no holds barred. He knew he had to open himself up to love again. The same way Claire did. Whether she admitted it to herself or not.

And, as hard as it had felt initially to push forward, he knew Lisa would want him to put aside his grief, and move on with his life, just as he would have wanted her to move on with hers, had their situations been reversed.

So there was no reason to feel guilty anymore.

Only hopeful…

As Claire now seemed to be, too.

While she slipped off her shoes, and settled in one corner of the long leather sofa, he got out two plates and a couple of sparkling waters from the fridge.

She'd had her hair up in a clip on the back of her head while at work. Now she took it down. Her black hair fell in a cloud of silky curls around her face. She used her fingers to comb it back into place. "So are you worried about getting ready for the move?" she asked softly, fastening the clip to the hem of her blouse.

He brought their dinner utensils over to the coffee table in front of the sofa and set them down. Noting how the sage print of her blouse brought out the green in her eyes, he went back for the rest. Quickly returning to her side, he said, "I'm not worried about that. I don't have all that much stuff, aside from my books. My family will help."

Claire nodded, seeming a little nonplussed she hadn't thought of that.

They opened up the box and each helped themselves to a slice brimming with pepperoni, ham, sausage, beef and cheese. "So did you find a place?" She bit into her pizza with relish.

He had.

And he hoped she would like it.

Not a person to jinx something by talking about it too soon, however, he shrugged, and took a big bite of pizza as well. "I'll know by Saturday."

Claire couldn't say why she was a little hurt by Zach's refusal to talk to her about what was clearly his decision to make. Maybe it was because he had been so forthcoming with her earlier, when talking about which Realtor to hire, what things to consider, and even what she thought of all the listings he had been sent to peruse.

All she knew for sure was that he was holding back. And she didn't like feeling shut out, any more than she had ever liked being abandoned.

"So," he changed the subject smoothly, "how did your meeting with my mom go today?"

"She was very helpful," Claire admitted, taking an equally matter-of-fact tack, "just as you predicted."

"Good to hear."

His husky response sent a thrill down her spine. She shifted in her seat to better view his ruggedly handsome profile. "I just wish…"

"What?" Zach continued looking at her as if he hoped this evening were a start to something more.

Figuring as long as they were talking candidly, she may as well admit, "…that I wasn't having to move so fast. Your mom set up a meeting with Danielle and Charlene for tomorrow, so I could interview them, and I don't even know what I'm going to ask."

His lazy quip brought heat to her cheeks. "Oh, that's easy."

Claire slid him another look. If only he weren't six feet four inches of masculine perfection, and didn't kiss like a dream, and rescue her at every opportunity, it would be a whole lot easier to keep the stronghold around her heart. So she'd never be hurt or abandoned again. "You think so, huh, doc?"

He grinned and looked deep into her eyes. "Absolutely, I do, yeah."

What was it about his innate confidence that made her want him all the more? "I'm going to hold you to that," Claire teased lazily.

"I'm sure you will," Zach joked back, as they helped themselves to another slice. "But first...we have to enjoy this while it's hot..."

"Agreed." They ate in companionable silence for a few minutes, enjoying the meal and one another's company.

Finally finished with her pizza, Claire put her plate aside. She pulled out her cell phone, prepared to record them there. "Okay, smarty-pants, what would your first question be to them?"

He put his empty plate on the coffee table, too. "How do you feel about pineapple?"

Claire couldn't help it, she burst out laughing.

Zach continued with comically exaggerated solemnity, conducting the mock interview. He waved a lecturing finger. "Because if you don't like pineapple, or at least respect it terribly, there is no future for you in this household."

Claire typed that on the cell phone note. "As much as I hate to admit it, you may have a point about that."

He mugged at her comically. "Oh, I know I do."

"What else?" Claire prodded, her giddiness building.

"Oh. Let's see." He considered. "Should boys be forced to play with baby dolls or have tea parties with their sister? Or should the sister always have to play the games her brothers want to play?"

"Another good one."

"And if not, is it okay to kidnap the dolls and hide them away, to torture said sister, at least until Lucky finds them for her?"

"They actually have only done that one time. It just happened to be the night you arrived to talk to me about Sasha's case."

"I wouldn't worry about it. My siblings and I used to play pranks on each other all the time."

"Did you grow out of it?"

He had to think about how to answer that. "Sort of…"

Claire groaned. "You're not giving me a lot to feel hopeful about, doc…"

He shrugged his broad shoulders. "At least you have a sense of humor about it. I don't think you can survive raising them without one."

"I imagine you are right about that."

Their glances meshed. In that instant, Claire knew Zach would be a great person to raise kids with. As well as a great dad, too. And then there was his wonderful family. Not that she should be going down that road, even whimsically, when she had a very important interview to prep for. One that could determine the childcare for her kids.

He carried the leftover pizza and empty plates to the kitchenette. Leaving it all for later, he returned to her side, and sank down on the sofa beside her, facing her. "What do you think you should ask?"

"Oh…" Claire forced herself to be serious as she typed. "Can you come on short notice if I get called into the hospital? Can you spend the night when I'm required to be on call from six p.m. until six a.m. the next day?"

"I agree. Both are very necessary. But…" He stretched his arm along the back of the leather sofa behind her. "I want to volunteer to come by on short notice if you are ever in a pinch, and sleep in the guest room and care for the kids."

Caught off guard, she covered the biceps on his outstretched arm with her palm. "You don't have to do that…"

He laid his hand over hers. "I *want* to."

Claire shivered at the sensation of being skin to skin with him, and once again, felt herself being inexorably drawn to him. Even more powerfully this time. "Why?" she whispered, her heart skittering in her chest. "Why would you want to do that for me?"

Zach shifted her closer, all the way onto his lap. He wove a hand through her hair, tenderness flowing between them. "Because I care about you, Claire," he murmured back, his mouth hovering just above hers. "I care about your kids. And I want you all to have everything you need."

Claire had wanted to think she had been exaggerating the impact of their previous encounters. However, the moment his lips were on hers, drawing her in, she was as lost in him as ever before. He made her feel all woman to his man. As tempted by him as ever.

Ever since becoming a single mom, she had focused on two things, family and work. Zach made her feel as if she could have more. He made her feel sexy, vibrant, and…oh so alive.

She wrapped her arms about his neck, even as he tugged her closer. The tips of her breasts pressed against his hard muscular chest. She felt the pounding of his heart, as he kissed her deeply, irrevocably. His lips seducing hers apart, his tongue tangling with hers, she tasted the essence that was him. Lower still, she felt the hardness of his desire. A low moan rose in her throat, echoed by him.

She wanted this.

Wanted him.

So very much.

Zach knew Claire was vulnerable. That was why he had planned to just spend tonight sharing a meal, talking, getting to know each other better. But remaining physically aloof from her was proving to be an impossible task, especially when she melted against him, kissing him back, again and again.

Her skirt had hiked up over her thighs. Revealing inches of silky skin. The blood thundered through him. He reveled in the soft surrender of her body cuddled against him. She unbuttoned his shirt, kissed the underside of his jaw.

"Claire…"

"I know. We need to get a lot more comfortable." She kissed him again with a wildness beyond his most erotic dreams, slid off his lap and led him toward his bed. They undressed each other swiftly.

Drunk with pleasure, they caressed each other, until she was damp with desire and shuddering, almost there. He laid her back on the bed and slid between her thighs. She gasped as his lips found the feminine heart of her, then shuddered again as she found the release she sought.

Claire helped him roll on a condom that would protect them both. Then he shifted over her once again. Lifting her, finding entry, diving deep. She closed around him, velvety and hot, and together they soared toward a climax more stunning and fulfilling than anything he had ever felt. And he knew, whatever this was now, whatever it could be, he didn't want to let her go. The two of them had something special. All he had to do was find a way to make Claire see that, too.

Thursday at 6:00 a.m., Claire and Gwen finally caught up with each other after playing phone tag for several days. Claire walked out to the backyard patio, a steaming latte in her hand, Lucky at her side. "So what's going on with Bette?" Gwen asked. "Did she ever get back from her last-minute trip to Fredericksburg?"

"Yes, but not until Easter Sunday evening," Claire reported solemnly.

"You're kidding!" Gwen sputtered.

"I only wish I was."

"Did you *know* she was going to be gone that long?" Her sister sounded as indignant as Claire had felt.

"No. Which made it all the more hard on the kids, because we had plans for the holiday weekend." As had Gwen and her crew, who had hosted her in-laws from Arkansas for an extended holiday weekend.

"So, what did you do?"

Claire heard Gwen making coffee. "Well, Zach McCabe went with us to the Easter egg hunt in the town park, on Saturday, and then we went to his family's ranch the next afternoon, for dinner on Sunday."

"Wow. I didn't realize you were such good friends."

Which was what made everything that had happened so darn crazy! She watched Lucky head for his favorite corner of the yard. "We were only casually acquainted until about ten days or so ago, when we started working on a case together." And she realized what she had been trying to ignore from the first moment she had caught a glimpse of him when she landed in Laramie, over a year before, which was how very attracted she was to him. And perhaps, vice versa...

"Hmmm." The sound had a wealth of implication.

Knowing her sister's romantic inclinations, Claire demanded, "What is *that* supposed to mean?"

"Just..." Gwen paused, as if taking time to shrug. "He must be nice if you're spending all that time with him, and letting the kids get to know him, too."

"He is. Really nice." And handsome. And chivalrous. And smart. And kind. And too many other things to mention.

Gwen paused. "Is that all that's going on? Friendship?"

No. We're now friends with benefits. But not about to reveal that, Claire said nothing.

Gwen got the hint. She moved on. "What about Sebastian?" she asked gently. "Any news on that front?"

Claire caught her older sister up on the latest there, too. "So right now we're in a holding pattern, and we'll stay that way until, or if, Sebastian decides he wants to have my attorney there with me to witness and advise."

"Good for you for sticking to your decision and not letting him push you around the way he used to do."

She flushed in embarrassment, as Lucky trotted back to her. "Sebastian never really…"

"Come on, Claire. When you were with him it was always about what Sebastian wanted and needed. Your feelings didn't matter. As was evidenced when he took the job in Antarctica without even consulting you and—"

"Handed me a puppy on his way out the door? Yeah, that was a bad move on his part. Although I have to say—" she reached over and petted her Newfie fondly "—that did turn out to be a very good thing." Her heart swelled with love as she looked into his big, handsome face. "I don't know what the kids or I would do without Lucky."

"He is such a sweet dog. So, is everything else okay now?"

"Not exactly." Claire told Gwen about Bette's resignation.

Her sister gasped again, then said a few more choice words. "What are you going to do?"

Claire caught her up on the new nanny search, too. "Anyway, Zach's mom—Mitzy Martin McCabe—is a social worker here in Laramie. She recommended two local women I'm going to interview later today. If it works out, I'll have them meet the kids, and then if they click, Bette and I will tell the kids she is leaving in another week."

"How do you think that's going to go?" Gwen sounded as worried as Claire privately felt.

"Terrible. In fact, I'm tempted to just wait until Bette is about to leave and then announce it, so we don't have a week of nonstop tears and acting out." *Where all I want to do is cry, too.*

"So why *don't* you handle it that way?"

"Because I had a long talk with Mitzy about it yesterday. And she thinks the kids need to be prepared and not be so blindsided this time, the way they were the last time Bette took off without warning. That this would give them time to process everything properly as we all prepare to say goodbye."

Gwen murmured approvingly. "I can see that."

"Anyway, Zach's mom also suggested that you and I get our families together as soon as we can. So I was hoping you and Patrick and the kids could come here for a visit."

"We absolutely can. But it will have to be when school is out in late May. When all the end-of-year stuff like dance and piano recitals, T-ball and soccer league playoffs are over. But then we would love to come."

"Sounds good," Claire said, going back into the kitchen.

They conversed a little while longer, each promising to do a better job of staying in touch with each other, and said goodbye.

The rest of Claire's day went by quickly.

She was about to leave the office that evening when Zach stopped by to see her.

"Sasha Donnelly's results came back."

Claire sat down at her desk and pulled up the proper screen on the computer. Not sure whether to be relieved or frustrated, she asked, "Has Harriett Donnelly left for the day?"

"Let's find out." Zach made the call.

Zach covered the speaker. "She's still there."

"Want to go talk to her together?" Claire asked.

He nodded, promising, "Harriett? We'll be right there."

By the time they reached the dietician's office, she had her husband Geoff on the phone, FaceTiming with them from Alaska. Both of them had logged in and looked at the online system and were familiar with the results. "So if I'm understanding this correctly," Geoff said, like the geo-scientist he was, "the heart monitor report showed no abnormalities."

Claire nodded. "Sasha was in normal sinus rhythm the entire seven days she had it on."

Harriett said, to confirm, "And the repeat blood work looks fine, too?"

"Yes, everything that second day was completely normal. Her A1C, or the three-month average of her blood glucose levels, is within normal range, too," Zach said.

Geoff frowned. "So Sasha's not diabetic or anything like that."

"No."

"Then why," Harriett persisted, "was she having brief periods of heart arrhythmia? To the point she fainted on the playground one day?"

"We don't have an answer on that yet," Claire said. "Arrhythmias aren't that uncommon in children, many times they go away on their own. Which seems to be what has happened here. But just to be sure, I'd like to order an echocardiogram. The test uses sound waves to take pictures of Sasha's heart, and look at the heart's structure and function. I'm not expecting to see anything there either, but it would be good to have the information as a baseline."

"When can that be done?" Sasha's father asked.

"I'll set it up for next week," Claire promised. "In the meantime, as always, let me know if anything changes…"

She exited the FaceTime chat and waved goodbye to Harriett, who was still talking with her husband on the call. Zach walked out with her. "I wish we'd had something more defini-tive to tell them," he said.

Claire nodded. "Except that if we had, it also would have meant an abnormality. So…"

"Maybe not knowing right now is a good thing?" he said, turning toward her.

"Maybe." She sighed as her phone vibrated to signal an incoming call.

"Got to take it?" Zach asked, looking ready to step away.

Claire nodded. "I do. It's your brother, calling me from his law office, which can only mean one thing."

"More on the situation with your ex?"

"Would have to be," she said grimly.

Chapter Fourteen

Claire moved a slight distance away to take her call. Zach waited until she had finished. He could tell she was upset and his heart went out to her.

Once she returned to his side, he wrapped his arm around her shoulder, pulling her in close, and asked, "Everything okay?"

"Well, be careful what you wish for, I guess," she muttered. "Sebastian's apparently had a change of heart." She huffed out a breath. "He decided he will talk to me with my attorney present. And Gabe says Sebastian wants to do it thirty minutes from now."

"Are you going to do that?"

She eased away from him. Flexing her shoulders and linking her hands behind her neck, in a way that made her fatigue all the more apparent, Claire frowned. "Gabe said we could reschedule for some time next week, if I would prefer, but honestly, I think I'd rather just get it over with."

"Understandable. Do you want me to go with you?" Zach asked. He didn't want her to have to face this alone, and having her lawyer with her didn't count.

She sent him a surprised glance.

He shrugged, belatedly aware he might have overstepped. Yet not sorry he had. "For moral support."

For a moment, he thought she was going to take him up on his offer. Then she seemed to shake off her momentary vulnerability. "Thanks, but I'm sure Gabe and I have got this."

Much as he loathed to admit it, he imagined they did.

"Do you need any help with the kids?"

Claire shook her head, already starting to text. "Bette was already planning to be there tonight, to help me with the triplets. And spend a little more time with them before she leaves. So it will be fine."

Zach did his best to quell his disappointment.

Then he reminded himself Claire was a single mom, well used to handling everything by herself. He was the one who needed to be there. To protect and care for them. Unfortunately, she wasn't asking. "Call me if you need me," he said anyway.

Claire flashed him a quick, officious smile, the kind you gave a colleague you knew only vaguely. "Will do. And thanks." Claire hurried off in the direction of her office. He headed down another long hallway, and up two floors, to his. Still wishing he could do more.

Gabe was waiting for Claire when she reached his law office. His secretary and paralegal had already gone home for the day, so it was just the two of them.

He handed her a chilled bottle of water. "I've set up the camera, so Sebastian will be able to see both of us while we're talking."

"Is he also going to have legal representation?"

"He didn't say. Although, as a matter of course, I did advise him to do so."

Claire sighed and settled in the chair at the conference table. "He probably won't…"

Her prediction was right. Sebastian was by himself when he appeared onscreen.

His hair was longer and a little unkempt, and he seemed to have gained some weight, but otherwise, he looked pretty much the same as when he had left, nearly five years before.

He appeared to be wearing several layers of expensive cold-weather clothing. And he radiated an air of impatience she recalled well.

"Okay, let's get this over with," he said abruptly, as soon as Gabe had introduced himself. "I want to get married. But Marie won't say yes until we have it in writing that I will never be saddled with child-rearing, no matter what. So I want to officially sign away my parental rights."

Gabe stopped him with a stern, lawyerly look. "It's not that simple."

"It certainly should be," Sebastian huffed. "I'm sure that's what Claire wants!"

Actually, now that she had seen her ex again, and realized what a colossal mistake she had made ever getting involved with the selfish jerk, it was.

"And we will definitely get there," Gabe continued smoothly. "But before you can surrender your rights, officially, you first have to prove they exist in the first place. Which means you're going to have to take a paternity test. And present it to the Texas court."

Gabe had prepared her for this, so Claire wasn't as shocked as her ex was. "The kids already have theirs," Claire told Sebastian calmly. "I had it done shortly after they were born, in case there was ever any issue."

"Fine. I'll get one done, pronto, and send you the results." Sebastian started to get up out of his seat. "And we'll be done here."

"Again, not that simple," Gabe countered, in a voice that pretty much commanded Sebastian to sit down again. "Because as soon as you are proved the biological father, in Texas court, child support will have to be dealt with, in accordance with Texas Family Code. There's no getting around that in the state of Texas. Even if Claire wanted to waive it, she couldn't."

Sebastian sat back in his chair with a thud. He glared at Claire. "You set me up," he accused.

"No," Zach's brother countered before Claire could speak. "My client did *no* such thing. But if you want to get your own lawyer now…as I advised you the first time we touched base with each other…it would be a good idea."

Sebastian sat there in stony silence. "I'll get you-all the DNA results as soon as they come in," he said, and the call went dead.

Claire stayed to talk to Gabe a few more minutes. Not sure what she was going to do next, she headed out of the office, toward the parking lot, still feeling shaken to the core. And that's when she looked up and saw Zach, leaning against his pickup truck.

Her insides trembling, she headed for him. Amazed at how much it meant to see him there. As well as how much she wanted to be with him right now. She gulped around the lump in her throat. "Waiting for me?" she asked hoarsely.

"You bet," he said.

For a moment, Claire looked so stressed-out and upset, Zach thought she was going to burst into tears and fall into his arms. He stood ready to comfort her. Then, she exhaled slowly, and pulled it together with fortitude and grace, the way she always did in traumatic situations.

"Any particular reason?" she murmured.

As always, he admired her strength. "I thought the call with your ex might be rough, and I wanted to make sure you were all right." *Was she?* He still couldn't tell. Leaning closer to search her face, he cupped her shoulders and asked, "Are you okay?"

Acting as if that were the most ridiculous question she had ever heard, she wrinkled her nose at him. "Um…you know, I don't usually say this, but I think I need a mom's time-out."

Noticing he was still holding onto her, he dropped his hands. He let their glances collide, then linger. Aware that everything but the possibility of making love to her again, had left his brain, he said gently, "I can help with that. Want to go to dinner or have a drink together…?"

Looking adorably flustered, and off-kilter, she shook her head. "I'd rather go some place private." Her upright posture emphasized the soft swell of her breasts. His body hardened in response. "So I don't have to worry about running into people, or being social if we do…"

He tore his eyes from her sensational legs, and the feminine curve of her hips. "How about the lake? It's pretty quiet during the week, this time of year."

She grinned. "You're talking picnic?"

"At sunset," Zach joshed back, "yeah."

Despite the apparent grimness of the situation, her smile widened. "Let me call Bette, make sure all is okay there."

Once again, he waited, while she made the call. This time, hitting the speaker and putting the phone out in front of her. So both could hear. "Hey Bette," she said when her soon-to-be-gone nanny answered, "how are things going?"

Zach tried not to think what it meant to have her allowing him to witness this particular conversation. Although, he had to admit, he was honored to be included however Claire chose to involve him in her life.

"Great!" Bette said, sounding chipper as ever. "So if you need more time to handle whatever that situation was with your attorney…"

Claire met Zach's eyes, radiating a mixture of turmoil and relief. "Actually, Bette, I do."

"No problem," the nanny responded genially in a way that had Zach understanding what Claire had seen in her children's caretaker. "But if you're going to be past nine thirty or ten, do you mind if I crash in the guest room again?"

"I'd love it if you would," Claire said.

So would Zach.

This way, they could talk as much and as long as Claire wanted. And if she wanted any other kind of comfort, well, he could provide that, too.

They picked up some dinner from a place in town. Claire parked her car at Zach's apartment, climbed into his pick-up truck and they were off.

Claire was quiet during the thirty minute drive to Lake Laramie. Partly because she needed some time to collect her thoughts. And partly because it was one of the rare times she wasn't driving herself, and hence was free to take in the beautiful scenery. As they went from town to ranch land, to the woods and rocky bluffs that surrounded the parkland.

At Zach's suggestion, they bypassed the picnic areas close to the lodge, and adjacent cabins, and headed for the eastern side of the water. It wasn't long before the perfect picnic area appeared. It was quiet and private, with a wooden table and benches. It also afforded a spectacular view of the shimmering blue lake, and the big Texas sky. Which was nearly as blue. Zach parked in the gravel next to it, and they got out. Taking their gear with them.

"We've got an hour or so until sunset," he told her.

Which was more than enough time to eat their dinner.

"But just in case..." he went back to his truck and returned with a camping lantern, and set it on the middle of the table.

Claire smiled. "Good thinking."

Together, they spread out the beach towel he'd brought to serve as a tablecloth. And set their dinner on top of it.

Zach glanced over at her, concerned. His hair was tousled. An evening beard rimmed his jaw, adding to his overall masculinity. "Are you okay?"

Was she?

Trying not to replay the virtual meeting with Sebastian in her head, or worry about what came next, she shook off her unease. "Yeah," she fibbed. "Sorry I've been so uncommunicative."

He flipped open the top of a bottle of hand sanitizer, poured some on his palm, then handed it to her.

"I've just been thinking…"

His dark brow quirked. "The meeting with your ex was that bad?" He watched as she disinfected her hands, too.

Claire nodded. "Yeah, actually, it was."

He gazed at her kindly. "You don't have to talk about it. I know it's none of my business. But if you need to vent, I can listen. Or we can just relax and eat and talk about other stuff."

She knew she needed the kind of support only he seemed to be able to give her. Especially tonight.

She met his gaze, drawing in a shaky breath. "I think I do need to get it out."

"Okay." He got out the two grilled southwestern chicken salads to go and two bottles of sparkling water. Waiting until she had spread her napkin onto her lap before he said, "Where do you want to start?"

Claire twisted the cap off her water and took a sip. "At the beginning of the meeting, I guess."

While they dug into their dinner, she went on to tell him everything Sebastian had said until abruptly ending the call.

Finished eating, Zach sat back in his chair. "So you don't know for sure if he is going to go through the process to legally terminate his rights? Given the process isn't nearly anywhere as easy as he thought it was going to be. Assuming he does go on to get a paternity test…?"

Claire knew Zach was right. There were a lot of "ifs" in the situation right now. That was likely the source of her anxiety. She liked things clear, and settled.

She set her napkin beside her plate. "I think Sebastian will eventually follow through...because it seems like he really wants to marry this Marie person he talked about. And she apparently won't say I do unless she can be absolutely certain the two of them would never be expected to take on the care of the triplets."

Zach nodded. As relieved as she was to find that her ex wasn't interested in trying to take the kids from her.

"But..." She took another sip of water to ease the dryness in her throat, "Sebastian wasn't happy about the idea of having to claim them, before he could legally sever ties with them. Nor did he want to pay the child support he will then owe the kids under the Texas Family Code."

"Can you waive that?"

"I talked to Gabe about that possibility after the call. He said in extreme cases the court can order that, but it is really only in situations where a parent is disabled, and can't work, or the child turns eighteen, stuff like that. Otherwise, the law states parents have an inherent right to support their children. Not feeling like forking over the money isn't what the courts would consider an acceptable reason for cancelling child support." She shrugged. "And I guess that makes sense. Because at the end of day, it would be the kids who would likely suffer."

Zach brought out a dessert flight, and two specialty coffees in insulated cups. "Wow, who thought it would be so complicated?"

Claire selected a lemon bar, Zach took a brownie. "I know."

He came around the table, and sat down on the bench next to her. They were both facing the lake now, their bodies close together. The sun was drifting toward the horizon. Pink, gray and pale blue streaks filled the Texas sky, adding to the peaceful mood. And a spring-scented breeze drifted over them. "Did you ever hope he might feel differently about the triplets?"

She sensed he was also asking if she had ever hoped that Sebastian would feel differently about *her*. And although that had been true, briefly, after her ex had left her in the lurch, her ex's abandonment of her had abruptly ended any lingering feelings she'd had.

Figuring all they needed to talk about now was the dilemma facing her, she turned her glance to his, and admitted in rueful honesty, "Sometimes when I look at them, or we're just sitting around having dinner, or hanging out in the yard, or taking Lucky on a walk together, I wonder how anyone could not fall in love with them. You know…?"

"They are adorable." Affection in his low tone.

He gave her no choice; she had to test that sentiment. "Even at their worst?"

Her teasing made him laugh. "Especially at their worst."

They exchanged grins.

"You're really good with them, you know. They adore you."

For a moment, he went silent.

She wasn't sure what he was thinking.

Only that he seemed… troubled somehow.

Wanting to support and encourage him the way he had her, she pushed on. "You'll make a really good father some day."

To her surprise, he didn't seem to want to go there. Conversationally or any other way. Which was a problem if the two of them got any more serious. Because she and her kids were a package deal. He had to know that.

His mood turned even more contemplative. As did hers. He wrapped one arm around her shoulder, covered her hand with his, and gazed at her as if he were suddenly no longer sure where he stood with her, under the circumstances. "You stated what Sebastian hoped he would get out of this," he said in a low, probing tone. "What do *you* want from this situation?"

As Zach waited for Claire to reply, the silence between them lengthened dramatically and Claire's lower lip trembled. He knew he had hurt and disappointed her just now, by not admitting how much he had always wanted to be a father, or confessing how much he already loved her kids. But he just wasn't ready to go there yet. Given how badly he had failed at the end of his last relationship. He had to be certain he could go the distance. That he wouldn't let any of them down, the way he had Lisa. Because they all deserved so much better than he had been able to give in the past. Especially Claire. Who was without a doubt the most incredible woman he had ever met. And had the privilege to spend time with.

"Have you thought about what you need from Sebastian?" Zach continued.

"Good question," she said softly. "To be honest, I don't want to need anything from my ex. Nor do I know exactly what I want to see happen in this situation." The depth of her despair only made her look more vulnerable. Still caging her loosely in his arms, he kissed her temple.

Tears suddenly shimmering in her eyes, she splayed her hands across his chest. Their knees bumped beneath the picnic table. Worry clouded her low voice. "I guess I haven't really thought about it beyond not wanting to share custody with him because I worried he wouldn't appreciate the kids. Or know how to love them."

Zach stroked a hand down her spine. "And as long as Sebastian was in Antarctica, pretending like his biological link to the kids did not exist…"

Twin spots of color appeared in her cheeks. "I was safe from being hurt," she confirmed in a low, agitated voice. "And so were the kids. At least in a way."

"And now…?" Zach asked.

A contemplative silence fell. For a long moment, she remained in the circle of his arms. Then suddenly got up and paced away, her mood restless. Agitated.

She spun back to face him. "Let's say tomorrow I get another email or message from my ex saying that he has changed his mind and decided not to take a paternity test, that we should forget the whole thing."

Bad move. Zach got to his feet, too. He walked over to stand next to her in the grass. Overhead, a half moon appeared in the darkening night sky. The breeze increased and the lake lapped rhythmically against the shoreline, adding to the romantic aura of the early evening. "Would you agree to that?"

"Probably not." Claire lifted her chin. "Because now that this Pandora's box has been opened, I'm not sure it can be closed again."

She threw up her hands in frustration.

"Not with any kind of certainty that it would remain closed. And then…" She drew in a jagged breath, eyes glittering with a complex welter of emotions he couldn't begin to dissect. "There is the fact that I haven't really had to discuss their biological origins with the kids."

He nodded at her, gently encouraging her to elaborate.

"Right now, they accept we are just a family where we only have a mom and kids. Just like there are families with only a dad and kids. And so on." She sighed. "But when that changes, and they realize there is a daddy out there somewhere and they want to know all about him, then I am going to have to figure out how to handle it. And that will require me being honest without hurting them or making them feel like it's their fault Sebastian left, or that they were unlovable."

Zach shared her concern. But because of the way he had been brought up, he still held an optimistic view of the future. "Maybe by then it won't be such a bad thing, when they find out about Sebastian."

She crinkled her brow. "How so?"

"Maybe when that time comes the triplets will already have a dad in their life that they trust and love."

Someone…like me… If I am really, really… lucky… and can

figure out how to give them everything they need and deserve to have, over the long haul...

Claire, too.

"So even if that dad isn't their biological father—the way my dad wasn't for me and my quadruplet brothers, because our mom went to a sperm bank and had her kids on her own...at least until my dad came into the picture and adopted us—your kids will still have everything they need in the way of family." *Especially if things work out between the two of us the way I am hoping.* He lifted his shoulders in a nonchalant shrug, hoping not to reveal *too* much. "So hopefully by then, Sebastian will just be kind of the footnote to the story of their lives, just the way he is now."

Looking stunned by his admission, Claire propped her hands on her hips, drawing his attention to her slender waist.

"How old were you when Chase came into your lives?" she asked.

"Four months or so."

Claire blinked, absorbing that. "And he's been there ever since?"

Zach nodded. "Even though my three quadruplet brothers and I aren't technically related to him by blood, he's been our father in every conceivable way. My sister Sadie, who came along four years later, is my mother and father's biological daughter. And they have loved us all equally."

Her smile bloomed slowly. "I'm really happy you and your siblings had role models like that in your life."

"Both our parents are pretty amazing, and they really love each other, too. Which provides a solid foundation for our family, and is a very good example to set."

Her slender body relaxing even more, Claire met his gaze. Seeming a lot happier now. "You're really making me feel better about all this. Not to mention, giving me hope for the future."

He closed the distance between them and took her into his arms once again. Loving the way she surged against him, he pressed a kiss to her lips. "That was definitely my plan," he murmured. "And you know what else might make you feel better?" He tunneled his hands in her hair and brought her mouth even closer to his. Feeling poured from his heart, followed by a need that went even deeper. Their lips met in an explosion of heat and need, passion and yearning. Sliding his hands down her spine, he brought her even closer, molding her supple curves to the demanding hardness of his body.

And still the sweet, mesmerizing kisses continued. Her lips parting beneath the pressure of his. She tasted like coffee and the dessert she had just consumed, and the tantalizing essence that was uniquely her.

He held her even tighter, as their kisses melded one into another. He luxuriated in her surrender, taking full possession. The night around them grew ever darker. Stars glowed overhead. Claire's breath became as shallow as his.

She drew back slowly. "I think we need to get out of here. Go somewhere private," she said, kissing his neck.

Somewhere comfortable where they wouldn't have to worry about being interrupted, Zach thought. "I think you're right," he agreed.

They'd barely gotten in the door to his apartment when he reached for her again, wanting her more than ever. "Now where were we?" he teased.

Eyes softening, she let out a shuddering sigh. "I have a feeling you're about to show me…"

He sure was.

All too willing to let passion lead them where it might, he bent to slip a hand beneath her knees. Lifting her up into his arms and against his chest, he carried her to his king-sized bed. Then setting her down, gathered her close, and began kissing her feverishly once again.

Claire had thought she could separate love and sex, but as they continued kissing and touching each other, she realized with Zach, it was all one and the same. She couldn't make love with him, without falling for him. She couldn't confide in him and bare her soul to him, without taking him into her life and into her heart. When they were together like this, all she wanted was to throw caution aside, and think about the possibilities inherent in the present. The future right here in Laramie.

It didn't matter that she had never behaved so impetuously in her life, or even that she was afraid these dependent tendencies toward him could be history repeating itself. All she knew was that the connection between them was changing for the better, each time they were together. And that she wanted to be soulmates with him, as well as friends, and colleagues.

And as they moved, naked, onto the bed, she began to suspect Zach wanted more than a secret friends-with-benefits arrangement, too.

The realization triggered a rush of emotion that overwhelmed her. In the feminine heart of her, the tingling started. He looked at her lovingly as he traced the bow shape of her lips with his fingertips. Then his hand dropped, to her breast. He caressed the round shape, her pouting nipples, the valley in between. Went lower still.

She had never felt more beautiful than she did at that moment, seeing herself reflected in his gaze. She gave herself over to the hot, languid lovemaking to come. Arching against him, whispering his name. "Now..." she said.

Zach slid up her body, pausing only long enough to find protection, then kissed her as if he had always known they had something special and were destined to be together like this.

He was hot and hard all over. All warm, satin skin and sinewy, delectably muscled male.

She moaned against him, kissing him ardently. Even as she

surrendered, she took. Even as he gave, he found. And then there was no more prolonging the inevitable. No more denying what they had discovered in each other. Trembling, they succumbed to the heady pleasure.

Afterwards, Claire lay in bed with Zach, as always enjoying the soul-deep satisfaction of snuggling with him in his big comfy bed. The garage apartment was small, and in some ways utilitarian, but it was also *so him*. Looking around, she murmured wistfully, "I am really going to miss this place." It was where she had started to get to know him. The first place—the only place—where they had made love.

And that made it special.

Oblivious to the deeply sentimental nature of her thoughts, Zach leaned down and kissed her temple. "I predict you'll like my new place just as well, sweetheart, if not better."

His low, gravelly voice sent a new thrill spiraling through her. Claire rested her head on her raised fist. "Speaking of which…" She paused to look into his eyes. "Did you put an offer on the home you were interested in earlier in the week. Was it accepted? " She realized he hadn't exactly said.

His expression was inscrutable. "I'm still working on it. I'll let you know soon as there is something to tell."

He looked so happy. She couldn't understand why he was being so mysterious. Especially when he had been so open with her about so many other things. It made her feel a little left out. Like maybe she didn't know as much about him as she thought. She regarded him closely. "Is there a reason you are keeping everything so hush-hush?" she asked curiously. "Some dicey negotiations going on, or something?"

Because that she could understand.

They locked eyes.

"You want the truth?" Zach asked.

Adopting a studied, casual look, she extricated herself from his arms, rose and began to dress. "Nothing but..."

He regarded her with rueful contemplation, something hot and sensual shimmering in his eyes. Throwing back the covers, he strode toward her in all his naked glory. "As soon as they heard I was looking for a house, everyone I know had advice for me."

Claire sighed her regret about that. She sent him the kind of glance meant to presage a quick and uncomplicated exit. "Including me." She hadn't meant to butt in.

"I asked for your opinion, if you recall."

More attracted to him than ever, Claire wiggled into her skirt. And blouse. "I do remember," she said as he pulled on his clothes, too. It was one of the reasons they'd had to spend time together, in the beginning.

Finished dressing, he took her hand and continued with a mixture of intrigue and practicality. "Anyway, there are always as many reasons *not* to do something as there are *to do* it. Either way, I didn't want to hear about it. I know what I want," he said firmly.

Apparently so, Claire noted, impressed by his inner grit. Even as she felt a little frustrated at being shut out, along with everyone else in his orbit.

He drew her all the way back into his arms, laying claim to her, as he vowed, "And I plan to get it."

Chapter Fifteen

Zach was just finishing up the day returning phone calls, on Friday afternoon, when the office manager popped her head in. "Dr. Lowell on line one. She said she can call back if—"

"I'll pick up. Thanks." Zach put the phone to his ear.

"Hey," he said. "What's up?" Talking to Claire was the best way to end what had been a very busy day.

"I realized I forgot to tell you that the kids and I accepted an invitation from your mom and dad this evening, at their house in town," she said in her soft, melodious voice.

Zach rocked back in his chair, phone to his ear. "Pizza Friday…"

Claire let out a laugh. "Yes! Gabe, Alex and his boys, Sadie, Joe and Ellie and the babies, and Miss Danielle and Miss Charlene are all going to be there."

Sounded like quite a crew. He didn't mind as long as he got to spend more time with Claire and the kids. He thought about one of the reasons for the get-together. "Will you be meeting Miss Danielle and Miss Charlene for the first time?"

"No. I guess I forgot to tell you, with all the Sebastian stuff going on. I met them yesterday at noon, on my lunch hour, over at the house. I showed them around, and we talked about kids in general and then did the whole formal interview thing."

He couldn't resist teasing. "With or without the questions about pineapple?"

"With!"

Zach could hear the smile in her tone.

"And you'll be as happy to know, as I was, that they both *adore* pineapple."

"Good," Zach quipped back, aware they were flirting again, "because if they work for you, they'll be eating a lot of it."

Claire chuckled. "The important thing is," she continued more seriously, "they both had a very healthy sense of humor, and they also understood how important it is to treat multiples as individuals, since they had twins and triplets."

"So you think it might work out?" He hoped so. More than anything, he wanted to see Claire and the kids as happy as they all deserved to be.

"I do and so does your mom. Which is why we are introducing the kids this evening in a casual, no-pressure situation, where they can get to know both women before finding out they are going to lose Bette again."

Zach thought about that prospect. "When do you plan to tell them?" he asked.

"If all goes well this evening, with Charlene and Danielle, Bette and I will both sit down with the kids tomorrow morning. And then starting next week, her replacements will come in, one at a time, to help learn the routine before Bette actually leaves at the end of next week."

It was a lot more structured than the last exit from Bette. "Sounds like a plan."

"Anyway," she drew a deep breath, "if I'm going to get to your folks' on time, I need to get the kids."

"Want me to pick you-all up? Street parking is kind of limited over there."

"Good point," Claire said immediately, still sounding as cheerful and optimistic as he felt. "We don't want to irritate all the neighbors, do we?"

"No, we do not," Zach agreed. He stood, ready to clock out. "So I'll see you in about half an hour?"

Again, he could sense Claire smiling. "Sounds good."

This was definitely *not* a date, Claire told herself as Zach escorted all three of her kids down the sidewalk to her SUV. But if it had been, it would have been an especially G-rated one, unlike their time together the night before.

She still tingled, thinking about the ferocity of their love-making. Her heart warmed, too.

It didn't seem to matter how challenging her life was these days. She always had Zach nearby, checking to make sure she had everything she needed.

And what she seemed to need most was *him*.

Claire climbed into the passenger seat, next to Zach. She checked on all three kids. "Everybody safely buckled in?"

"Yes, Mommy!" came the unified response.

Oliver declared, "I am so excited we get to see our cousins tonight!"

Zach shot her a puzzled look. "Gwen and her family are coming, too?"

"No, silly," Andrew said. "They all live in Dallas. Not here."

"We're talking about Max, Marty, Michael and Matthew!" Isabella explained.

Recognition lit Zach's smile. "Ah. Alex's boys."

"Yes. *The cousins*," Oliver said.

Tamping down her embarrassment, Claire drew a breath. "I tried explaining, but they think because there are two sets of siblings, one from Alex's family, and one from ours, and you and Alex are brothers, and the kids all get along and like playing together and seeing each other, that they are officially cousins."

Zach's eyes twinkled merrily. "Makes sense to me," he said solemnly. He parked at the curb.

"Wait for us to come around and help you out," Claire said.

Somehow they managed to get the kids up to the front door without incident. Once inside, they went through Chase and Mitzy's lovely bungalow, and out to the backyard where the quadruplets were already playing in a public-playground-sized sandbox. Miss Charlene and Miss Danielle were already there, too, handing out plastic dump trucks and excavators, buckets and pails, sifters and shovels.

She was about to go over to make formal introductions, but Mitzy put her hand on Claire's elbow. "Let them take it from here."

Realizing Zach's mom was right, her presence would only have her children turning to her, instead of getting to know their future part-time nannies, Claire hung back. Watching.

As expected, the kids all got along great with their two helpers slash dinner guests. Charlene and Danielle had no trouble managing all seven preschoolers, even when there was a temporary upset over an accidentally knocked-down sand building.

And by the end of the casual dinner, all three of Claire's kids were talking animatedly to the two experienced moms of multiples.

They even hugged them goodbye, along with everyone else.

"Well, that went well tonight," Zach remarked, when they had returned to her home around seven thirty that evening.

Claire smiled, relieved, as her kids raced up the stairs to pick out their pajamas. "It did."

Without warning, the sound of overtired kids arguing radiated through the upstairs. Claire winced. So much for peace.

"Want me to stay around and help?" he asked.

She knew she shouldn't ask. He had done so much more for her this week than was fair. But honestly, she didn't care. She wanted to be with him, consequences be damned. So, taking a deep breath, she nodded. "Would you?"

* * *

Was this what it would be like to be a dad? Zach wondered a few minutes later.

All he knew was that he enjoyed walking Lucky while Claire got her kids in and out of the shower and into pajamas. The grime from the sandbox gone, the triplets dashed downstairs, to choose their bedtime storybooks from the basket in the living room.

They rushed in to jump on the sofa next to him. "Can you read to us tonight, Zach?" Oliver asked.

"Yes, please!" Isabella clapped her hands.

Andrew promised with a grin. "We'll be good listeners!"

Zach was sure they would. The trio loved story time.

He sent a glance at Claire who was coming down the stairs with an overflowing laundry basket full of sandbox clothes and damp towels. "What does your mommy think?" He didn't want to overstep.

"Their mommy thinks it is a wonderful idea." She paused a moment, taking in the three preschoolers snuggling up to him. A poignant tenderness softened the features of her pretty face. An answering love, that somehow seemed deeper than just friendship, or what you felt for family, sifted through him, warming him through and through.

Claire smiled. "I'll be in the kitchen, if you need me."

He nodded. And opened the first book, a story about renegade trucks, and began to read. The next was about a stuffed elephant who went to explore a real jungle, before deciding to go back home, with his child-owner. The third was the classic, *The Little Red Hen*.

By the time he had finished that last one, the kids could barely keep their eyes open. Yawning, Isabella asked, "More stories…?"

Claire—who'd evidently been listening from somewhere behind them—came toward them. "Definitely in the morning. We will read as many books as you like. But right now, everyone needs to say good-night to Zach, and come upstairs to bed."

Andrew, who was usually the most reserved, tucked his little hand into Zach's. "You come, too."

"Yeah," Oliver was suddenly on his other side. "You can help tuck us in," he told Zach.

A little touched by the invitation, Zach turned back to Claire. She had Isabella's hand. "What do you think?" he asked, surprised to hear his voice had turned a little gravelly.

This was definitely what it would be like to be a dad.

And he more than liked it.

He could see it quickly becoming a part of his life he would not ever want to be without.

"Help with the tucking-in of kids absolutely sounds good to me, too," Claire murmured, breaking into his thoughts.

Together, the five of them trooped up the stairs. It was the first time Zach had seen where the triplets slept. Although there appeared to be four bedrooms on the second floor, their beds were all in one room, next to Claire's. Lined up side by side with nightstands in between.

Oliver had a *Star Wars* bedspread. Andrew, *Lion King* bedding. Isabella's featured *Beauty and the Beast*.

Their favorite loveys—giraffe, zebra and baby doll—and baby blankets were already on their pillows.

"Hug!" Isabella held out her arms.

His heart in his throat, Zach knelt down to hug her. He pressed a kiss to the top of her head. "Good night, Isabella."

Oliver was next. He hurtled into Zach's arms with customary exuberance. Squeezing Zach tight. "'Night!" he said.

Andrew came last. As reserved as usual. He went into Zach's arms and hugged Zach shyly.

"Good night, buddy," Zach told him.

"Okay, everyone in bed!" Claire said.

Suddenly, it was a race. The triplets leapt onto the mattresses and scrambled toward their pillows, shimmying beneath the covers.

By the time their mom had kissed and tucked them all in, too, and turned on the night-light, they were sliding into much-needed sleep.

She tiptoed out of the room.

Zach followed her downstairs. Wondering if now that the chores were done, she was going to kick him out.

Instead, she turned to him and said, "I was thinking about opening a bottle of wine, and making some popcorn, and watching some Netflix. What do you think, doc? Want to stay?"

Hell, yes, he wanted to stay! "Sounds like the perfect way to spend a Friday night." With the woman and her kids, who he was quickly finding it difficult to live without.

Claire met his gaze. "To me, too," she admitted softly.

Admiring the enticing way she looked in her snug white Capri leggings and a loose-fitting peach tunic, he followed her to the kitchen. She got out a bottle of Chablis. While he worked on opening that, she put a bag of popcorn in the microwave.

Noting how happy and relaxed she was, he said, "After the week you've had, I would have figured you'd be crashing hard this evening."

She wrinkled her nose and gave him a teasing once-over that upped his pulse another notch. "Normally, I probably would have. But, as it turns out," she murmured as she came toward him with two wineglasses, "being with your family tonight was just what the kids and I needed. I'm serious, Zach. They have been so wonderful, warm and welcoming to us this last week."

She returned for a big bowl of popcorn for them to share, and they settled on the couch, side by side. "They've enjoyed spending time with you, too," Zach said gruffly.

Her expression wistful, she handed him the controller for the TV. "You're lucky to have them."

He poured wine for them both. Then handed her a glass. "You miss your family."

"Yeah." She clinked rims with him in a silent toast, then her green eyes darkened. "It's hard, being several hours away. Hard for the kids, too. They miss their real cousins—eight-year-old Seth and Sam, who are twins, and five-year-old Regan. So being around your nephews and niece has helped a lot." She tucked her legs beneath her and settled more comfortably against the cushions, her shapely knee bumping his thigh in the process. "And of course the kids adore you, too."

"It's mutual." He lifted an errant strand of her hair away from her cheek, and tucked it behind her ear.

She paused to study him. For a moment, she seemed to struggle with whatever it was she wanted to ask him. "You really aren't ever going to have a family?"

Clearly, she recalled what he had said to her, when they had first started getting to know each other. He saw how short-sighted his attitude had been. "That's what I thought, when I first met you."

She took a sip of her wine. "You thought those dreams died with Lisa."

He nodded, swallowing a lump in his throat. The memories were still painful no matter how much time had passed. That was why he had built a life for himself that was so different from the one he had imagined with Lisa. Why he had refused to pursue another romantic relationship or open himself up for more hurt. Until Claire came along, that was.

"So you weren't ever going to try to have a family of your own after you lost her..." she guessed.

He knew she deserved an explanation. Especially if she were ever going to see how being with her was changing him, for the better. Albeit sometimes more slowly than he would like.

Pushing aside his residual grief, he admitted, "First, at that time, I had already had the love of my life and was definitely not looking for another." Although now he could see himself opening up to the possibilities she presented. "And second, I guess I had convinced myself that caring for kids as a pediatrician, plus being around my brothers' kids, would fill the void that came from not having a family of my own."

Her head-to-toe survey of him was as serious as his confession. "But it hasn't."

Zach frowned. "Not really. And that has made me understand that I do still want a fuller, more satisfying life."

Claire sent him a curious glance. "Do you think kids will be a part of that?"

How to answer? Without promising more than he could currently give? "I hope so. Eventually. When the time is right."

The truth was, he'd like to have a *family like Claire had with her kids.*

He'd like to have Claire...

And to know things weren't moving too fast...for either of them.

Leaning in closer, he couldn't help but inhale the familiar post-evening-routine, baby shampoo and soap scent of her. Damn, she was beautiful. Feminine. And sweetly maternal and loving in a way he found incredibly nurturing and sexy, all at once.

Like she was his dream woman.

Dream life partner, actually.

But knowing it was way too soon to be mentioning that, when she already thought they were getting intimately involved too quickly, he continued, "Even if it's not exactly what I had envisioned when I was with Lisa."

Claire nodded, seeming to understand how life could force you to grow and change. "I think my wishes are evolving, too."

He turned to her in surprise. "How so?"

"I don't know." She used humor to lessen the seriousness of the situation. "Maybe to an existence…that includes more of a personal life for me?"

"Not just as a mom and physician…"

"But a woman, too."

He could see that.

Support it wholeheartedly.

Especially if said *personal life* included him. In whatever way seemed comfortable for them both right now.

Claire took another sip of wine. "Now what would you like to watch? Comedy? Drama? Documentary?"

Zach hit the On button and handed her the remote. The truth was he didn't care what they viewed, as long as he got to sit there, close to her. "You pick."

She turned on the classic romantic comedy *You've Got Mail*.

By the time it ended, she was yawning and struggling to stay awake.

He helped her carry the things to the kitchen, then walked toward the front door, with her at his side. "What are your plans for the weekend?" she asked.

Was she nailing down their next meeting?

He hoped so.

That would mean she was as into him as he was into her. Not wanting to ruin the surprise he had planned for her and the kids, he kept his response purposefully vague. "I've got some stuff to take care of tomorrow morning. After that, I'm free. Not on call this weekend. You?"

"Nope. But Bette's promised to work all weekend anyway. To help ease the separation anxiety after we tell the kids she is leaving tomorrow."

Claire switched on the outside lights. They stepped out on the porch. "You're going to do that tomorrow morning, together?" He recalled what she had said earlier.

"Yes." Claire exhaled. "Neither Bette or I are looking forward to it, of course, but," she sighed, "at least they have met and liked Miss Danielle and Miss Charlene, so they will know who is going to take over their before- and after-school care. They won't be hearing about two new people they've never spent time with or met."

"I can be around to help, during the transition, too."

For once, she didn't tell him she could handle it on her own. Instead, she looked more receptive to his help than ever. Satisfaction roared through him.

"Thank you," she told him softly.

The next thing he knew she was initiating a sultry, sweet good-night kiss that eventually turned inexplicably tender.

When it came to an end, Zach drew back reluctantly. He loved the direction their relationship was taking.

He also wanted more.

Much more.

Needing one more thing from her, before he bid her adieu for the night, he clasped her hands in his. Gazed down at her. "To aid with your quest for a more fulfilling personal life... when things settle down, I want to take you on a proper date. Dinner out. Somewhere quiet and romantic. Just the two of us."

Once again, she didn't even hesitate. "I'd like that."

He kissed her again. "I'd like it, too."

Chapter Sixteen

"That was fun," Oliver said at the conclusion of breakfast on Saturday morning.

Andrew nodded, sitting back in his chair at the kitchen table. "Mommy makes the best pancakes."

"And Bette helped us make good fruit faces." Isabella grinned.

Banana slices for eyes, halved strawberries for noses and lines of blueberries for the mouths.

"I'm glad you all liked it," Bette murmured as she got up to clear the plates.

Claire used wet wipes to get the sticky off the kids' faces and hands. Then motioned for the triplets to stay put, as the adults sat down again. "Bette and I have something to talk to you about," she said seriously.

All eyes were upon them.

"Bette has a new job in Fredericksburg, working for an art gallery that is also going to sell her paintings. So, this is going to be her last week with us," Claire finished gently. "Before she says goodbye."

Isabella's lower lip trembled. "But who will take us to pre-school?"

"And come and get us in the afternoon!" Andrew wanted to know.

"Miss Danielle and Miss Charlene are going to be help-ing us out."

Oliver vaulted out of his chair. He ran to Bette's side and held on tight. "I don't want you to leave!"

"I don't want to say goodbye either." Bette stroked the top of his head and cuddled him close. "But I'm still going to be here for another whole week," she promised.

"And we have special things planned for all five of us, for the entire weekend," Claire soothed.

"No!" Isabelle began to wail. Tears slid down her face.

Andrew pouted and kicked the table.

His tail at half-mast, Lucky came racing in to see what was the matter.

"I don't want anyone else!" Oliver pushed away from Bette. "*You're* our nanny," he told Bette.

Isabelle cried harder. "Please...please...please...stay," she begged.

"Don't go!" Andrew began to sob, too.

Oliver joined in. Tears streamed down his little face. "Mommy, do something!" he shouted. "Tell her she can't go."

"I can't do that," Claire said, and gently began to explain again. But the more she talked, the more the kids sobbed, until Bette broke down, too, and ran out of the room. Lucky trotted after her. He let out a lonesome bark, as the front door shut quietly behind her. The triplets were so wrapped up in their misery, they barely seemed to notice she was gone.

Hoping the young artist had just stepped out for a minute to pull herself together, Claire stayed with the kids, trying to calm them. A minute later, Claire got a text from Bette:

I can't do this. I'm sorry. Please let them know I will miss them.

Her spirits sinking all the more, Claire typed, You're not coming back? Hopefully, she'd just misunderstood.

No. This is just making it worse, Bette texted back. And

I don't want to hurt them anymore than I already have. Say goodbye for me...

Behind Claire, Isabella's distraught wails reached a fever pitch. Oliver was lying face down on the floor. Sobbing and kicking both feet as hard as he could. Andrew was crying silently and hurling toys onto the middle of the living room floor. One after another.

Claire knew from experience, there was no talking to them when they were this worked up. She was going to have to wait until they calmed down. It would also be easier if she had help from the one and only knight in shining armor in her life. She reached for her phone again. And began to type.

"Sorry," Zach said, from his place at the conference table. "I have to read this."

It was an SOS from Claire. Need help with kids. Any chance you can come over ASAP?

He recalled what she had told him about this morning's plans.

Bette isn't there?

She left. For good, this time.

Which meant telling the kids of their nanny's departure had not gone well. Zach looked over at Gabe and his brother's paralegal. "How long before we finish?"

Gabe assessed the unsigned stack of papers. "Fifteen, twenty minutes."

Zach typed, I can be there in thirty.

Claire sent a relieved emoji back with a thumbs up.

Zach returned his attention to business. The rest of the appointment went smoothly. As soon as they were done, he thanked Gabe and the paralegal for meeting with him, and headed out.

When he reached Claire's house, all seemed quiet on the outside. The minute she opened the door, however, he took in her red-rimmed eyes, her slender body slumped with exhaustion and defeat, and realized just how badly the day must have gone for them all so far. Lucky's depressed posture and the tearstained faces of all three kids confirmed it.

Zach walked over to where they were sitting on the front stair steps. All of the triplets had their lovies and special blankets in their arms. Things that usually only got attention at bedtime these days.

"Whoa," he said, and hunkered down in front of them, searching each of their faces in turn. "What's going on here?"

"Mommy's mean," Andrew said.

"She made Bette leave," Oliver complained bitterly.

Isabella pouted. "And she's not ever coming back!"

Sharing in their distress, Zach nodded. "Bette leaving makes me sad, too. Because I really liked her."

"We did, too!" Isabella cried.

"But it wasn't your mommy's fault. She wanted Bette to stay if she could. I know that for a fact," he said firmly.

He moved up to sit on the fourth stair step. The next thing he knew, he had all three kids snuggled up against him. Eyes still full of tears, they continued to listen.

He nodded at Claire, who was crying openly now. "See how sad your mommy is?" he asked gently.

They nodded emphatically. He gestured for her to join them on the stairs. When she snuggled in, too, the kids cuddled against her, as well.

"But that is not the only reason I'm sad," he said, inhaling the pancakes-and-syrup scent of them.

Claire wiped her eyes and sent him a puzzled look.

"I had a big surprise for all of you today, and now it looks like you aren't going to be able to see it, because you're too upset."

Andrew straightened. He puffed out his chest. "I like surprises, Dr. Zach."

"So do I!" Oliver agreed.

Isabella clutched her baby doll closer. "Mommy and I like s'prises, too."

Aware this was the best way he knew to change the trajectory of their day, Zach asked softly, "Should we all take a walk then? Together?"

Having declared that Lucky could accompany them, too, Claire snapped a leash on her still-distressed Newfie, and followed Zach and the kids out the door.

"Any hint where we're going?" she asked. The downtown area and parks were too far away for her kids to walk. The only things close to her home were more houses. Although she supposed that someone could have put up a fountain or something of interest in their front yard. She glanced over at Zach, who looked happy and handsome in the light of the gorgeous spring day. Despite the utterly miserable morning she'd spent with the kids, her heart skipped a beat. He just had a way of making her feel better no matter the circumstances. "Are we going to a yard sale?" It was Saturday, after all. He might have driven past one, en route to her home.

"Nope." He smiled mysteriously. "You'll see."

And she did when he stopped five houses down, in front of the large Victorian with the wraparound front porch that had been on sale just a few days ago.

The Realtor sign was gone. So was the lock box on the front door.

Zach reached into his pocket and brought out a key.

"Let's go check this place out," he said, beaming.

* * *

"I don't understand." Claire lagged behind slightly, as the kids raced on ahead. They darted up the porch steps and scrambled onto the big chain-hung swing, sitting side by side, grinning from ear to ear, the trauma of the morning all but forgotten.

She struggled to understand. Zach had just begun looking at homes on Tuesday evening, four and a half days earlier. "Did you put a contract on this house? Are you purchasing this home?" she asked, not sure how she felt about that, if he was. Thrilled, or wary.

What if things didn't work out?

If he walked away from her, the way Sebastian had?

They would still have to see each other all the time. When the kids rode their tricycles on the sidewalk, or they all walked Lucky together. It would be unavoidable.

He tilted his head. "I signed the papers this morning. It was an all-cash transaction so I didn't have to worry about getting a mortgage."

Claire blinked, feeling even more stunned. "Wow. That was fast," she breathed. Much faster even than the speed of their relationship!

"Yeah. It was." Still looking happy and proud, he motioned the kids off the swing, then opened the front door, ushering everyone in. The foyer was big, the staircase leading up to the second floor, grand. The kids gazed around in awe.

Zach walked them through the formal living room, into the dining area, and then to the combination kitchen/breakfast room. There was a big bay window, with a cushioned window seat. Spying that, the kids ran over and tested it out, the same way they had tested out the swing on the front porch.

"I know what you're thinking. It needs an entirely new kitchen, including appliances."

"Actually..." Claire wandered into the mud slash laundry room that led onto the back of the wraparound porch. Then down into the spacious backyard. "I was thinking it's a really big place for a single guy."

"And you're wondering why I bought it."

She nodded, her tummy suddenly doing flip-flops.

"I'll show you..." He led the way back to the front of the house. Opposite the living room were two closed double wooden doors.

He opened them with a flourish and stalked on in.

Following, Claire could only gasp in amazement. It was a huge old-fashioned library, with tall windows, fireplace and shelves that went from floor to ceiling. "This wasn't in the listing, was it?"

He shook his head. "Apparently, one of the reasons it was on the market for so long was that people didn't know what they were going to do with a room like this."

Claire laughed, unable to resist teasing, "I'm sure you do!"

"Yep. Finally, a place to put all my books. And even get some more."

She walked the length of the room, thinking about how it would look with his handsome leather sofa, club chair and ottoman. With a nice rug, a fire blazing in the grate, the shelves filled with tons of books, it would be so cozy. And masculine. Perfect for a guy like Zach.

She swung back to face him, really happy for him. "This room will be a great place to unwind after a long day at the hospital."

His lips curved in satisfaction. "Or have you all over, on the evenings or weekends."

Claire could envision going back and forth between their two homes, too—if they continued to be close friends, that was.

"I could see putting my leather furniture in here, just hanging out with you sometimes, when we snag some alone time, and or reading stories to the kids in front of the fire, when we're all together."

That would be wonderful, Claire couldn't help but note.

From the expression on his face, Zach seemed to think so, too.

With a shake of his head, he cleared his throat. "Anyway, you know how you told me when you walked into your house, you knew right away it was the place for you and the kids? Well, when I walked in here last Tuesday evening, I knew, too."

Claire went over to give him a hug. "I'm glad you got it." She stepped back. Smiling.

And she knew she would continue to be, as long as their friendship grew, and deepened. Instead of waned....

Without warning, all three kids barreled through the double doors. "Mommy, can we go upstairs? Please?" Oliver asked.

Claire looked at Zach. He nodded, explaining as he escorted them to the second floor. "There are six bedrooms, and three baths. Plus a powder room tucked beneath the stairs that I forgot to show you all..."

The bedrooms all needed work, but it was mostly cosmetic. Refinished floors, new paint and window treatments should give them a nice facelift. The bathrooms were retro, but charmingly so. Claire figured he might want to have the master bath redone, but only because that was likely the one he would be using.

"So what do you think?" Zach asked, when they had made their way downstairs again.

"I love it." It was way too big for one person, especially someone who didn't plan to ever get married, but somehow she could see him being really happy there. Plus, it was big enough for him to host his entire family if he wanted to have them over for dinner or whatnot. So in that sense it seemed practical, since they all did plan to have spouses, and or kids. And Joe and Alex already did...

"Are you going to live here?" Andrew asked. He sat down on the floor to pet Lucky, who had done the tour with them.

His brother and sister collapsed beside them and affectionately stroked Lucky's silky black fur, too.

"I'm moving in tomorrow afternoon," Zach said. "Which is the second thing I wanted to ask you. My whole family is going to be here, helping, including Max, Marty, Michael and Matthew."

"The cousins!" The kids whooped and yelled.

Zach grinned at them affectionately. "If you and your mom aren't busy, I'd love it if you would come, too."

Which would definitely assuage the sting of Bette's absence, Claire thought. Something he clearly realized. She sent him a grateful glance.

"Can we, Mommy?" Isabella asked.

"Please?" Andrew added.

"We love the cousins!" Oliver said.

Claire swung back to Zach. He was watching her, a pensive look on his face. He closed the distance between them in two steps. She could feel his body heat and breathed in the enticing scent of mint and man.

Their eyes met and held.

She said, "I think that would be a great thing to do." Then she turned back to her kids. "Zach has helped us out a lot the last couple of weeks. Now we can return the favor and help him."

Chapter Seventeen

"Mommy, can we sit on the porch swing one more time?" Isabella asked, short minutes later.

Zach grinned. He had known the kids would love that. "Fine with me," he said, when his phone chimed. He looked at the screen, saw it was a message from his answering service. "Sorry. I have to get this." He walked to the other end of the wraparound porch, while the kids scrambled onto the swing with Claire.

Lucky settled in front of them, his tail wagging.

He called the patient's mom back. Harriett Donnelly answered on the first ring. "I'm sorry to bother you on a Saturday, Dr. McCabe. It's Tucker. He has terrible indigestion that's been going on since late last night, off and on. He said he feels like he's going to throw up."

"Has he?"

"No."

"What about pain? Fever? Diarrhea?" he asked.

"Nothing. Just this persistent sour feeling in his gut."

"But nothing higher, around his sternum?"

"No. It doesn't seem like reflux, which I've had upon occasion. But he hasn't."

"Has he eaten anything spicy? Like jalapenos? Or done the hot sauce challenge that some of the seniors have been doing?"

There was a muffled sound on the other end. Harriett was

back. "Tucker says not. In fact, he thinks it's probably just the stress of all the AP tests and so on he has right now."

"I'm glad you called me. And your son could be right. Anxiety could be enough to trigger something like this. Let's try some over-the-counter liquid antacid." Zach told her which one to get. And the dosage to take. "See if that works. If he is still feeling bad, or anything changes, call me back."

"I will." Harriett sighed her relief. "Thank you, Dr. McCabe."

Zach pocketed his phone and strolled back to Claire. She eased off the porch swing. While the kids continued swaying back and forth, he caught her up to speed. Like him, she was relieved it hadn't been Sasha this time—whose own arrhythmia episodes had yet to be explained. But hadn't returned, either. "That poor young man," she said. "You can tell just by looking at him that he puts way too much pressure on himself."

Glad to have her to confer with, she was such a fine physician in her own right, Zach asked, "So you think it could be a stress reaction, too?"

Her gaze radiated casual affection. "Most likely. Hopefully, the over-the-counter antacid will take care of it."

Zach could tell the kids were starting to get a little wild. Which meant it wouldn't be long before they were out of control. Or worse, focused once again on Bette, and her unexpected departure.

He moved in a little closer, loving the way she looked in a simple navy T-shirt and coordinating Bermuda shorts, and sneakers. "So what's next for you and your crew of little ones?" he prodded.

"Well," she murmured so the kids could not overhear. Taking him by the elbow, she guided him a little further away, whispering conspiratorially, "We did have plans, before Bette decided she couldn't handle a long goodbye, or any goodbye at all, to go to Lake Laramie for the rest of the day. But now…"

Her soft lips twisted into a moue of frustration.

He let his gaze drift over her. "You're not sure you could handle that on your own."

"Exactly."

He shrugged, downplaying his protectiveness. "What if I tagged along with you?"

Claire couldn't help but recall the hot kiss they had shared at the lake, a few days earlier. "You'd really do that?" She searched his eyes, the barriers around her heart lowering, one by one.

He reached over and gave her hand a brief squeeze. "All you have to do is invite me."

To Claire's relief, the kids were delighted to hear Zach was going with them, and they spent the rest of the day at the lake, having a picnic lunch, and then visiting the hands-on-learning Nature Center for kids.

It was dinnertime when they got back to town.

Zach volunteered to help out with that, too. Unfortunately, the kids only wanted one thing. Their favorite restaurant comfort food.

"You're sure you don't mind having pizza so many times in the last couple of weeks?" They'd had it at her house, when she had to think fast after her Crock-Pot disaster with the pineapple chicken. Plus, they'd shared a Lugazzi's pie, after being at the hospital one evening. And it was what they'd had at his folks' place the night before.

He shrugged, rolling with the punches, as always, and retaining his genial sense of humor. "First, I think I have lived on pizza my entire life. I love it. Second, every time I pick up one for myself, I eat half the first night, hot, the rest the second day, cold. So I'm used to having it two nights in a row, too."

Reminded what a bachelor he was, Claire smiled and shook her head. "Cheese for them? The works for us?"

"Sounds good to me."

Zach went off to pick it up, while Claire ushered the kids upstairs, to get cleaned up. All three were in their pj's, their hair smelling of shampoo, when Zach returned with dinner.

As they sat together for the next half an hour, eating and chatting about their very busy day, she couldn't help but think how wonderful it would be if Zach were her children's father. Never mind how much happier her kids would be, if they had a traditional family unit. A loving daddy there for them, all the time. And that was, of course, when her phone rang. Jarring her out of her romantic fantasy.

She looked at the screen on her cell phone. "It's Gabe."

Suddenly, her palms were damp.

He seemed to know it would drive her crazy if she didn't find out what this was about. He stood, his expression benign. "Want me to read some stories to the kids in the living room, while you take care of things in here?"

"That would be great, thanks."

They moved off.

Claire led Lucky into the backyard, to take care of his after-dinner business while she called his brother right back. When she came back in, ten minutes later, the kids were yawning and rubbing their eyes.

Zach finished the last few pages.

"Okay, bedtime everyone!" Claire said.

"Can Zach tuck us in, too?" Andrew asked.

"Please, Mommy?" Oliver added.

"We want him to say good night, too," Isabella added.

Zach caught her imperceptible nod of approval, even as she wondered if she was doing it again, leaning on someone more than she should, just because times were hard and she needed someone to be there for her. Physically, emotionally. Worse, was she inspiring her kids to do the exact same thing...because things were difficult for them right now, too?

Claire didn't know the answer to that.

She *did* know it would be cruel to deny the kids one request this evening. "Sure," she said.

They trooped up the stairs.

Blankets were tucked in. Lovies snuggled close. Forehead kisses delivered, one by one.

All were snoozing before they even got out the door.

Zach and Claire quietly retreated to the first floor and took a seat at the kitchen table. "Everything all right?" he asked.

Was it?

Claire wasn't exactly sure.

"The DNA test came back." Claire forced herself to say the rest. "Sebastian was a match for the kids."

Zach took her hand in his. Held it warmly in his firm, comforting grip. "You knew that was the case."

"I know. But…" She struggled to put her fears into words.

Unable to sit still a moment longer, she headed for the laundry room, and the mountain of dirty clothes awaiting her there. Spying the picnic hamper she'd left by the mudroom door, she picked it up and carried it back into the kitchen. "This just makes us that much closer to a custody…" she searched for the right word, and unable to find it, finally said, "…battle."

His expression concerned, Zach watched her empty the bento boxes she had packed for the kids and put them in the top rack of the dishwasher.

Her hands were trembling as she took apart the thermos of coffee she had packed for the adults. And put the parts into the sink to hand-wash later.

"Did Sebastian tell Gabe he intends to fight you?"

Aware her heart was pounding, Claire shook her head. "All he said was we needed to get this settled ASAP. So he can get on with his marriage to Marie DuBois."

Finished, Claire wheeled around and headed back to the laundry room, where more dirty clothes awaited her.

She started plucking light-colored items off the floor and dropping them into the washer.

Joining her, Zach bent to help her, too. Making the chore go twice as fast. Their bodies bumped occasionally as they worked, sending a little thrill through Claire.

"Anything else?" he said, locking eyes with her.

She swallowed at the effort it took to meet his dark, assessing gaze. "Yes. Sebastian decided we were right, he needs his own counsel representing him, so he's going to get a family law attorney next week. As soon as he does, he wants us to set up a virtual conference to hammer out the details of the severing of his parental rights and the issue of child support. Although Gabe said Sebastian is still hoping—unrealistically—the court will let him off scot-free in that regard."

Zach's gaze narrowed. His expression was patient, but grim. He folded his arms in front of him. "From what I understand of Texas Family Code that is not likely to happen."

A myriad of emotions gathered inside her, tightening her gut. "I know. Which is where the battle might come in." Claire added detergent and started the washing machine. "What if he uses the kids as a bargaining chip?" She turned back to Zach.

He lounged against the wall opposite her, his hands braced on either side of him. She loved the fact he took everything related to her kids' happiness and well-being so seriously. "You mean, he says if he has to pay to support them, then he wants visitation after all?"

"Yes."

Zach told her gently, "I don't think that is very likely, given what I know about your ex. But say he did request it, he would have to come here to see the kids. No judge is going to make them get on a plane to Antarctica to see him. If they would even be allowed to be at the medical research facility where he works."

His tranquil tone made her realize how riled up she was getting. Thankfully she had him here to reel her in. As always, he was a calming presence in her sea of chaos. "You're right."

Her eyes drifted appreciatively over him. Even in a cotton shirt and shorts, he looked impossibly sexy.

"Is that all that's bothering you?" he asked gruffly.

Despite herself, she found herself melting against him when he bent down and kissed her tenderly. "It's silly."

He stroked her cheek "Tell me, darlin.'"

Claire absorbed the heat of his body pressed up against hers. "It's just…the entire time Sebastian and I were together, I thought we were the same. That we both liked being in a relationship while still being completely independent, too. That neither of us wanted to live together or get married."

She took him by the hand and led him out of the laundry room. Back into the kitchen. "Only to find out now that he does want those things. He just never wanted to be married to *me*."

He squeezed his fingers around hers. Tingles spread outward, through not just her entire arm, but her entire body. "And that makes you feel…?"

Claire gulped around the tightness in her throat, while the casual affection in his eyes deepened all the more. "Unlovable."

He flashed a ferociously protective smile her way. "Oh, Claire. There's never been a woman more lovable than you."

The next thing she knew she was all the way in his arms. His lips were on hers, making way for the sexy tangling of their tongues. And she was too caught up in the moment to think rationally.

All she knew was that she wanted him, and he wanted her, and she had never felt so beautiful and so wanted as she did then.

Unfortunately, this time the two of them weren't alone. The way they had been the previous times they had made love.

Realizing this couldn't continue, not with the kids in the house, Claire put her hands across his chest.

He drew back. Studied her face. "Time for me to go?"

Quivering with a yearning unlike any she had ever known, she reluctantly nodded. Kissing him once more, sweetly and tenderly, this time. "Sadly, yes. I promised my sister Gwen I would call her tonight, before it got too late, so we could catch up."

Taking obligation to family as seriously as always, he said, "Well, then you need to do that." He kissed her again, then lifted his head, looking as reluctant to go as she was to see him leave. He flashed her an amiable smile. "See you tomorrow?"

"Yes. The kids and I will be there, to help you move in," Claire promised.

But even as he left, she longed for more.

"Sounds like you had quite the day then," Gwen said when Claire had revealed all the events. "Actually, make that quite the week!"

"Probably explains why I am so exhausted." She snuggled against the pillows on her bed.

"And worried about what's to come," Gwen mused.

"Honestly, I don't know what I'm going to do about the kids and the nanny situation. I mean, I know they will eventually adjust to new childcare arrangements."

"Especially with the handsome Zach McCabe there pitching in right and left," her sister quipped.

Claire paused. "How do you know what he looks like?" She hadn't said!

"His photo is on the hospital website. I have to say I can see why you're so smitten." Gwen's voice dropped a conspiratorial notch. "He's really cute."

"I don't think I would describe him as cute…"

Gwen laughed with a big sister's intuition. "How would you describe him then?"

"Nice." *Sexy.* "Charming." *Charismatic.*

"And lately, always there for you?"

"Pretty much." Claire fell silent.

"What's the matter?"

She stared into her tea. Exhaled again, a little miserably this time. "I worry I'm getting involved with him way too fast."

"Sometimes that is the way it happens. At least it was for me and Patrick. One or two weeks in, we both knew, and we've never looked back."

If only she and Zach would be so lucky, Claire thought wistfully.

"Anyway, back to the kids and new part-time nannies," Gwen said with her usual sunny disposition. "Want my advice?"

Claire perked up. "Always, you know that."

"Being forced into a situation you didn't ask for is always hard, no matter how old or young you are. Feeling like you have at least some choice in the matter, can do a lot to make things bearable."

Claire had an idea where this was going. "So you're saying I should find some way to let the kids have a say in what happens next?"

"I think that would go a long way to bringing back peace in your household. Or," her sister teased playfully, "you could just keep calling in Doctor Sir Galahad to lend a helping hand…"

If only that could happen without fear of wearing out their welcome. But that was a real risk…

Especially when it came to a confirmed bachelor, who had been hurt deeply once before, and claimed he never wanted to marry.

On the other hand, he seemed interested in continuing their

current arrangement. And it was working well. Or had been. She would just have to hope and pray it continued to do so, no matter what the days ahead held for them.

Chapter Eighteen

"Amazing, isn't it," Sadie said to Claire, Sunday afternoon. She nodded at the seven preschoolers sitting on the chain-hung swing on the front porch of Zach's newly purchased home. "How mesmerized kids can be by the simplest things?"

Affection welled inside Claire, as she took in the homey scene. The perfectly behaved children. Whoever would have thought that move-in day at Zach's could go so smoothly? "Yeah, I wouldn't have predicted that Alex's quadruplets and my triplets could sit still for over an hour, watching the guys unload the U-Haul, and bring everything inside."

"I know, right?" Zach's sister chuckled warmly. "I thought we were going to have to round 'em up time and time again, too."

"We still will probably have to, once the guys are done with the truck." Right now, though, she was just as fascinated as the kiddos by the sight of Joe, Gabe, Zach and Alex, moving stuff as if it were all light as feathers. The grown quadruplet brothers were not identical, but all were handsome and buff as could be.

Sadie smiled and waved at one of the neighbors across the street. "Mom said Miss Charlene and Miss Danielle are coming by in a little bit."

"Yeah. I asked them to help out with the kids today. So mine will get to know them a little better before tomorrow. Which will be their first official day on the job."

The other woman nodded. "I'm sure they will adjust."

Claire knew they would. The question was how long would it take.

"And speaking of adjustments," Sadie continued, giving Zach a thoughtful glance. "Whether he realizes it or not, this is going to be a really big change for him."

Her concern for her brother sent off an answering alarm in Claire. She moved to the other side of the portal, out of earshot of the kids. "What do you mean?"

Sadie trailed after Claire. "Zach's always lived in small, compact places. I was surprised he purchased such a big house. Six bedrooms, and three and a half baths! As well as a sprawling downstairs. Most of which will be completely empty, since he has very little furniture and belongings. And then there is the fact it needs work. Remodeling and updating has never been something that interested him at all."

They watched as the men maneuvered Zach's king-sized mattress and box springs through the front door. Up the stairs. Forcing herself not to think about how much she and Zach enjoyed that particular piece of furniture, Claire said, "I think it was the library that sold him."

Oblivious to the ardent nature of Claire's thoughts, Sadie smiled at the guys as they went back to get the bed frame and head and footboards out of the truck as well. "I can see that, given Zach's love of books. Still, I thought when he found out he needed to move that he would continue on with the bachelor tradition, and pick one of the historic shotgun houses near the hospital, where Gabe lives now. Or maybe a townhome in the new subdivision east of town."

Claire would have thought so, too, had she not gotten to know him as well as she had.

He was starting to want a family of his own.

Maybe even a wife...?

"How do you feel about the two of you being such close neighbors?" Sadie asked.

She was definitely protective of her brother, Claire thought.

"Well," she answered honestly, "like you, I was surprised when he told me he had purchased this place." Enough to wonder if familiarity would ever breed contempt. "But I also know he is really going to love that library, and that it's a solid financial investment. Any home in Laramie is."

Sadie turned back to survey the large Victorian with the wraparound porch and the big yard. "As well as the perfect place to raise a family," she murmured with a thoughtful frown.

Was that what Zach had actually been thinking when he made the purchase? Was he that close to moving on...? Claire knew he'd be a great dad, if he ever put aside his residual grief over losing Lisa and all their dreams, in one tragic moment, and went that route.

But in the meantime, would hers pester him to death? With him now living so very close? Or pester her, asking to go and see him all the time?

Only time would tell.

As Claire had predicted, all seven kids jumped off the porch swing, the moment the moving truck drove out of sight. They raced inside.

Luckily, Chase and Mitzy were right there to intercept them. Herding them all into the library, which was filled with boxes. Within minutes, they had the kids carrying a book or two at a time, over to the bookcases, where Claire and Sadie shelved them.

Satisfied all was well, Chase and Mitzy went upstairs to help put together the necessary rooms up there.

They all continued on tranquilly, until Sadie received a FaceTime request from her best friend, Will—a Special Forces soldier, deployed overseas.

Apologizing, she ran outside to take it, in private.

Upstairs, Claire could hear a lot of activity and things being moved around.

Noticing, the boys began edging toward the sounds, one at a time. The next thing she knew, her two boys were sliding down the banister, with two of Alex's boys. While the remaining two boys had figured out the ladder in the library had wheels on the bottom, and they were pushing it back and forth, while an impressed Isabella laughed and clapped her hands with glee.

Not sure where to direct her attention first, Claire went out in the front hall. "Boys! I don't think Zach is going to like you doing that."

"Sure he will!" Marty declared, racing up the stairs to hop on and slide down backward again.

"Yeah, he likes us to have fun," Max agreed, following suit.

Unsure of how much authority to exert over children that weren't her own, Claire nevertheless caught hold of her two boys, keeping them by her side.

Behind her, there was a crash. She ran back to the library, and saw the ladder had hit an open box of books that had toppled onto its side.

"Stop!" she told Marty and Matthew, who were both halfway up the very tall ladder.

Isabella was holding onto the sides at the bottom. Apparently, she had been doing the ladder-pushing.

"You, too," Claire scolded her daughter.

Isabella regarded her stubbornly.

The front door opened. A glance out the window showed Sadie still on the phone. Joe and Zach walked in, closing the door behind them.

Both took in the scene.

Joe reacted like the former military Special Forces Officer he was.

In a loud, commanding voice he said, "*Everyone. Down. Now.*" He waved at the three still in the library. "Find a seat on the steps and sit down."

They all followed his directions.

He took a moment to survey them all. "Okay, what's the first rule of climbing?" he asked the kids.

Marty raised his arm, requesting permission to speak. "Save it for the climbing gym."

Joe nodded approvingly. "Why?"

"So we won't get hurt," Matthew said.

"And because the climbing gym is the best place to learn to do things right!" Max declared.

"We're sorry, Uncle Zach," Michael said. All four of Alex's boys looked contrite.

"Yeah, we're sorry, too," Oliver chimed in soberly.

"We didn't mean to get in trouble," Andrew agreed seriously.

"I won't push the ladder anymore," Isabella promised.

Zach smiled in a way to let everyone know all had been forgiven. "Good to know," he told the seven kids enthusiastically. "Now—" he met Claire's gaze, and winked before turning back to the kids, confident as ever "—who wants to help us finish unpacking all those books?"

With all those hands, the task of ripping open the boxes and unpacking the books went quickly and efficiently. Zach didn't care what was shelved where. He just wanted the boxes collapsed and taken to the recycling center.

This time, the kids were able to stay on task.

At least until Miss Charlene and Miss Danielle showed up, art supplies in hand. Then they all went off to the picnic table out back, to work on decorations for the outside of Zach's very bare, very old fridge.

Watching, Claire was relieved to see her kids happily welcome the two women. Whatever resentment they'd had previously didn't appear to be there today.

Meanwhile, over the course of the next two hours, the guys got the small café table for two put back together, the chairs in place, and the big leather furniture where Zach wanted it, in the library. Mitzy, Sadie, Ellie and Claire had plenty to do as well, wiping down the inside of his fridge, unpacking his dishes and organizing Zach's meagerly outfitted kitchen for him.

Claire realized she had never felt so much a part of a family, as she did that afternoon.

She wondered if Zach realized how lucky he was, to be part of such an incredible clan.

The proud new homeowner had ordered food for all the helpers. Mitzy had brought quilts, which were spread over the grass in the backyard. They ate buttermilk fried chicken with all the fixings, picnic-style in the backyard—with all seven kids sitting at the picnic table—because it was a little easier for them to manage their plates there. Then they topped it off with peach cobbler and vanilla ice cream. Paper plates made the cleanup quick and easy, and by five thirty, everyone was on their way out the door.

Miss Danielle and Miss Charlene stopped by to speak with Claire as they headed out. "Still on for tomorrow morning?" Miss Charlene asked.

Claire nodded, more hopeful than ever that her plan to get her children on board with the new childcare arrangement would work. She kept her voice discreetly low. "I'll see you both at six thirty."

Luckily, the kids missed the exchange, since they were busy saying goodbye to "their cousins." Mitzy and Chase left next, then Joe and Ellie, followed by Sadie and Gabe.

Finally, it was just Zach, Claire and her three kids. Who showed no sign of being ready to get off the front porch swing, where they had again taken up residence.

Claire knew she had a choice. Take a firm, disciplinarian approach, and risk the meltdown of all meltdowns. Or let them have a couple more minutes.

She looked at Zach.

"I think they've earned a few more minutes of swing time," he murmured in a low, conspiratorial voice. "Then I'll help you walk them home."

Gazing up at him, she couldn't help but note how his eyes looked more blue than gray in the spring sunlight. It was all she could do not to move into his arms and rest her head against his broad shoulder. Only worry how a move like that would be perceived by her kids kept her firmly in place. "You are so incredibly understanding."

He nudged her elbow playfully with his. "I'm a pediatrician, remember?" he said, stepping reluctantly away. "I know what overtired looks like."

Already beginning to feel better about the possible meltdown looming on the horizon, Claire went to perch on the railing that edged the wraparound porch. He followed her and sat beside her.

He turned slightly to face her, while still keeping an eagle eye on the kids. The empathy on his handsome face gave her the courage to go on. "I'm sorry I let the kids all get out of hand when you and your brother were taking the U-Haul truck back."

Zach let out a chuckle. "Hey, I'm just surprised they stayed calm for that long." Respect laced his low voice. "I mean, for a preschooler, it was an incredibly exciting afternoon."

For me, too, Claire thought. Just being with him, his family, getting a glimpse of how things might be if she and Zach ever moved beyond the friends-with-benefits zone, had been incredibly intoxicating for her, as well.

On the swing, the kids began to yawn. She touched Zach's

wrist lightly, letting him know it was time. "Hey, kiddos, we have to get home to let Lucky out. It's his dinnertime."

The triplets slid off the swing, one by one.

Oliver took one of Zach's hands, Isabella the other.

Andrew wearily latched onto Claire's outstretched palm.

Together, they headed down the front porch steps and down the street to Claire's home. Giving Claire yet another glimpse of what it would be like to have Zach as a permanent part of their lives.

"Mommy, when is Bette coming back?" Isabella asked, short minutes later, as they all walked into the house.

Lucky came to greet them and Zach knelt to pet his head.

"Honey, she's not." Claire poured kibble into Lucky's bowl and put fresh water in the other dish. She moved away as he began to eat. "You know that. We talked about that yesterday morning."

"But you got her to come back last time," Oliver said.

"Yeah," Andrew agreed. "Do it again."

Claire realized this was why they had been so calm the last thirty-six hours. They thought it was all going to work out the way they wanted, just like it had before.

Zach gave her a look that seemed to say: *Do you want me to stay or go? I realize this is a private family matter.*

"Please stay," Claire mouthed.

He nodded.

"We need to have a talk," Claire said firmly. She led the kids into the living room.

They all climbed onto the center of the sofa. Snuggled together. Zach took a place on the end, his expression as serious and kind as the situation required. Feeling bolstered by his unwavering support, she pulled up the ottoman and sat in front of them. Looking each child in the eye, she began matter-of-factly, "Bette has a new job as an artist in Fredericksburg. She has worked very hard for this, and it will make her very happy. So I am happy for her, and you all should be too."

Zach nodded, even as Isabelle teared up. "But who is going to take care of us?"

She leaned into Zach's side.

"Yeah, when you're not here?" Andrew added.

"Can Zach come and help us?" Oliver asked plaintively, looking over at him.

I wish, Claire thought.

For a moment, Zach seemed to share her wistful sentiment.

Determined not to take advantage any more than she already had, she shook her head. "Zach has to work at the hospital, taking care of sick patients, just like I do. Miss Charlene and Miss Danielle are going to come and help us. Starting tomorrow."

"But we don't want them!" Oliver said.

"We want *you*!" Fat tears rolled down Isabella's cheeks.

Feeling betrayed, the little girl moved away from Zach and toward her brothers.

"And Zach!" Andrew scowled.

"I know that," Claire said, remembering the advice she had received from her sister. Briefly, she met Zach's eyes, before returning her attention to the kids. "Which is why I'm going to give you all a choice." She paused to give what she was saying a moment to sink in. "I can still take you kids to school, and pick you up after I get off work, but that means you have to go to early care and late care again. Both. Every day."

No one looked thrilled about that. Sighs abounded all around.

"So if you want to do that, we will do that, starting tomorrow. Or," she continued, "if you decide you want Miss Charlene and Miss Danielle to do the preschool drop-offs and pickups the way Bette did, then we can do that, too."

The kids pouted in unison. While Zach gave her a subtle

thumbs-up. But at least, Claire noted, they had stopped arguing.

"In any case, Miss Charlene and Miss Danielle will be coming here tomorrow morning, and again tomorrow afternoon, and every day after that, because whether you want them to take care of you or not," Claire palmed her chest emphatically, "*I* need their help. With all the other stuff that has to get done, like laundry and lunch-packing, and dinner and dishes. Because I can't do it all by myself."

The kids fell silent, thinking about that. They knew how hard she worked, how much there was to do.

"So what's it going to be?" Claire asked gently. She needed to know tonight, so she could email the school.

"I want you to take us to preschool," Isabella said finally, marshalling her strength.

"Me, too," Oliver said firmly.

Andrew shrugged and sighed, making the best of what he clearly still thought was a bad situation. "Early care is kind of fun."

"Okay...then it's settled," Claire told them.

This next week was going to every bit as difficult as she had imagined it would be.

But they would get through it.

Hopefully, with Zach by her side.

Chapter Nineteen

At eight thirty the next evening, Claire heard a soft rap on her front door. Lucky jumped up and trotted to the foyer, his silky black tail wagging.

A peek through the window showed it to be Zach on her portal, some sort of bag in hand. Trying not to think how relieved she was to see him standing there, she swung the door wide. He smiled and regarded her in a way that left no doubt they would be making love again first chance they had. Keeping his voice deferentially low, he murmured, "I heard you left work early today."

Boy, had she. "Yep." A thrill sweeping through her, she took him by the sleeve and pulled him across the threshold. How was it he always knew exactly when to show up?

"I thought you might call me for assistance." His voice was a sexy rumble in his chest.

She had wanted to. More than anything. But she had also worried she was leaning on him a bit too hard these days, and that sooner or later, he would feel taken advantage of or begin to feel used.

Which was the last thing she wanted.

As she swiveled to face him, her shoulder bumped his. She gazed at the bag in his hand. "What's that?"

"Ah." Grinning, he walked with her through the kitchen and set in on the island. "I thought you might need a little pick-me-up." With a triumphant flourish, he brought out half a dozen pints of gourmet ice cream.

Claire salivated just reading the labels. "Marionberry pie. Mocha coffee almond. Milk chocolate toffee. Coconut pecan. Key lime pie. And bourbon vanilla bean truffle." She shook her head in amazement. "This is quite the assortment, doc."

Slanting her a sidelong glance, he settled whisper-close. "No choice." He flashed her a sexy grin, pausing to let his words sink in. "I realized when I went to the store to pick some out, that I had *no idea* what you liked when it comes to ice cream."

But he sure knew enough about other things.

Like exactly how to touch and hold and kiss her...

Claire swallowed and pushed the erotic thoughts away. Reminding herself that her kids were just upstairs, she returned, "I guess there's a lot we don't know about each other." So much she wanted to learn. "But," she continued playfully, "for the record these are some darn good guesses."

She got two spoons from the drawer and pulled up a stool, gesturing for him to take the other. Then worked off the tops of all six containers. When she had finished, they both took a spoon and started sampling.

"So what happened today?" Zach asked, moving the conversation back to why she had left earlier than expected. "No one was hurt at preschool or anything I hope...?"

Claire savored the sweet-tart taste of frozen marionberry on her tongue. "No, no one was hurt. Except maybe a few eardrums of nearby bystanders."

He chuckled at the accompanying expression she made. "Well, at least you have a sense of humor about it."

"Now." Claire made another face. "Not really then..."

He sympathized with her lingering frustration. "So what happened?"

Claire decided to start at the beginning. "Well, you know

how the kids promised to cooperate yesterday with the new routine."

"Let me guess. They changed their minds."

"Oh yeah."

She paused, while he gave her a spoon of toffee ice cream. She offered him the bourbon vanilla truffle in return. Both of them moaned sensually as the sweet treats melted on their tongues.

"Well," Claire continued with a sigh, figuring it would help her to talk about this with someone. And Zach was as close to a surrogate father in this situation, as she had. "Isabella complained she was wearing the wrong outfit—even though that was what she picked out. Andrew didn't like the way Miss Danielle was packing their lunches. And Oliver thought Miss Charlene's pancakes were *not nearly* as good as Bette's. And he *could not* eat them."

Zach tempted her with a bite of the mocha coffee almond. "Yikes."

"Yeah, anyway," she offered him some of the key lime pie, "when it was time to leave for early care all three of them could not have been more uncooperative. Toothpaste got smeared on clean clothes, shoes were lost. There was a sudden wave of separation anxiety. You get the picture." Remembering the stress, she put her spoon down and rested her chin on her upraised palm.

Having had enough of the rich dessert, too, Zach began recapping the pints. "How did Miss Charlene and Miss Danielle take it?"

Appreciating his strong, sexy presence, Claire helped with that, too. "They both took me aside and told me not to worry about the rocky start. They had seen far worse from their own kids at this age. We just all had to be patient and things would get better."

Zach leaned intimately close. "Did you believe them?"

"Time will tell, I guess…" Their eyes met. Realizing all over again just how much of a comfort Zach was to her in challenging moments like these, she forced herself to continue matter-of-factly, "Anyway, they helped me get them in the car, and I drove the kids to preschool. Then they stayed behind and cleaned up the mess here."

His eyes twinkled with his usual good cheer. Even more interested, he asked, "How did it go when you got to the pre-school?"

Claire groaned, making no effort to hide her feelings about that. "As terrible as you can imagine. They wailed when I took them inside, like they had never been there before in their life. But I was already late, and I couldn't let the inmates run the asylum, if you know what I mean, so I left them in the capable early care teachers' care. Of course," she waved a dismissive hand, "I cried all the way to work, because it was my fault we were in such a terrible mess—"

Zach frowned, interrupting, "Yours…why?"

Claire fought back tears of guilt and regret. "I hired Bette, knowing this could happen," she admitted miserably. "But all I could think about when we met her was the kids' happiness in the moment, how they related to her from the get-go, so I was willing to take the risk. And look how it has all turned out."

Zach shook his head. "There's no way you could have pre-dicted this," he told her firmly.

Wasn't there? "Mmm. Well, that's a discussion for another day. Anyway, I worked all through lunch, seeing patients early, so I could try and get home an hour early. But before I was able to finish up with all my patient appointments, I got an urgent call from the preschool. The kids were in complete meltdown in aftercare. Their hysteria was so bad, they had all the other kids in preschool aftercare crying, too. So I had to ask a colleague to see my two remaining patients, which he happily did. And rush over to the preschool to collect them."

Zach sobered, his concern evident. "I'm guessing their distress was genuine." Standing, he helped her gather up all the ice cream. Together, they put them in the freezer.

"Yes, it was." Claire turned to face him, her back resting against the fridge. She gazed up at him, confessing, "Which made it impossible for me to be upset with them. I realized how hard this has all been for them. Abandonment is always hard, no matter what your age, or the situation. And they feel completely abandoned by Bette."

Zach wrapped his arms around her and drew her close. He stroked a hand through her hair. "I get that. But that doesn't mean there aren't other people in their lives, who will love and support them, given half a chance. And the kids need to know that, too."

She snuggled closer, needing the intimate contact as much as he apparently did. She wreathed her arms about his shoulders and turned her face up to his. "I feel you're about to suggest something."

His gaze roved her languorously before returning to settle on her eyes. "I'm that obvious, hm?"

Her vulnerability began to fade. She knew in her heart that she—and her kids—could count on him. That he'd never let them down if he had any say in the matter. But still...the lingering fear that what was happening between them could still go terribly wrong was hard to relinquish. "You're definitely in hero-to-the-rescue mode. All the delicious ice cream you brought me tonight, proves it."

He sifted a strand of her tousled curls through his fingers. "The question is, are *you* in damsel-in-distress, ready-to-be-rescued mode?"

She tried unsuccessfully to contain a blush. "This morning I would have said no, I need to start working things out on my own. Now—" she released a sigh, still meeting his eyes "—after the day I've had, and…given that tomorrow is yet another work and school day, I am definitely listening…"

Noticing Lucky had gone to the back door, he followed, hit the patio light switch and let her Newfie out into the backyard.

Claire and Zach stepped outside with him.

The night was warm and breezy, fragrant with blooming trees and bushes. Overhead, a crescent moon shone against a backdrop of stars in the black velvet night.

Zach strolled to the edge of the patio. He shoved his hands into the pockets of his jeans. "Well, you know how the kids didn't really mind being around Miss Charlene and Miss Danielle as long as there were other adults around, too?"

"Mmm-hmm. It put a lot less pressure on the whole situation. The kids could allow themselves to warm up to Charlene and Danielle, without feeling disloyal to Bette. Or so mad at me."

Zach edged closer, inundating her with his brisk soap-and-man scent. He gazed at her as if she were the sexiest, most desirable woman on earth. "So maybe what we need to do is mix it up a little. Starting tomorrow."

Claire's heart thundered in her chest. "How?" she asked hoarsely.

"What do you say we both work through lunch, until things settle down? That way one of us can be around the kids before school, the other after school, helping out Miss Charlene and Miss Danielle. Sort of like you and I are assisting Charlene and Danielle. And they in turn are assisting us. So it's not so obvious what we are really doing is helping the kids adjust to new nannies.

"Then, once the kids all realize they like Miss Charlene and Miss Danielle after all, and can trust them not to up and desert them, then you and I can gradually ease back into our normal schedules."

Claire could see his plan working. But…

She held up a staying hand. "I can't ask you to do that."

"Yeah, you can, Claire," he interjected gruffly, taking her palm affectionately in his. "It's what people who care about each other, do for each other."

She drew a quavering breath, ignoring the warmth spiraling through her. "You're saying…?"

His eyes crinkled at the corners. And his lips took on a compelling tilt. "You matter to me." He kissed her knuckles, in turn. "So do the kids. So much."

She knew he was being serious. He mattered to her, too.

But was that the same as love? Was it too *soon* for love?

Was it crazy to even want love from him? Or want him to accept hers in return?

Claire didn't know.

He tilted her chin up in his palm. "It's okay to need someone, Claire," he said softly. "And when you do, I want that person to be me."

She studied him, her heart racing in her chest. "Are you sure about that?" she asked. Wanting him to really think about this, too.

He nodded. "Yes." He stroked her cheek with the pad of his thumb. "I am." He paused, then seeming to sense she wasn't entirely convinced, went on to admit in a moment of raw vulnerability, "I know you think this is all one-sided. That I'm doing all the giving while you're doing all the taking. But it's not that way at all." He brought her closer, wrapping his arms around her. His voice dropped another husky notch. "I need to be there for you as much as you need me. The time we spend together is helping me heal and start to live life fully again, and I can't thank you enough for that."

"It's helping me, too," Claire replied softly. So much.

He kissed her tenderly. "So we're agreed? Going forward, you and I will be there for each other, whenever, however, we're needed?"

Claire nodded, stunned at how quickly and effortlessly their lives were meshing. Although the more reserved side of her still worried it was all a little too good to be true. But the romantic side of her knew it was all so perfect, she couldn't—and wouldn't—turn away.

"Yes," she promised, wreathing her arms around his neck and bringing him closer still. "That is exactly what we're going to do."

Tuesday morning, Claire and Zach switched vehicles, the way she and Bette used to do. Zach went in an hour late, and was there to help drive the kids to preschool in her SUV. Miss Danielle rode along in the passenger seat. As agreed, both he and Claire worked straight through lunch. Then swapped cars again. Claire picked the kids up at preschool an hour early and was home to help continue to show their two new helpers the ropes, as they all worked together to prepare dinner before Miss Charlene and Miss Danielle headed home to their husbands.

Not soon after, to the kids' delight, Zach stopped by for dinner. As he had predicted, the seemingly improvised slate of unexpected activity kept the kids' mood happy and relaxed.

He and Claire took the triplets and Lucky on a walk through the town park afterward. Acting as if he were having the time of his life, he hung out through the bedtime routine. Reading stories to the kids. Helping her tuck them in.

As they both went downstairs, Claire remembered to tell him the latest about their mutual patient. "Sasha Donnelly had her echocardiogram this afternoon. Everything was normal. I called Harriett before I left work to let her know."

Zach briefly locked eyes with Claire, reminding her all over again what a good team they made—medically and otherwise. Compassion colored his low tone. "Harriett must have been relieved."

"Yes. She was." She paused at the bottom of the newel post then leaned over to pet Lucky, who had wandered over to greet them. "Although I think she would've felt better if we had some explanation as to why Sasha was having brief, intermittent arrhythmia a few weeks ago."

Looking in no rush to leave anytime soon, Zach joined her at the bottom of the stairs. He petted her pooch, too. "It may very well never recur."

"I know." She led the way into the kitchen, where her evening chores awaited. "That's the best-case scenario. It can still be hard, just waiting around for the other shoe to drop, though."

Falling into step beside her, Zach acknowledged this with a tilt of his head. "True. On the other hand, borrowing trouble never really helped anyone."

"True," Claire agreed. Unable to help but think about the way she kept worrying that her affair with Zach was too much, too soon, or would not last. Was this her own form of self-sabotage that definitely needed to go…?

While Lucky trotted over to his water bowl, for a long thirsty drink, Claire surveyed the dishes she had insisted on leaving 'til the kids were asleep. She immediately felt overwhelmed. The way she often felt at the end of a long day.

Zach, however, was still raring to go. Looking as ready to pitch in as ever, he said, "How about I clear while you load the dishwasher?"

Was there no end to this man's generosity? Especially when she knew she was already taking advantage. "You don't have to stay."

"Oh, Ms. Claire, you're not kicking me out now." He closed the distance between them and made an exaggerated show of examining her visually. "Before I've had some of your secret stash of adults-only ice cream?"

She grinned. "Ah… Now I see. It's not my company you want, it's a sugar fix."

His gaze tracked the careless way she had piled her hair on top of her head, with a few strands escaping, and she could tell he was thinking about taking it right back down. "Sugar's good." He took her into his arms and delivered a hot kiss. "So is this…" he murmured in that sexy-gruff voice she loved.

His lips covered hers again. Exploring sensually. Tempting her. Just enough…

"Zach…" Yearning swept through her. Powerful and real.

She moaned again, this time in frustration.

Reluctantly, he let the kiss end. "I know." He sighed his frustration, too. Pulling back slightly, he mumbled, "We really have to have that date you've been promising me. How about Friday night?"

Time alone sounded wonderful. But… "The kids—"

"I'll get Sadie or my parents to sit for us. We can have dinner in San Angelo."

Where it would be easier to steal time alone together and get some privacy at the same time.

He had no idea how good that sounded.

Especially given how much her kids loved spending time with any and all of the McCabes.

She took both his hands in hers. "If the rest of the week goes as smoothly as it did today, then yes, okay. We can finally have that date."

He nodded, seeming to understand there would be no relaxing or enjoying their time together for either of them if her kids were in meltdown.

He winked at her. "As long as you're looking forward to it, too…"

He wrapped his arms around her and brought her against him, giving her another kiss. This one tender, evocative. So full of promise she felt another thrill run through her.

She wound her arms about his neck, not ashamed to admit, "I am looking forward to our first official date...more than anything."

To Claire's relief, Wednesday proved to be an even easier day than the one before. She stayed with the kids in the morning and Zach took over in the afternoon, with Miss Charlene and Miss Danielle helping out both times.

"Mommy, Zach learned to cook!" Isabella announced as she walked in the door at five thirty. She ran up to hug Claire fiercely. "The ladies taught him. And we all helped!"

She set her bag down on the foyer table. Taking her daughter's hand, she moved toward the kitchen, able to see the table was set for five, the prep mess all cleaned up. Which would make the after-dinner tidying a breeze. She smiled her approval. "It certainly smells delicious."

"It's pasta with chicken in it!" Oliver clapped his hands with excitement. He and his brother came up to hug her, too.

"And pineapple muffins!" Andrew added helpfully.

That were golden-brown and delicious, Claire noted. "Yum."

Looking like he wanted to kiss her hello as much as she wanted to hug him, Zach stayed where he was. He lounged against the sink, his muscular arms folded in front of him. One of her chef's aprons was wrapped around his big, sturdy body. She sucked in an appreciative breath. He couldn't have looked more masculine or enticing if he tried.

The new nannies were ready to head home. Grateful for both their patience and assistance, Claire walked both out to the hall. "Everything go okay this afternoon?"

"Much better," Charlene replied happily.

Danielle slung her carryall over her shoulder. She inclined her head slightly, in the direction where Zach was still standing, chatting with the kids. "Although how that man has stayed single as long as he has, is a mystery to me," the older woman murmured cheekily.

Charlene nodded her approval. "He's definitely a keeper."

Danielle looked at Claire meaningfully. "Some lucky lady should snatch him up…"

If only finding a forever love were that easy. Unfortunately, she knew from experience it wasn't. Although she could also see why Charlene and Danielle might think that there was the potential for a more serious romantic relationship. With Zach going above and beyond for them, day after day.

Still, better not to let anyone—even herself—harbor false hope. Friends with benefits was as far as they were likely to go. Why then did her heart long for so much more?

"From what I've heard around the hospital, many women have tried," Claire said, diverting the attention away from herself. "But I don't think anyone will ever take the place of his late fiancée," she concluded, as much for herself, as for them.

Zach had told her at the outset, he had already had the love of his life. The reason he had stayed single was because he had decided that was the path he wanted. Had that changed, as the two older women seemed to want to believe? Or not? Because so far all he had talked about was wanting a fuller, more satisfying life that he hoped would eventually include kids, if and when the time was right. And hanging out together, at their two houses, being there for each other whenever needed, and continuing their friends-with-benefits arrangement. All of which were great, but still a far cry from a permanent, committed relationship and or marriage with her. Which was what, she was beginning to realize, that she and the kids were eventually going to need.…

As he had the night before, Zach stayed around to help with evening chores and put the kids to bed. Claire hadn't asked him to do this. He had done it anyway even though he knew he risked wearing out his welcome. He also knew she needed his help, even if she didn't want to actually come out and admit this to be true. Which could have been why she was less cheerful than usual. And also maybe why, more than once, he caught her looking at her phone. Finally, needing to know, he asked, "Everything all right?"

Claire knelt to pull clean clothes out of the dryer. "Gabe texted me as I was leaving the hospital."

He picked up the laundry basket for her and followed her into the living room. "And...?"

She motioned for him to set it down on the middle of the sofa. "Sebastian, his fiancée and his lawyer want to meet with me and Gabe at six p.m. on Friday evening."

She sat down and started to fold.

No stranger to laundry, he pitched in with that, too. "Which is when we were supposed to have our first date."

Disappointment glimmered in her eyes, making them an even darker green. "Right," she said, sounding even more conflicted, "but..."

As they both reached for more clothing, their hands brushed, reminding him how silky her skin was. With effort, he turned his attention back to the conversation at hand. "You want to get this business with your ex over with," he guessed. Figuring if he were in her place, he would want to do the same.

Claire wrinkled her brow. "Actually, it's a little more than that. You know how last time I told you I could handle this situation on my own?"

He nodded.

She bit her lip. "Well, it helped having you there when I came out of the building and saw you waiting on just the chance that I might need something."

Hope flared. Maybe they were getting somewhere. "You want me to do that again?"

"Actually, if it's okay with you, I'd like you to go in and

attend the meeting with me and Gabe, be my moral support." The corners of her lips turned down. "But that would mean we would have to put off our date, *again*."

Zach watched as she put the neatly folded children's clothing back in the laundry basket. When she was done, she set it aside. And he moved close to her. "Not necessarily." Their knees touched as they faced each other on the sofa. "We could go out to dinner after the meeting."

Interest flared in her expression, and he pushed on persuasively. "I talked to my parents and Sadie. They all said they would help watch the kids at my parents' place. Maybe even host a sleepover with the cousins. You could swing by to pick the triplets up early the next day. Then they could all go to Saturday Morning Climbing Club together."

Claire touched her forehead. "Oh, I forgot about that." She let out a regretful little moan that was nearly as sexy as the ones she made when they made love. "I did tell Joe that I would let the kids come by the climbing gym and at least check out the preschool classes."

"Which they will love, by the way."

Her smile bloomed slowly. Their gazes locked. "I imagine so," she said softly.

"So what do you say?" he asked, more certain than ever that something good and lasting was happening between them. And that he was finally ready to let the ghosts of his past go, once and for all. "Can the triplets have their Friday evening pizza party and sleepover? While we have our first official date?"

Chapter Twenty

Claire spotted Zach outside bay number 12, the moment she walked into the ER at five o'clock the next morning. Wanting to be brought up to date on the teenage boy who was now their mutual patient, she rushed to Zach's side. "What's going on?" Like her, he appeared to have been pulled out of bed just a while ago, but was wide awake now.

His eyes a smokier blue, thanks to the gray shirt he was wearing, Zach steered her against the wall and out of the path of the empty EMS stretcher now leaving the area. He suffused her with his familiar masculine scent as her heartbeat picked up even more. "Harriett Donnelly called me an hour ago. Tucker—their seventeen-year-old—was suddenly having chest pain, an irregular heartbeat and difficulty breathing. I called an ambulance and they brought him in. His mother is in with him, talking to the admitting ER doctor now. Apparently, he just vomited, too."

Glad Zach—and the ER doc—had called her to consult, rather than waiting til later to catch her up on the situation, Claire went into diagnostic mode. It could be so many things. "What about his sister Sasha?" Their other mutual patient. "Where is she?"

"She came with."

Not wanting to get ahead of herself, Claire asked, "Was Sasha having any of the same issues?"

"No." Zach's gaze narrowed. "She's just fine. Upset, of course, to see her brother brought here in an ambulance, but otherwise, okay."

"What is Tucker's heart rate?"

Zach guided Claire over to an open staff computer. As they both sat down at the desk, he logged in and pulled up Tucker's chart. "In the 150s. And he's been in A-fib since he was picked up by the EMS. As well as before they arrived."

Just like his little sister had once inexplicably been. "Murmurs, rubs or gallops?"

"None."

"BP?"

Zach pointed at the screen. "118 over 80."

Which was normal. Claire frowned, momentarily stymied. "Have they done workups for thyroid function and serum electrolytes?"

Zach nodded. "Yep. Still waiting to hear back from the lab."

"What about an echocardiogram?" *The one Sasha had the day before had been normal. Would Tucker's be?*

"Harriett's giving permission for that now."

"What about a toxicology screen?"

"Still waiting on results from that, too," he informed her. "Although Tucker told the EMS he didn't take any medications—legal or otherwise. And he has no known history of drug use."

Which was good. Although it didn't help them with a diagnosis.

Just then, the ER doc came out of bay number 12. Harriett Donnelly was right behind her, eyes red-rimmed and teary. "I've got to call my husband," she said.

Claire looked at Sasha, who was still in her pajamas, hair tousled and her expression worried, her little face streaked with tears. Just beyond, inside the patient room, a nurse and lab tech were still bustling around Tucker. Claire knew that she and Zach would need to talk to him as soon as they finished. See if they could get any further information from him and ascertain whether the excessive pressure he had been putting on himself at school had anything to do with this. In the meantime, there was one way to help.

Knowing what it was like to be the only parent on duty in a situation like this, she smiled at Harriett Donnelly reassuringly. "How about Zach and I keep an eye on Sasha while you go do that? See if we can rustle up some juice and graham crackers for her?"

"Would you? Thank you." Still looking extremely distraught, Harriett hugged her daughter, instructed her to stay with Zach and Claire and rushed off.

Claire grabbed the aforementioned snacks from the fridge and cabinet in the break room. Sasha stood next to them, her small shoulders slumped in misery. Fresh tears leaked from her eyes.

Claire and Zach exchanged sympathetic looks. Reminded yet again what a kind man he was, Claire turned back to their small charge.

Sasha continued to cry silently. "I wish my daddy were here," she sobbed.

But he wasn't.

And right now that couldn't be fixed.

Zach hunkered down in front of her and suggested gently, "Maybe you can talk to him later, on the phone."

Sasha's lower lip trembled. It didn't look like that was going to be much comfort.

Claire understood that, too. Once you'd had a daddy in your life all the time, which had been the situation until recently for Sasha and her family, it was hard to not have him there.

Especially in situations where two parents were best.

Like now...

Her heart going out to the child, Claire took Sasha's hand

in hers. Zach took Sasha's other hand. A siren in the distance indicated another ambulance was coming in. "Want to see where we doctors look at x-rays?" he asked.

Sasha nodded and Zach led the way. They settled in an empty viewing room. All taking a swivel chair or stool. "Scary morning, huh?" Zach said softly. He opened up a carton of juice for Sasha and put in a straw. Nodding, the five-year-old took a long, thirsty gulp.

Claire handed her a tissue and she wiped her face.

"Is my brother going to be okay?"

"Yes, he is." Claire opened the individual packet of graham crackers. Gave Sasha that, too. "We need to know more about what happened, though, to be able to help him." She watched the child tense in alarm. She knew, as did Zach, they were onto something. That Sasha could help. She leaned in, using the same gentle regard she used with her own kids. "Do you know if Tucker was taking any medicine that maybe your mommy doesn't know about?"

A look of guilt immediately crossed her little face. Beside Claire, Zach gave the upset little girl a look that encouraged her to keep going. "Like ADHD meds?" he continued affably, in a voice that said it would be okay if she gave them information. Better than okay, actually. "Or Ritalin? Have you ever heard Tucker talk about anything like that?"

Sasha chewed on her thumb. Claire looked at Zach again and coaxed, "We need to know, honey."

"I don't want him to get in trouble." Her voice took on a determined edge. "And Mommy will be mad if she finds out."

"About what?"

Sasha crumpled the end of her straw and pushed her orange juice away. She looked at the door, and seeing no one else within earshot, said, "His special drink and the candy."

Now they were getting somewhere!

"What kind of candy?" Zach sat back, looking concerned.

"Chocolate." Sasha wrinkled her nose. She shook her head, complaining, "But it doesn't taste very good at all."

"Have *you* had some?" Claire asked.

Sasha nodded emphatically. "When he wasn't looking. I took some," she told them proudly, suddenly looking and acting very grown-up, "because I wanted to be smart and study good, too."

"I see." Zach nodded, taking that in. "Did you drink some of his special drink too?"

Sasha nodded. "I didn't like that, either. It was too fizzy. It burns here." She pointed to the center of her chest.

"What does the special drink look like?" Claire asked.

Sasha stared at them blankly.

"Is it in a bottle or a can?" Zach prodded.

"Can."

Claire locked eyes with the child. "What color is on the can?"

"It's blue. With an animal on it."

She and Zach exchanged looks. Both of the same mind. "Does this drink give Tucker lots of energy?" Zach asked.

Sasha nodded. She leaned forward confidingly, "My brother says it helps him stay up late to study and take good tests, so he drinks *a lot* of it, but he doesn't want Mommy to know."

Curious, Claire asked, "You mentioned that you tried some of his special drink. Did Tucker share it with you?"

Sasha made a face as if to say that was a silly question. "No. I just take-d it when he wasn't around," she told them cavalierly. "But I didn't like it, so I stopped."

Without warning, Harriett Donnelly appeared in the open doorway, cell phone in hand. "Sasha honey, Daddy's Face-Timing with me, and he wants to talk to you, too."

Claire and Zach rose. "You can have the room," she offered. "We're going to go and check in on Tucker."

Harriett nodded.

Tucker was alone when they went into his bay, his face trained anxiously to the monitors next to his bed.

As Zach told him what they had learned from his little sister, he began to cry. Confessing easily to consuming multiple cans of energy drink and large dark-chocolate bars a day—for months—all without his mother's knowledge or permission.

He gestured at the leads of the heart monitor attached to his chest. "I didn't mean for this to happen," he sobbed. "Or know it had anything to do with what was going on with Sasha's intermittent arrhythmia. But there is so much pressure… Especially since my dad took that job in Alaska so he and Mom could pay for me to go to an Ivy League school…"

He threw up his hands and cried harder. "A-all I was t-trying to do was compete with the other kids…and see if I could get in. But then it looked like it was actually going to happen and everyone got so excited…"

He shook his head.

Claire handed him a box of tissues.

"But you're happy you got into Yale?" Zach asked quietly.

"Yes, but…that doesn't mean I really want to go. It's so far away. All my friends are going to UT-Austin. And I kind of want to be with them."

Claire paused. "Have you told your parents that?"

"No." Tucker burst into tears again. Finally asking, "Am I going to be all right?"

"Yes. Although you're going to have to spend the day here, and go through a few more tests, while we wait for your heart rate to lower, and the rhythm to convert back to normal, which could take a while, too," Zach told him. "And you definitely have to promise to stay completely away from highly caffeinated foods and beverages…"

They talked to him a little more, then went to find Harriett and filled her in. She was relieved and upset. But mostly relieved the medical mystery had been solved.

She also said Geoff was getting the first flight home, to help her deal with things.

And they had already talked about her husband not going back to Alaska, but rather seeking work in west Texas again. Because they realized now that their kids needed them both. And Geoff and Harriet needed each other.

"Speaking of families," Zach said a few minutes later, after Harriet and Sasha had returned to Tucker's room to keep him company. Crisis averted, he and Claire took scones and coffee into the courtyard before their regular office hours started. They settled at a wrought iron table in the warm morning sunshine. "How was your crew this morning, when you had to leave them, without warning, in the capable hands of Miss Charlene and Miss Danielle?"

"Well, it was so early, I didn't wake them. But they also know that sometimes one of my patients gets sick in the middle of the night and I have to go to the hospital. And when that happens, I always make sure someone is there to take care of them and be there for them, when they do wake up."

Zach looked thoughtful. He settled back in his chair, his knee briefly brushing hers, before withdrawing once again. "Part of being a doctor's kid, I guess."

"It is," Claire admitted, tingling where they had touched. Although under the circumstances, she really hadn't been sure how it was going to go this morning. Reminding herself they were in a public space, she pushed the awareness away. Sat back, too, sipping her vanilla latte.

"Anyway, I got a text a little while ago. It said the kids were fine and had decided not to go to early care today, but rather stay there with Charlene and Danielle, and they were busy making new pictures for my fridge before school because we should have some, too."

Zach's jaw dropped in happy surprise. "Wow. That *is* progress."

Joy flooded Claire, too. "It is." She took a bite of delicate, buttery scone.

"Does that mean I'm fired from my duties as part-time fill-in manny?" he teased.

She returned his flirtatious glance with one of her own. "Do you *want* to get fired?"

"No. Not at all." He studied her, his eyes darkening. "I'm liking the arrangement we have now," he told her softly.

So was she. And so were her kids. Way, way too much.

And it was easy to see why.

Zach had a way with kids. He had been so good with Sasha and Tucker this morning. Every bit as good as he was with hers. And he had been correct in his recent realization. Being a doting uncle or a pediatrician was never going to be enough to fill that void in his life. He needed to love with his whole heart again. He needed his own children. And would never truly be happy without a big, loving family like the one he had grown up in. There were times when she could see herself and her triplets fitting the bill. Others, when she wondered if he was going to want to fall deeply in love again—the way he had with Lisa—and have his own biological kids to give him that fuller, more satisfying life he yearned for. Instead of someone else's ready-made family, rife with complications not of his making, taking up his time....

Zach's gaze narrowed. "Why the frown?"

Claire shook off her own worries and concentrated on what they could discuss while they had the chance. "I was just thinking about the Donnelly family. How difficult their life has been the past few months." With her troubles on the back burner—for now anyway—she relaxed and gave herself permission to enjoy the easy camaraderie she had come to expect with him. The feeling that she could confess anything to him, and he would understand. She flashed a rueful smile. "Here,

I thought when my kids got a little older, that it would all get easier for me to do it on my own."

"And now…?"

As their glances held, she felt her heart take on a heavy beat. "I'm starting to think it will never really be that way. That being a single mom will always be a rougher road to travel."

He leaned toward her, and for a moment, forgetting where they were, clasped her hand with his own. "It doesn't have to be, sweetheart. If you accept assistance from me, and all the many others, who care about you and the kids."

Claire figured that was true.

She had Gwen and Patrick in Dallas.

All the people she was beginning to get to really know here. *And Zach.*

The question was, would their relationship eventually turn to one of simply friendship? Stay one of friends with secret benefits. Or become something else entirely? Right now, there was just no way for either of them to predict.

Like it or not, they needed time. To see where this was all going to go.

Later that afternoon, Mitzy McCabe came by cardiology. "I got your text," she told Claire, pleasant and cheerful as always. "And thought I would stop by in person to answer any questions you might have about the setup for the 'cousin' sleepover at our place tomorrow night."

Claire settled behind her desk and gestured for Zach's mom to take a seat, too. "Are you sure you and Chase want to do that? I mean, it would be plenty if you could just watch them while Zach and I went to the meeting at Gabe's office."

Mitzy tilted her head. "I thought the two of you were supposed to be having an official first date."

"We were. Until the virtual meeting with my ex, his fiancée and lawyer got scheduled. Now," she said, and released a regretful breath, "I don't know…"

Mitzy immediately seemed to understand why Claire was on the fence. She guessed gently, "You're worried it will spoil the mood for the two of you?"

"Yes." Claire rubbed at her forehead, and the headache beginning to start there. When the tension began to ease, she dropped her hand to the desk. "Although Zach doesn't seem to think that should necessarily be the case. He thinks we might be celebrating."

"Only a man who has yet to have children would think that," Mitzy said drily.

"Which is kind of why I want to reschedule the date." Without discouraging Zach in any way.

"It's also the reason why you should keep the time to yourself." The older woman paused, her expression kind. "I've seen a lot of families go through these custody and child support conferences. Even when things go smoothly, it can still take a tremendous amount out of you."

No kidding. Claire sighed. "I know what you mean. I feel drained already, just thinking about it. Worrying about what might lay ahead."

Mitzy hesitated. "You think your ex is going to try and pull a fast one on you, change his mind and suddenly demand at least partial custody, or visitation?"

"No. But to be honest, I haven't expected anything of what has happened so far, to occur either."

Zach's mom nodded, mulling that over. "Have you thought about what you want out of the situation?"

Not sure what she meant, she countered, "Besides full custody?"

"Mmm-hmm."

There was something. She just didn't think she could get it. Which made her wary.

"Think about it," Mitzy advised, with the wisdom of her thirty-plus years as a social worker. "Your kids' future is at stake. And this is the time to anticipate what the triplets are going to need from here on out. So if you want something off the table, or on, *now* is the time for you to mention it. Not further down the road…"

"Sebastian has never responded well to demands from anyone else."

Mitzy shrugged. "Maybe it's time he started being more open to the needs and wants of others. In any case, it's been my experience that these situations go better when *both* sides bring something to the table. And leave with something, too."

That was true of everything, Claire thought. Wishing once again she still had her mother here to protect and advise her, and if not, someone as loving and understanding and wise as Zach's mother to steer her in the right direction.

But she and Zach weren't connected in that way.

Not yet, anyway.

"But…back to the sleepover," Mitzy continued, deftly switching gears. "Chase and I host Alex and his boys every Friday night for dinner anyway. It's no trouble to add three more, and Sadie, Joe and Ellie and their babies are going to be with us, too. The kids play so beautifully together, and bonus—they tire each other out!" She flashed a comforting smile Claire's way. "It will be super easy to get them to bed down in sleeping bags on the family room floor. Alex and Sadie are going to stretch out on the sofas. So there will be adult supervision right there. And if anyone wakes up in the middle of the night and needs their mommy, not to worry, you *will* be getting a call."

She laughed at Mitzy's comical expression.

"Otherwise, you can come by for pancakes at eight on Saturday morning, and then take them to the climbing gym, for their introduction to the Saturday morning preschool climbing camp."

"Oh. I almost forgot about that."

"Well, don't." Mitzy winked. "Because Joe and his team are wonderful instructors, and it might be just what you need for your Saturday mornings from here on out…"

Soon after the social worker left, Zach showed up to get the update on Tucker Donnelly—who had been discharged from the ER, after the rest of his test results came back okay and his heart had spontaneously converted back to a normal sinus rhythm.

"I heard my mom was here?"

Claire nodded, noting how good he looked in the gray button-up and casual slacks, despite the very long day. Her gaze drifted upward to admire his rumpled, dark brown hair, and the hint of evening beard lining his jaw. Wishing they weren't still at work, she suppressed an appreciative sigh. The man really was the epitome of masculinity. "She was. She convinced me to go with the sleepover tomorrow night, whether you and I go out on an official first date or not."

He looked as piqued as any man his age would be to find his mother had been interfering. He dropped into the chair opposite her. "For the record," he said, lips pressing together sternly, "I did *not* ask her to do that."

Claire chuckled, enjoying the humor of the situation. "I am sure you did not. She did it anyway. In any case, I enjoyed talking to her. Just like I am enjoying talking to you now. So no worries. All is good."

"What about Isabella, Andrew and Oliver? Are your kids still doing okay?" he asked in concern.

He really was going to make an excellent father someday.

Claire nodded, knowing as well as Zach that things could turn on a dime. In this case, however, there really was no reason for worry. Happily, she informed him, "In the spirit of continuing to mix things up, Charlene and Danielle took the kids to the playground at the park, after preschool pickup, where they met several of their classmates. Charlene texted a brief video a while ago, showing them all having a great time. They should get home about the same time we do." She paused, hoping he didn't already have plans. "To celebrate their adjustment to a very difficult week, I was thinking maybe you and I could take the kids to the Dairy Barn for dinner, eat outside tonight."

"You and I." He seemed to like the sound of that. "Does that mean I'm invited to this family shindig?"

Always, Claire thought. Aware it was really too soon to be saying that, though, she murmured, instead, "Yes. You are."

Friday was going to be a tough day for her.

She wanted to enjoy the rest of Thursday—with Zach and the kids—while she could. She had the feeling it would give her the strength she would need to get through the scheduled meeting with her ex.

Chapter Twenty-One

"Ready to go in?" Zach asked, shortly before six o'clock Friday evening.

Claire paused outside Gabe's law office, her hand tucked in Zach's.

Was she?

Right now, all she wanted to do was run as fast and far away as she could.

And that wasn't like her. Normally, she could handle anything that came her way.

"It's going to be okay," Zach soothed. He turned to face her, shifting position, so her back was against the corridor wall. She tamped down the whisper of desire and the need to make love with him again. Whenever she was in his arms, swept up in the heat of passion, the whole world always managed to slip away. "You've got Gabe to handle all the legal issues," he reminded her. "Me and the whole McCabe family to protect you and the kids."

Claire inhaled shakily. "I know." Plus, the kids were safely ensconced at Mitzy and Chase's home for the night. Moving forward, she gathered him in close, hugging him tight, absorbing his warmth and his strength. "Thank you for being here for me," she murmured, breathing in the brisk, woodsy scent of him.

He squeezed her in return. "Thanks for allowing me to

help…" He drew back. Briefly, tenderness and an understanding that seemed to go soul-deep reverberated between them.

Their eyes locked.

Claire took another deep breath and they went in.

Gabe and his paralegal were set up in the video conference room. Soon thereafter, Sebastian, his attorney—who was calling in from her own Houston law office—and Sebastian's fiancée, Marie DuBois, were all pictured onscreen, alongside Gabe, Zach and Claire.

It was her first time catching a glimpse of Marie, and she could see instantly why Sebastian was so smitten. She was French, gorgeous, with a medical-scholar aura that matched Sebastian's own scientific brilliance.

"Who are you?" Sebastian asked Zach, as introductions were being made.

Claire winced, aware how tactless and rude her ex could be. Especially when he was under stress.

"Zach is a close friend of mine, here for moral support," she answered, wanting to leave it at that.

Sebastian frowned. Leaning closer, he peered at the monitor. "Which means what? The two of you are dating?" he asked, with his usual lack of social grace. He looked at Claire, more curious than jealous. "Are you getting married, too? Because if you are," he continued abruptly, over his own attorney's muted objections, "I can see where that might change things…"

"I'm *not* getting married," Claire interrupted. Beside her, Zach did not move, his expression inscrutable. Yet she knew him well enough by now to sense how irritated he was, whether with her or Sebastian or the whole situation, she couldn't really say.

Not that she blamed Zach.

Sebastian was treating him as if he were an interloper, when he clearly was not.

"Let's get back to the agreement at hand," Gabe said.

"Agreed…" The other attorney nodded.

For the next thirty minutes, they went over the terms of the draft settlement both lawyers had drawn up. Eighteen years of child support for all three children had been calculated. The total would be paid in advance into a general welfare trust in their names. No further financial obligations would be demanded of him. In exchange, he wanted to surrender all legal rights and or visitation from here forward.

"So if that is all right with your client…" the Houston attorney said.

Claire looked at Gabe. He nodded, giving her the go-ahead to speak on her own behalf, about what she had briefly discussed with him earlier.

"Actually, it's not," she said.

Sebastian scowled.

Beside her, Zach looked as if he felt equally blindsided.

Claire straightened and forced herself to go on. "Right now, the kids have only been told that we live in a family that has a mom and no dad. They know there are families that have dads and no moms. And families that have both moms and dads."

"I told you, Claire!" Sebastian interrupted on a huff. "I'm not, and never will be, parent material."

Zach shifted in his chair, his broad shoulders flexing against the starched fabric of his shirt. His mouth thinned, as if it were taking every ounce of self-control he had not to jump in and tell Sebastian what a jackass he was being.

Which was exactly why she hadn't warned him beforehand what she planned to do, because she had instinctively known he would go all protective on her. Like the stand-up McCabe he was.

She leaned toward her ex's image. Continued calmly, "But you *are* a scientist. And because you are, you know firsthand what it is like to have nagging questions that must be answered." She gave him and Marie a moment to consider that. Then went on. "Right now, this is fine. They haven't questioned the facts of their existence, or even asked for a daddy..."

Except for Zach, whom they adored...in an informal way. But that was neither here nor there.

"But one day, this will change. They are going to learn science and biology, just as you and I did, and they will know they are linked to someone else's genetic material, too. And then they will have very specific questions that are going to have to be answered."

A pall of silence fell over the videoconference. "What are you suggesting?" Sebastian asked warily.

"I want you to agree—in writing, as part of this custody and child support arrangement—to meet with them once, when they are eighteen. It can be a virtual meeting. But they are going to want and need to know who their biological father is. And I want us to work together to provide that for them, when the time comes."

Claire reached over and took Zach's hand in hers. Squeezing it tightly. He squeezed back.

Infused with strength, Claire looked her ex in the eye, and said, "One thirty-minute meeting, Sebastian—that will save us all a lot of bitterness and heartbreak. That is all I am asking."

Sebastian was silent.

So was Marie.

"I can see where they will eventually have questions," he allowed finally.

Marie looked at her fiancé, her analytical side clearly kicking in once again. She touched his forearm persuasively. "We would as well, if we were in their place."

"Preparing for this eventuality will give us all some control over the situation," Gabe added with lawyerly calm.

"And specific parameters under which to handle it," the Houston attorney said.

Which would be a lot better than her kids seeking out their biological daddy on their own, Claire knew.

"Okay," Sebastian finally said. "Let's add this to the agreement…"

Everyone wanted it done that evening, so they stayed late, and sent the drafts back and forth until at last everyone was satisfied. The documents were electronically signed. A bill was prepared. Claire wrote Gabe a check, and then she and Zach left Gabe and his paralegal to close up the law office.

They walked out into the dusky parking lot.

Zach hadn't said much during the two-hour-long meeting. But she had felt his strong, sturdy presence beckoning her like a port in the storm the entire time.

She knew it hadn't all been entirely comfortable for him. But he had provided the needed support nevertheless.

He turned his head in her direction, giving her a brief view of his handsome profile. "You look tired," he murmured.

She acknowledged this with heartfelt emotion. "I am."

He wrapped an arm around her waist. Aware how comfortable—*how domestic*—this all suddenly felt, she leaned into him. Savoring the sensation of their bodies pressed together.

He cupped her chin in his palm, lifting her face to his. Searched her expression. "Want a rain check on our date?"

His low voice was as intensely sexy and inviting as the rest of him.

Making Claire want only one thing. Time alone with him. *In bed.* The way he was looking at her told her he wanted that, too. She leaned a fraction closer and stroked his chest. Knowing him well enough to answer honestly, "If we're talking a fancy dinner out, where I go home and get glammed up in a pretty dress, then we have to head right back out to a place crowded with other diners, then yes, I'd like to put that off another day or two, if we can." She slid her hand lower, letting it rest just above his waist, as they locked gazes. "I would also like to be with you tonight. So," she inhaled a deep, shuddering breath, "I was thinking… Maybe we could revise our plans and go back to my place, and whip up something together?"

A happy gleam made his eyes seem an even smokier blue. "Sounds great to me."

Short minutes later, Claire was silent, her gaze turned toward the passenger window as Zach drove them through the quiet streets of Laramie. Back to her home. He knew the meeting with her ex had wiped her out, physically and emotionally. His heart went out to her and the kids.

None of them deserved this…

Yet it was what it was. And they were all just going to have to deal with it. Put the potential for heartache aside, and move forward, one day, *one step*, at a time.

Lucky was waiting for them when they came in the front door. Claire knelt to greet her beloved pet. Rising, she turned toward Zach. "Thank you again for being there with me tonight," she whispered, pressing her slender body against his and winding her arms around his neck. He held her close, breathing in the sweet feminine scent of her.

The next thing he knew, her mouth was lifting. Lingering just under his. He captured her lips with his. Reading her heart as readily as her mind. Everything they had held back came pouring out. She moaned softly, opening her mouth to the plundering pressure of his. And once they had made contact, there was no stopping with just one kiss. He explored her tongue with his. She tempted and cajoled with hers.

Again and again. In one hot, steamy kiss after another. Reminding him that she was all he truly wanted—or needed—in his life.

And if they were damn lucky…determined and willing to compromise…they could have it all.

Taking him by the hand, she led him up the stairs, to the sanctuary of her bedroom.

The air between them vibrated with escalating passion. Emotion rose as he dropped kisses along her cheekbone, the delicate shell of her ear, and the pulse in her throat. Their mood achingly sentimental, they undressed. Letting their clothes, the day, fall away. He guided her to sit on the edge of the bed. Parting her thighs with his hands, he knelt before her and leaned in to kiss her. His fingers paved the way to the heart of her, in a manner that left her writhing against him.

"Zach..." Pulling him with her, she shifted onto her back. He rolled on a condom and stretched over on top of her. Penetrated her slowly, then deeper still. Gripping her hips, tilting her in a way that pleased them both. She opened herself up to him and he claimed her with unchecked abandon. Again and again. Until all that mattered was the here and now. The two of them. The chance to spend another evening together, at long last.

Claire lay with her head on Zach's chest. Little tremors of sensation rocked her body, head to toe. Yet she felt safer, more secure than ever before.

Aware she hadn't quite kept her part of the bargain, she lifted her head, and looked into his eyes. "You must be hungry," she said.

He seemed willing to stay and play some more. "Are you?"

"I wasn't earlier." Before they had made love. "But now," as it turned out, "I am ravenous."

He threw back the sheet, revealing a tempting amount of sinewy hair-roughened skin. "Then let's go rustle up some grub."

She grabbed a hairbrush on the way into her bathroom, already restoring order to her curls. When she stuck her head back out again, he had his boxer briefs on again. She was in bra and panties. "How do you feel about paninis?"

He surveyed her with a sexy smile. "Love 'em."

It was amazing how handsome he was. Even with his hair delectably rumpled and a shadow of a beard lining his jaw. She could really get used to having him around like this. Feeling so much a part of each other's lives…

Was this what it would be like to live with him?

To be…*married*?

She pushed the unexpected thought away. The events of the evening had left her feeling unsettled, that was all. Zach wasn't any more interested in marriage than she was, was he?

She watched as he drew on his own khakis and button-up, leaving it untucked. "Do you care if I put on pajamas?"

He shrugged. "Whatever is comfortable, darlin', is fine with me."

Together, they went downstairs, once again working together with ease.

He spread the chipotle mayo and layered roast turkey and swiss on multigrain bread, while she sliced up tomato and avocado. By the time the sandwiches came out of the panini press, she had opened up a bag of chips and dressed the spring greens with vinaigrette.

They sat at the kitchen table. Their schedules were usually both so busy that she treasured their time alone together. It felt so good just to be with him tonight. To have the meeting with Sebastian, Marie and their attorneys behind them. Zach, however, did not seem as relaxed as she was starting to feel. In fact, she was pretty sure he had wanted to say something to her all evening. "Something on your mind?"

He avoided her eyes. "Nothing we have to discuss tonight."

Well, now she *had* to know. "Tell me what's on your mind." She leaned toward him imploringly. "Please. Otherwise, I'll fill in the mystery gap myself and who knows what crazy theory I'll come up with."

For a long moment, he gave her nothing. Just sat there,

watching, waiting. Looking cautious. *Way too cautious.* Finally, he said, "Can I ask you something?"

She moved in even closer, searching his eyes for some flicker of emotion that would let her know they were on the same page. "Sure," she said, just as warily.

With a measured stoicism that seemed to come straight from his soul, he asked, "Has Sebastian ever asked you anything about the kids? Why you named them what you did, for instance? Or what they are like as individuals?"

Claire stared at him in confusion. "No…"

Determination lighting his eyes, he continued, "Does he know how analytical Andrew can be? Or that Oliver is one fearless little kid who always says exactly what is on his mind? Or even how sensitive…but brave and strong… Isabella is?"

Why did she suddenly think he felt this was her fault? "No." Emotion trembled inside her.

"Don't you think a daddy should know these things?"

She dragged in a breath and pulled herself together with effort. "What are you getting at, Zach?"

"I know it's probably too soon to talk about adoption, but… just the same…"

Claire did a double take, feeling like the slightest thing might knock her over. *"Adoption,"* she repeated slowly, sure she hadn't heard right.

Zach shook his head in disapproval. "Your kids deserve a helluva lot more than one meeting when they turn eighteen."

Maybe so but wishing for something was not going to make it happen, either. She lifted a staying hand, starting to feel annoyed. "Even if it were the right thing to do, which in this case I do not believe it is, there is not going to be any visitation between them, Zach. Neither Sebastian nor I nor Marie want that."

"Which leaves a gaping hole in their lives."

"That I have tried very hard to fill."

"It's not about what you haven't done. It's about what more *could* be done." He reached out and cupped her shoulders between his palms. "Listen to me, Claire. We were both lucky enough to have two parents in our lives when we were growing up. You had a dad until your mom died, and even though he wasn't all you wished he had been, he was still there, still part of your world. My dad was fantastic. He was and is everything to me and my siblings."

"I know." Claire still didn't have a clue where this was all going. Except that Zach was very serious about what he was going to say next. "Your mom and dad are wonderful. Your whole family is. You are very lucky."

"That's the point, Claire. Your kids could be, too." He paused to let his words sink in as his eyes searched hers poignantly. "I want to be there for them, Claire. I want to be there for all of you."

If she didn't know better, she would think he was working up to some sort of proposal. But that couldn't be. Could it? "What are you talking about?" she ascertained slowly, her emotions in turmoil.

He took both her hands in his. "I love the kids. You know that."

Tears clogged her throat. "Yes. I do. They love you, too."

"And I love spending time with you."

Which wasn't the same as falling in love with her, or even being in the process of falling in love, Claire realized miserably, as his confession fell horribly flat.

But what had she expected? Zach had already told her he'd had the love of his life, with Lisa, and had never expected to have another.

She was the one who had kept insisting a friends-with-benefits arrangement was going to be good enough.

And it had been, until her feelings had inexplicably begun to change…

She disengaged their palms, and needing time to think, stood up and stepped back a pace.

He remained seated but continued, "We make a good team, the five of us."

A team. Of five. Was he proposing what she *thought* he was, she wondered, still floundering under his steady regard?

Worse, how had she gone from being involved with a man who wanted nothing to do with having children of his own, to one who seemed to want them in his life just as much as her?

"I know it would take time," he said thickly. "And a lot of careful maneuvering on both our parts. But we could do it." His low tone turned as earnest as his expression. "Gradually merge households and lives. I've already got the house for it."

OMG! Was that why he'd bought that six-bedroom three-and-a-half-bath house? Just half a block from hers? Not because of the fabulous library, to store all his books, but because it was convenient? And would make it that much easier to merge lives?

The heat of rejection moved from the center of her chest, into her face. She regarded him in shock. "You want us to move in there?" she asked numbly. As what? Roommates? Secret lovers? A borrowed family to give him a fuller, more satisfying life?

His expression still maddeningly impassive, he got to his feet too. Arms folded in front of him, his gaze roved over her face before returning with slow deliberation to her eyes. "Eventually, when the renovations are all done." He stared at her persuasively. Jaw set, he moved toward her, hands outstretched. He stopped just short of her, gazing down at her as if, in his view anyway, this were already decided. "In the meantime, I could spend a lot of time over here, and you and the kids and Lucky could all come over to my place, too. And then," he shrugged his broad shoulders casually, "when we did eventually make things official and become a real family, you could sell this place."

Tears filled her eyes. "Please tell me you're not suggesting I marry you after just a few weeks!" She gaped at him, even more distraught. "Just so you can become the daddy my children need."

"I'm proposing we seriously think about it."

Claire's temper flared, the heat of that emotion morphing into razor-sharp hurt. Worse, as she studied him, she realized he sincerely thought there was nothing the least bit wrong about what he was suggesting.

Disappointment roiled through her.

She realized she had done it again.

Seen what she wanted or hoped to see in someone, rather than what actually was…

Zach was a good man…gallant and caring to the bottom of his soul…but he was never going to love her. Not the way she wanted and needed to be loved. And that meant that whatever they had now was not going to last. Not over the long haul.

The problem was…making him see that. Getting him to realize that continuing to move in that direction would not just hurt her children, but leave them feeling emotionally discarded and abandoned all over again.

The way *she* was feeling right now!

Aware they weren't on the cusp of something truly wonderful and fulfilling after all, she spun away from him. Pacing even further away. "So let me recap." She moved so the kitchen island was between them.

Her knees were shaking.

"My kids need a daddy," she said, her own humiliation and anger mounting, "and you have begun to realize you still want the family you always thought you were going to have."

"Right."

She flattened her hands on the cool granite. Steadying herself. "And you and I are good together. Personally."

With a nod, he looked at her and added, "Professionally too."

She couldn't pretend to be even the smallest part okay with this. "And let's not forget in bed."

His expression grew harsh, resentful. "Why are you making all this sound bad, like it's *not* a good thing?"

Her heart shattering, she stormed out of the kitchen. Tossing the words over her shoulder, "Because sex and friendship and an ability to work together are not all a successful relationship is based on, Zach."

A successful marriage needed a forever-kind-of-love. For the spouse, as well as the kids!

He followed her to the foyer, and out the front door onto the porch. As aware as she that they had neighbors, he kept his voice low and irritatingly reasonable. "I'm not trying to shortchange you or offer you less than what you deserve, Claire."

"No." Scoffing, she folded her hands militantly in front of her. "You just want to come into our lives for all the wrong reasons." Tears misted her vision. "You want us to replace the family you always wanted and never got to have."

Which was somehow worse.

It made her feel like a substitution. One that would never measure up.

He rested his hands on her shoulders, rasping, "You're not taking the place of anyone or anything."

"That remains to be seen," Claire said. Ignoring the hurt, disbelieving look etched on his face, she inhaled a tremulous breath. "Right now we don't even know if you will stick around when the going gets tough. The one thing I do know is that my kids can't handle another loss."

Mouth thinning, he watched as she moved away again, this

time toward her front door. "Your kids," he echoed softly, sarcastically, "or *you*?"

"Both." She stepped across the threshold. Pushed the hair off her face, and tried for a reset before they lost everything. "Look, I know you mean well, that you are trying to help, to be the knight in shining armor that you have concluded we all need—" When she stopped to think about it, she knew Zach was a good guy. One of the best, actually.

"But?" he prodded, his lips thinning in mute disapproval.

She stepped out onto the porch, and forced herself to go on. "I don't think you have moved on from your past, the way you say you have."

He joined her on the porch, as an unhappy silence stretched between them. "Tell me you're not accusing me of lying about that!" he countered, looking even more resentful.

"Of course not!" Claire threw up her hands and struggled to frame it in a way he would understand. "I just think… you're such a wonderful, giving person… that sometimes you get so caught up in helping others that you don't realize what is or is not in your own heart, Zach." *Like a deep, abiding romantic love for me. At least not yet.* "I know you're not deliberately trying to hurt me, or the kids."

"But I somehow am, anyway," he concluded bitterly.

Knowing how much was at stake, Claire paced back and forth and chose her words carefully. "All I am saying is that I think if we continue down this path, of quickly trying to turn…our…" She struggled for a way to frame it. "…friendship… into something serious, that we will hurt the kids. And we'll both be hurt, too."

He stepped closer, his strong body radiating tension. Weariness etched his handsome features. "So what are you saying, Claire?" His low tone took on a defiant edge. "You want us to just stay in the friends-with-benefits zone? And not get any closer?"

Put that way, it didn't sound so great. Tears welled in her eyes. Even as she told herself to be as cautious as they needed to be. "Would that be so bad?" she choked out miserably. *At least for right now?*

"After what we've started to have?" he volleyed back furiously. "Yeah, Claire, it would!"

With a shake of his head, he headed for the front steps, then paused, and swung back to her, his attitude as set and immovable as her own.

"I'm sorry I haven't offered what you want, Claire, but I am not going backwards."

And she wasn't recklessly leaping into what he wanted, either.

Which left them at a devastating stalemate.

"Then I wish you luck," she told him sadly.

Their eyes met and held one last time, and her fragile heart broke all to pieces. "Goodbye, Zach."

Chapter Twenty-Two

At nine the next morning, Zach found his parents on their back patio, drinking iced coffees. Unlike him, they looked as if they hadn't a worry in the world.

Adopting a casual attitude he couldn't begin to really feel, he ambled toward them and dropped into a cushioned patio chair. Until Claire had come into his life, whenever he had needed a sense of comfort and familial support, this was where he had come.

Was he really back to that?

Relying on his folks and sibs. Living vicariously through the joys and challenges in their personal lives? All the while being even lonelier and more shut off than he had been then...

Aware Mitzy was studying him with motherly concern, he mumbled, "How did it go last night?"

His mom smiled, happily recalling what it had been like to babysit all seven grandkids.

Not that Oliver, Andrew, and Isabella were actually their kin. They had just started to feel like McCabes...

Like his...

To love and care for.

"The kids had a wonderful time, playing together." She filled him in. "Everyone ate a good dinner, and they were all sound asleep an hour after that."

"In fact," Chase added, as if he could hardly believe it, "we actually had to wake them up this morning so they could eat pancakes before they all headed to the gym."

"Why aren't you there with them?" Mitzy asked. She rose and grabbed her bucket of pruning gear, going over to the rosebushes. "And why was Claire looking so pale this morning?" She paused to draw on her gardening gloves. "Did the meeting with her ex and his lawyer not go well?"

Zach watched her snip one perfect rose after another. "That went fine."

"So you were there with her, as planned?" Mitzy stacked them, for later arranging.

Wishing he'd found somewhere else to go this morning, Zach nodded. "Yes."

His mom and dad exchanged worried glances.

Mitzy went on to the next rosebush. Determined to get to the root of the problem, as always. "Did your date afterward go badly then?"

So bad there weren't any words in the universe to actually describe it. "We didn't go out," Zach admitted tersely. Wishing for the hundredth time he had just had an impromptu supper with her, made love to her and then gone to sleep, with her wrapped in his arms.

But he hadn't.

In a panic, over Claire and the kids' happiness and well-being, he'd had to push things way past where he knew they should be.

Try to talk about the future he knew now that Claire did not want.

His mother and father both waited patiently, wanting to know more. Yet letting him decide if he wanted to reveal what was really going on.

His emotions in turmoil, Zach stood and took one of the wicker baskets his mother used for cut flowers over to where she worked. "It was late." He gave his folks the facts. "We were tired. We just grabbed something to eat at her place and then I went home to mine."

Mitzy nodded. "Obviously, you don't have to tell us. But it seemed like a little more than that transpired between the two of you-all, because when I saw Claire this morning, when she came by to get the kids and take them to the climbing gym, she seemed off."

Figuring they would find out sooner or later, and they might as well hear it from him, Zach muttered, "We ah…" Damn, it hurt to admit. "Actually…*she*…ended things."

Mitzy's elegant brow rose. "Before your first actual date?"

Relieved to realize he wasn't the only one who thought the brusque breakup was unwarranted, Zach shoved his hands in his pockets. "I told her I was serious, that I wanted to raise the kids with her. And be the daddy the triplets should have had all along, so they wouldn't grow up feeling abandoned and unloved by her ex's disinterest."

"And Claire took offense at that," Chase guessed.

Zach nodded. "She got mad that I was even bringing up adoption." He shook his head bitterly, wondering how in the hell everything had derailed so badly. "Then she asked me to leave."

Mitzy brought the basket of flowers back onto the patio. She inched off her gardening gloves before saying, "That does seem a bit premature, given you have only been seeing each other a few weeks."

The pressure built in the center of Zach's chest once again. Aware he hadn't felt this way about another woman, since Lisa, he said gruffly, "I know how I feel, Mom." As if Claire and her kids were his everything. "I thought I knew how she felt, too."

"So you laid it all on the line," Chase reflected. Seeming to think, like Zach had at the time, that the discussion could easily have gone another way. If Claire had been the least bit open to a future with him anyway…

His mom, though, had other ideas. She planted her hands on her hips and gave him the same look she'd used whenever he had disappointed her in the past. "How did you think she was going to react to you bringing up even the idea of adoption right after she'd had a custody conference with her ex?"

Irritated to find himself on the hot seat, Zach shrugged. "I don't know." *Happy? Relieved? Intrigued?*

Mitzy huffed out a frustrated breath. "I think you might have had a clue."

Zach tensed. "What are you trying to imply?"

His mom laid a gentle hand on his shoulder. "That maybe the reason you made such a bad proposal to Claire was because you subconsciously *wanted* to wreck things with her."

Across town, Claire was sitting in one of the folding chairs set up for the parents at the Laramie climbing gym when Gabe walked in, in shorts and a T-shirt, a chalk bag attached to his waist.

He smiled at the sight of her three kids, in pre-k climbing gear and full-body safety harnesses. All were listening attentively to the teenage coach/instructors who were showing them how to approach the very first holds on the wall.

Further down the row, Alex's four boys were also participating in the Saturday morning camp and taking lessons.

Gabe sat down beside her and began switching out his sneakers for climbing shoes. He nodded at Claire's triplets. "They look like they are having fun."

"They are." She was glad Zach's brother, Joe, the gym owner, had suggested they come. She was definitely going to enroll them in the Saturday morning program.

"I'm surprised Zach isn't here, though. I figured he wouldn't want to miss this." Gabe stood and looked around. "Did he get called into the hospital or something?"

For the first time wishing her attorney was not also one of

Zach's family members, Claire kept her tone neutral. "Actually, I'm not sure where he is."

Gabe looked at her funny, as if trying to decipher what that meant. Then sat back down. "Did you two have a fight or something?"

The heat of humiliation crept into Claire's face. "Not exactly."

His eyes narrowed and she felt him sizing her up like the shrewd lawyer he was. "But *something* happened between when you left my office last night and this morning."

Yes, it certainly had, Claire thought sadly. Just when she thought she finally had it all figured out, her world had turned upside down and inside out. She frowned. "Let's just say we are not going to be spending time together anymore."

"So…" Gabe exhaled, looking disappointed. "You dumped him."

Why would he assume that she wanted this to happen. "First of all, we were never *actually* a couple. Second, the realization that our relationship wasn't going to work out as we hoped, was really mutual…" Or it had been, after they had argued for the first and only time.

He did a double take. "I find that hard to believe. I've never seen him as crazy about anyone as he is about you."

Claire had thought Zach was falling in love with her, too. Until he had delivered that half-hearted proposal, anyway. Then she had questioned why she was so willing to put her heart all the way out there, when it was clear he still had at least a partial wall around his. "I don't think he ever got over losing Lisa…"

"My brother loved his fiancée." Gabe looked her in the eye, his voice as solemn as his gaze, when he said, "But trust me, he never looked at her the way he looks at you."

Hope rose swiftly, only to be quashed back down by reality. Quietly, she replied, "That may be, but it doesn't mean what he feels for me is ever going to be enough to sustain a viable relationship, either." *Certainly nothing that would provide a foundation for long-lasting, satisfying marriage. And that's what she would need. What the kids would need. To have a happy life.*

"You want it all."

Claire swallowed around the ache in her throat. "If I ever marry, I sure do."

"And up to now, you thought you might get everything you ever wanted with Zach," Gabe continued gently.

"I *wanted* to think that," she confided, thinking how deeply and passionately she had felt about Zach. How connected they had felt when they'd made love. Worked together on patient cases. Taken care of the kids and Lucky. Done the simplest things, as a team.

It had all felt so right.

So how had it all gone so terribly wrong?

Claire sighed and shook her head, feeling more desolate than ever. "Until I found out we didn't want the same things in life after all."

Zach wanted a marriage of convenience. That would work on a practical level. She wanted the real thing.

"Which is why I'm guessing you were so quick to cut and run, instead of staying and seeing if it was possible to work things out. To fight for what you want."

He was making it sound like she was a coward. She wasn't. She would put her heart out there. If she knew her love would be received—and returned—in kind.

It was these one-sided unions, like the one she'd had with Sebastian, that she feared. Where she waited patiently for the intimacy to grow. Only to have it remain status quo.

Then fade…

And go away entirely.

She looked at Gabe, wanting him—and the whole McCabe

family, for that matter—to understand where she was coming from. "I have my kids to consider. They are already so attached to Zach. And he to them." Her eyes misted but she forced herself to go on. "If he and I were to continue on this path we've been on, and things don't work out, *all* of our hearts will be broken."

"Whereas now," Gabe presumed, with lawyerly pragmatism, "you'll all still be hurt, but it will be a lot less painful."

Would it though? Claire wondered.

Had she made the right decision where Zach was concerned? By pushing him away?

Or had she acted rashly and potentially made the biggest mistake of her life?

Zach stayed and talked to his parents a while longer, then went for a run to clear his head. By the time he had finished, he knew what he had to do. The first order of business was enlisting the assistance of his sister. Luckily, she answered on the first ring.

"I need your help," he told Sadie.

"As long as it's not tonight, you've got it."

Zach tensed. "What do you mean?"

"I already promised Claire I'd help her out this evening."

"With…?" he prodded.

There was a long pause. "Not a question you should be asking me, bro. If you want to know what her plans are, ask her."

If only that were an option. But given how he had screwed up their relationship the night before…by leapfrogging over the tried and true to what he wanted…

"That's the thing. I don't think she is exactly speaking to me right now."

Sadie snorted. He could hear her moving things around in the background, which meant she was probably doing some kind of chore. "Yeah, I heard how you botched things."

Zach winced. "She told you?"

Sadie paused. "Probably shouldn't be talking to you about that, either."

Desperation rose within him, stronger than ever. "Listen, sis, I've got to fix things. And to do that, I have to see her." In person and alone.

She made a dissenting sound. "I don't think this is something you can rush your way out of."

As much as he didn't want to admit it, he knew she might have a point. Especially since it was rushing things that had gotten them in this mess in the first place. "Meaning...?"

"Slow down. Think about what you really want to say to her this time. And then wait for *her* to reach out to *you*."

Easier said than done, Zach thought sullenly, as he ended the call and walked into his big, empty house. Especially when everything within him was telling him to just go back outside and hightail it five houses down the block, to her place...and beg her forgiveness.

But he couldn't do that in the middle of the day.

Couldn't afford another blowup between them.

Especially with the kids there to witness it.

So, he would have to wait.

And think.

And wait some more.

By eight that evening, Zach was so frustrated and impatient, and sad and lonely, he was about to climb out of his skin. And that was when the doorbell rang.

Hoping it wasn't his family, there to give him more unsolicited advice on how to get the woman of his dreams back, he swung open the door.

Claire stood on the porch, a bottle of wine in one hand, her wicker picnic basket in the other.

In a pretty dress and killer heels, she looked ready for the date they should have had weeks ago.

Would have if he hadn't been such a fool.

"Is this a good time?" she asked, her cloud of silky dark curls gorgeously framing her face.

He nodded. "Hell yes!"

Taking the picnic basket in one hand, her wrist in the other, he drew her across the threshold.

She scanned the shelves of military history books that had once given him such comfort, but offered not the least bit of distraction today, then swung back to him and asked, "The library okay for us to talk?"

It was his favorite room in the house, which she well knew. "Perfect."

She perched on the middle of the long leather sofa and set the bottle of wine aside. Glad he had showered and dressed nicely, just in case, he sat, facing her.

"Sadie's watching the kids tonight."

Which meant they had time that they damn well needed.

Suddenly tears shimmered in Claire's eyes. She put a hand to her heart. "I told her that last night was such a mess, I needed a do-over."

Relief mixed with gratitude. The determination to also get it right this time. "We both need one," he told her softly. He gazed deep into her eyes. "I'm sorry, too, Claire. I never meant to blurt out such an asinine proposal and hurt you like that. Never mind lead you to think that all I ever wanted from you, and the kids, was a ready-made family and a convenient arrangement of a marriage."

She shrugged like it didn't matter, but it did. "Then why did you?" she whispered.

"Because when we were in that meeting, in Gabe's office, all I could think about was how you and your family deserved so much better than what your ex was ever going to offer you," he told her hoarsely, shifting her onto his lap. "And I wanted you to know that you and the kids weren't going to have to weather the years ahead by yourself, because I would be there by your side every step of the way." He stroked a hand through her hair.

She swallowed but her gaze didn't waver. "Because you're the kind of guy who rescues those in need," she surmised, referring back to the guy he had been when they met.

"Yes, that is a small part of it," he admitted. "I'm a natural born caretaker. You are, too. All physicians are. But there's so much more to it than that..."

She hitched in a breath, waiting for him to continue.

"The truth is, I would never offer to seriously commit to someone without my heart being fully involved."

She shifted toward him, settling more intimately against him. Hope hung in the air between them.

"Good to know..."

"I'm glad you feel that way. Because I don't just love your kids, Claire. I love you. With all my heart and soul."

Happiness gleamed in her eyes. She snuggled closer, splaying a hand over the center of his chest. "Then why didn't you tell me that first?" she asked with an affectionate smile.

"I should have." He lowered his head and covered her mouth with his, drinking in the soft, womanly taste of her. His body heated and shuddered at the compliant sound she made. Aware his life was finally getting back on track again, he stroked a hand through the silk of her hair. Only pulling back when they were both breathless, and only then, because he needed to look deep into her eyes, he confessed, "I meant to...but I was afraid you weren't ready to hear it." He shook his head, recalling the panic he had felt in that particular moment. The sense that he was losing her...for good. "You already thought it was all happening way too fast."

"And it was," she reflected softly. "But that doesn't mean

it didn't happen, Zach." She kissed him tenderly. "I love you, too."

It was his turn to be confused. "Then why didn't you tell me that last night? Why just announce it was over if I didn't agree to keep things status quo, and kick me out?"

Claire hitched in a breath, gazed at him and admitted tremulously, "Because I was afraid that I was making the same mistake I'd made in the past, and just seeing what I wanted to see—that you were in love with me as I was with you." Her voice cracking, she confessed, "Your proposal, such as it was, seemed like proof that you *weren't* ever going to be able to really love me, not the way married couples should love each other anyway."

He could see how she had reached that conclusion. "So what changed your mind and brought you here tonight?"

"A lot of soul-searching. And the realization that what was really happening between us was not history repeating itself." She knit her fingers through his. "But me—being scared of getting hurt again—and refusing to let myself see what was really in my heart…and yours."

He nodded, accepting her mistakes as readily as she forgave his. He brought her even closer and kissed the back of her hand. "Whereas I was worried that if we waited for the exact right time, that it might never come. And we'd lose out. Or worse, that in the process of following some arbitrary timeline that you and the kids would need me, and I wouldn't be there. So I rushed everything." He looked deep into her eyes. "But I know now that we can take all the time we need to do this right and become husband and wife. And the family we were meant to be."

Claire wreathed her arms about his neck, her eyes brimming with joy. "Oh Zach, I love you so much."

He kissed her back. Tenderly. Reverently. Sure now all their dreams would come true. "I love you, too."

Epilogue

One year later...

Claire and Zach stood at the bottom of the bungalow stairs.

"Everybody ready to go?" she called up.

Lucky appeared first, tail wagging slowly. Oliver, Andrew and Isabella joined him in the upstairs hall. All three were clutching their loveys and favorite blankets.

"Did everyone say goodbye one last time?" Zach asked.

All three kids nodded solemnly.

Slowly, they started down the stairs of the completely empty house, Lucky leading the way. "When is the new family moving in, Mommy?" Isabella asked.

After the closing on Monday. Claire smiled. "Next week."

"Do you think they will like the house as much as we do?" Andrew asked.

Zach snapped the leash on Lucky. "I bet they will, buddy."

Claire and Zach waited while everyone had one last sentimental look around. With a sigh, the kids filtered out. They stood on the porch, then followed each other down to the sidewalk. Where they each turned and gave one last wave goodbye.

"Ready to go to our house?" Zach asked the kids.

Nods all around.

"It's bigger," Oliver reported cheerfully. He took off on the path he had taken many times over the last year.

"I like the new swings there," Andrew said, keeping pace.

Isabella smiled as they passed the second house on the familiar trek. In deference to the beautiful April weather, it sported newly full landscape beds. She skipped happily, her mind now on the day ahead. "Mommy, are we still going to the garden center today to buy flowers for our house?"

Claire grinned as she recalled Zach and Gabe stopping by midrun, to help with that the year before. What would she have done without them—indeed the entire McCabe clan?

"Yes, we are. As soon as we put on our gardening clothes." Overalls, T-shirts and sneakers for the kids. Jeans and tees for her and Zach.

It was going to be a new tradition.

To be added to a visit from Gwen, Patrick and their kids, on Memorial Day weekend.

Claire planned to get both extended families together for a barbecue in their backyard.

"And then tomorrow we get to go to the Easter egg hunt in the park? Right, Daddy?" Andrew affirmed.

Zach reached out to affectionately ruffle his hair. "Yes."

Oliver leaned against Zach affectionately, too. "And then on Sunday we get to go to Easter dinner at the Knotty Pine ranch, with all our cousins!" he concluded.

Isabella clutched her baby doll close and tilted her head thoughtfully. "Daddy, do you think we'll get to decorate Easter eggs again with stickers and stuff?"

Zach smiled, like the loving father he was. "Grandma Mitzy is counting on it!"

As they reached the Victorian they now all called home the kids scrambled up onto the porch, and piled on the long wooden swing. They grinned and moved back and forth.

Following behind, Zach and Claire took their time. She reached over to take his hand in hers. "Hard to believe it's been a year, isn't it?" she murmured. From one Easter weekend to the next.

He wrapped an arm about her shoulder, and kissed her temple. His voice a sexy rasp, he confessed, "I can't remember a time when you all weren't in my life."

Tears of bliss misted Claire's eyes as she watched him looking down at her as if he were the most fortunate man alive. "Same here," she whispered back, her heart filling with more love than she could have ever imagined.

"We took our time. Gave the kids and ourselves plenty of opportunity to adjust."

"And it has all worked out perfectly," Claire said. Thanks to a lot of thought and careful planning.

They had dated all summer, spending time at both their homes, and with both their families. Zach had proposed in late August. She had said yes and asked him to be her children's legal father. They had married several weeks later, beneath a beautiful flower arbor, at the Knotty Pine ranch. And, with Zach and the kids as extremely enthusiastic participants, begun the formal adoption proceedings. Giving Oliver, Andrew and Isabella the doting daddy they had deserved all along.

Zach had moved into Claire's bungalow with them, while six months of renovations were done on the big Victorian.

When the adoption was finalized in court at the end of February, they threw another big party to celebrate.

Then, in early March, they had begun the process of transitioning from one home into the other. Claire's bungalow had been put on the market, promptly sold. And now, Easter weekend, they were embarking on yet another transition, a very welcome one.

They would all be living in the big house Zach had found and bought on faith.

Faith that they belonged together and their bigger-than-life love would carry them through.

And it had.

* * * * *

Watch for the next book in Cathy Gillen Thacker's Marrying a McCabe Romance miniseries, coming October 2025 only from Harlequin Special Edition!

Harlequin® Reader Service

Enjoyed your book?

Try the perfect subscription for Romance readers and get more great books like this delivered right to your door.

See why over 10+ million readers have tried Harlequin Reader Service.

Start with a Free Welcome Collection with free books and a gift—valued over $20.

Choose any series in print or ebook. See website for details and order today:

TryReaderService.com/subscriptions

RSBPA2409